P9-EMR-803

Pictures at an Exhibition

PICTURES
at an
EXHIBITION

Sara Houghteling

ALFRED A. KNOPF · New York
2009

THIS IS A BORZOI BOOK
PUBLISHED BY ALFRED A. KNOPF

www.aaknopf.com

Knopf, Borzoi Books, and the colophon are registered trademarks of Random House, Inc.

Library of Congress Cataloging-in-Publication Data
Houghteling, Sara.
Pictures at an exhibition / Sara Houghteling.
p. cm.
"This is a Borzoi book"—T.p. verso.
ISBN 978-0-307-26685-9
1. Art treasures in war—Fiction. 2. Family secrets—Fiction. 3. World War, 1939–1945—France—Fiction. 4. Art dealers—Fiction. 5. Paris (France)—Fiction. I. Title.
PS3608.O8553P53 2009
813'.6—dc22 2008027138

Manufactured in the United States of America
First Edition

For Fiora and James Houghteling

and

Florence and Burton Waisbren

"Only in a house where one has learnt to be lonely does one have this solicitude for *things*."

—Elizabeth Bowen, *The Death of the Heart*

PART ONE

JOSSE BERNHEIM-JEUNE COLLECTION
(LOOTED DURING WORLD WAR II AND NEVER RECOVERED)

Almonds

ÉDOUARD MANET, oil on canvas (21 × 26 cm), 1861–1871

Chapter One

IN THE TWILIGHT OF MY LIFE, I BEGAN TO QUESTION if my childhood was a time of almost absurd languor, or if the violence that would strike us later had lurked there all along. I revisited certain of these memories, determined to find the hidden vein of savagery within them: the sticky hand, the scattered nuts, the gap-toothed girl grasping a firecracker, a cap floating on the Seine, flayed legs swinging between a pair of crutches, the tailor and his mouthful of pins. Some of these were immediately ominous, while others only later revealed themselves as such. However, whether or not another boy living my life would agree, I cannot say.

Of the humble beginnings from which my father built his fame, I knew only a few details. My grandfather, Abraham Berenzon, born in 1865, had inherited an artists' supply store. He sold tinctures, oil, canvases, palettes and palette knives, miniver brushes made from squirrel fur, purple-labeled bottles of turpentine, and easels, which my father described as stacked like a pile of bones. The shop was wedged between a cobbler's and a dressmaker's. Artists paid in paintings when they could not pay their bills. And as Renoir, Pissarro, and Courbet were far better with paint than with money, the family built up a collection.

When the value of a painting exceeded the price of its paint, Abraham sold it and invested the money with the Count Moïses de Camondo, a Jew from Istanbul with an Italian title and a counting-house that he named the Bank of Constantinople. Both men loved art, and they were fast friends. By 1900, Abraham could purchase an apartment on rue Lafitte, near Notre-Dame-de-Lorette, in a neighborhood known as the Florence of Paris. Soon afterward, Moïses de Camondo recommended that my grandfather invest in the railroads. Coffers opened by the beauty of paint were lined with the spoils of steel, steam, and iron, and my grandfather did not have to sell any more of his paintings.

As a teenager, I often passed by rue Lafitte and imagined the family home as it had once been, as my father had described it: each picture on the grand salon's walls opening like a window—onto a wintry landscape, a tilted table with rolling apples, a ballet studio blooming with turquoise tulle. The salon's chandelier shone onto the street through windows which, as was the case across the Continent, were made from high-quality crystal. On sunny afternoons, Grandfather's gallery was so ablaze with prismatic light that schoolchildren returning home for lunch thought they saw angels fluttering down rue Lafitte. They reported their sightings to the choirmaster at Notre-Dame-de-Lorette. When he could no longer bear to tell any more youngsters that they had not seen angels but just rainbows, and from a Jew's house no less, the choirmaster hinted to some older boys that perhaps they should break the windows, which they did.

At least that was how my father explained the attack on his childhood home in July of 1906. Then again, Dreyfus had just been exonerated, and there were many such outbursts across Paris. Abraham had followed the trial closely, nearly sleepless until the Jewish captain's verdict was announced. Two days later, hoping to spare a dog that ran into the road, he drove his open-roofed Delage into an arbor of pollarded trees on avenue de Breteuil. My sixteen-year-old father, Daniel, was pinned between the tree trunk and the crushed hood as Abraham expired beside him. From then on, my father walked with a limp, which eight years later exempted him from service in the Great War. So whether he was lucky or unlucky, I could not exactly say.

In 1917, my father purchased the building at 21, rue de La Boétie, after my mother Eva agreed to marry him. For this young Polish beauty, whom he hardly knew, and who spoke comically stilted

French, he bought a house in a neighborhood known for its tolerance of the creative temperament. Yes, as if in anticipation of the utter bleakness that would eventually follow, that block was home not only to my father the collector and my mother the virtuoso pianist, but also to a choreographer renowned for his collaboration with Diaghilev; the Hungarian trumpeter most preferred by European conductors to perform the second of the *Brandenburg Concertos;* a sculptor known for his works in bronze and his clamorous machines; and, three years later, though without the same fanfare, me.

From the well of my early childhood, only one half-lit event emerges: I am in the forest and a small girl shares a sweet bag of nuts with me. We dance on the mossy floor, and she holds my sticky fist in her own. Until late in my life, I supposed that the little girl in the white dress had been a dream, invented sometime in the crepuscular years before my seventh birthday. I remembered nothing at all before 1927, when Lindbergh landed at Le Bourget, on an airfield lit brighter than day. This absence of memory was natural, I imagined. I had no siblings with whom to compare my experience and was loath to press others into discussing my youth.

UNLIKE HIS OWN FATHER, MINE MAINTAINED NO PARticular attachments to the paintings that found their way into his possession upon Abraham's death. Father sold this collection as the first exhibition of the Daniel Berenzon Gallery in the early 1920s. He explained that, at the time, he had been under the influence of the German philosopher Goethe. "Remember the *Theory of Colors,* Max," he said, as he paced the gallery. "When you stare steadfastly at an object, and then it is taken away, the spectrum of another color rises to your mind's eye. This second image now belongs to the mind. The object's absence or presence is irrelevant. They're all up here"—he tapped his head—"so why worry about them out there?" He gestured to the carmine and gold gallery walls. "You'll have a museum of the mind."

And for him this was true. To hear my father describe the paintings he had sold—which I thought of as lost—was as if their watery images, quivering and illuminated, were projected on the dark walls of the gallery from a slide carousel. These pictures possessed a certain patina—of regret, of time, of absence, of value—which lent my father's descriptions a deeper beauty than I had been able to see when the paintings hung before me.

Indeed, my father was among a tiny group, the heirs to the patron spirit of Catherine de Médicis and the savoir faire of Duveen or Vollard, whose genius was not in the handling of paint itself, but in the handling of men who painted. They encouraged the artists' outrageous experiments so that they could paint without fear of financial ruin. They were not just rug merchants and moneymen. They were as devoted as monks to the beauty of their illuminated manuscripts. Or so my father said, in his most rhapsodic moments. And I believed him.

Pablo Picasso was my father's most famous artist, and he too came to live on rue de La Boétie, at number 23. When my father passed below on the street, Picasso would stand in the window and hold up canvases for my father's approval, and approve he always did. Father encouraged the Spaniard's experiments, understanding that Picasso's genius resided not in a single style but in his ability to reinvent himself. He was, Father said, our Fountain of Youth. Since Monsieur Picasso's art would never grow decrepit or stale, neither would Father and neither would their glorious world of paint. Yet Father kept not a single Picasso in our family collection; what hung over our dinner table would likely be sold the next week. Our walls were never bare, nor were they familiar. "We're trying to give what we have away," Father said. Though he hardly gave the paintings away, I wondered, sometimes, if he felt that he had.

Beginning in my earliest years, each night before Father locked the doors to the art gallery, I was called downstairs from my bedroom and, with my eyes closed, was told the name of a past exhibition and made to recite each painting's artist, title, and composition: a Morisot *Woman in White* looking like an angel with the dress slipping from her shoulder; the Vuillard odalisque *Nude Hiding Her Face* from 1904; an iridescent 1910 Bonnard, *Breakfast*, of woman, jam, and toast.

After we reviewed the present exhibition, we would recollect past ones, of Sisley and Monet's winter scenes; Toulouse-Lautrec's portraits on cardboard with low-grade paint; the occasion on which Father had furnished the exhibition rooms with rococo settees and ormolu chiffoniers and then hung above them the most wild drawings by Braque, Miró, Gris, and Ernst, so as to indicate that modern art could indeed decorate a home. Though Father's clients purchased mostly for this purpose, privately he scoffed at those who arrived with a scrap of drapery when choosing a painting. "The artist is an aristocrat, Max," my father told me. "He has suffered for his art. And yet still he is generous, because he offers us a new language that permits us to converse outside of words."

I often wished that Father would not converse outside of words but, rather, raise other subjects during these meetings and guide me on boyhood matters, such as girls in sweaters or my birthday choice of alpine skis. Once or twice, I sensed that he tried to. I waited patiently, nearly holding my breath so as not to break the spell when Father began, "Over the years, I have wanted to tell you—" But this sentence, though repeated, was never finished, and eventually I gave up hope. Still, the nightly recitations were treasured occasions with my father, a man for whose attention many people, including my mother, had to fight.

In my memory of those nights in the gallery with pictures orbiting around me, my father is splendid, luminous even. He had a brushy mustache, a neat chin, and a slim neck. He wore a white collar and a long tie the shade and sheen of obsidian: a lean, angular man, as if he had stepped out of a canvas by Modigliani and, dusting the paint from his dinner jacket, taken his place against the gallery's doorjamb. He parted his black hair on the side and his eyebrows looked penciled in. His face might have seemed too small were it not for the significant ears, the plane of his cheekbones, and his long, sloping nose.

As pictures were hoisted to the walls and then lowered, President Doumer was shot dead at a book fair, the Lindbergh son was kidnapped, and America choked in a cloud of dust. All of France seemed to be on strike. By eleven, I was expected to discuss various genres and artists.

"On still lifes," my father began, and walked to the back of the red divan.

"The lowliest of genres," I said. "Courbet painted his in prison."

"Yes."

"With landscape painting only slightly superior."

From upstairs, we heard Mother singing along with her piano playing. Sometimes she sang the orchestra parts to Brahms or Beethoven, or hummed along with the piano melody so as not to lose her place in it as her fingers whirled through their steps. If Father was rehearsing the art of recollection with me, we both knew that Mother, with her hundreds of hours of music committed to memory, reigned supreme. Whatever sensitivity Father and I might have possessed, Mother surpassed this, too: she heard sharps in the opening and closing of my dresser drawers and an unpleasant A-flat when the telephone rang. She thanked Father for choosing an automobile whose motor played an excellent C. When Mother traveled to Zurich and London to perform, I was left in the care of our housekeeper, Lucie, and our chauffeur, Auguste. Both loved music and, fortunately, both loved me.

I grew from a boy in pajamas to a young man who lit his father's cigarette before smoking his own. The fixed point in Father's collection was Manet's *Almonds*, painted in the years between 1869 and 1871. It was the one painting from my youth that had never left 21, rue de La Boétie, not in the first auction nor in the dozens that would follow. When Father bought Manet's *The Bar at the Folies-Bergère* before lunch and sold it by dinnertime to a British sugar magnate, *Almonds* stayed behind; Picasso's *The Family of Saltimbanques* was shipped to New York, but *Almonds* stayed behind. Even when Mrs. Guggenheim was on her campaign, as she told Father, to buy "a picture a day," *Almonds* remained. Father claimed that no one offered him the right price for it, though later I came to understand otherwise. Father loved the painting, though he would not say why, except that it was painted by a humbled man nearing the end of his life, when Manet's legs were weak with syphilis and the artist could no longer stand at his grand canvases, as he had done with *The Execution of Maximilian* or *The Bar at the Folies-Bergère.* The man whose life had begun to still began to paint still lifes. I did not consider Manet's *Almonds* beautiful. I found it morbid and sad to look at in the morning hours, when the light was clear and bright. In comparison to Cézanne, who often had to replace his pyramids of apples with wax versions because the real fruit rotted after a fortnight of study, Manet's almonds were the ones that had been passed over, deemed too inferior to eat, painted by someone who'd had his fill. Still, I averted my eyes from the painting with difficulty.

When the time came to take my winter exams, Father explained that he could not "with good conscience" pass his beautiful gallery down to me. The day before, there was news of Kristallnacht in Berlin; Mother had said, "surely your courses will be canceled," but they were not.

For a year, we did not rehearse the paintings. Rather, I rehearsed Father's sudden rejection: I lacked, he had said, the memory, the business acumen, the ruthlessness, and the lucidity of vision to predict what could be bought one spring and sold a dozen Junes hence. "I wish for you a stable life," he said. "*My* father drove too fast." This I did not hear. I was made to fill out the exams and forms for the schooling that would land me in the hospital, not as a patient like my father long ago, but as a doctor. I resolved to fail as brilliantly as I had once studied to inherit the gallery. Eventually, Father and I resumed our nightly study of the paintings, but it was never the same as before. I was seventeen years old.

PART TWO

1939–1940

Josse Bernheim-Jeune Collection
(Looted during World War II and never recovered)

Woman in White

Berthe Morisot

Chapter Two

I FIRST LEARNED OF ROSE CLÉMENT WHEN I WAS NINETEEN and she was twenty-one. In the end, she will prove the most indispensable of us all. In January of 1939, however, I understood her only as the object of my envy. I did not understand that we were living on borrowed time.

"Hide this from your mother," Father said, and handed *Paris Soir* to me. He smoothed his mustache. "I have to interview a new assistant tomorrow. The boss"—this meant René Huyghe, curator of the Louvre's department of paintings and sculpture—"says she's got the best eye the museum's seen since Louis Quatorze walked through the Salon Carré. That old adage. He insists she still work on some extravagant project of theirs for a few hours each week, stockpiling sandbags at the museum and refitting Notre-Dame's stained glass windows with putty so they are easier to remove in case the bombing starts. I suppose I must learn to compromise."

Before I was of the age to work alongside my father, I had greeted the arrival of his new apprentices with glee. Every two years, he took on one of the Louvre's young, underpaid curators. As a child, I enjoyed the uninterrupted stream of older-brother figures. They were debonair. Some spoke French with an accent; one came from as far as Delhi. They had excellent taste in clothing, cigarettes, women, and—I realized later—men. I learned to blow smoke rings, to discern between interchangeable Braques and Picassos (they said Braque's lines were blunter, Picasso's more fluid), to iron a shirt, and to say, "The night is beautiful and so are you. Kiss me," in Swedish.

In the years between the wars, the curators-in-training traveled with my father from the Prado to the Uffizi and from the Rijksmuseum to the British. They went to the Hermitage to discuss the acceptable humidity ranges for Byzantine triptychs and to the Vatican to examine the separation of soot from fresco. I had a dusty collection of trinkets and snow globes, one from each city Father visited. The apprentices occupied an apartment off the gallery, inexplicably called the Nurse's Room, which could be entered either from the gallery's main floor or through a separate door in the courtyard. My father liked his trainees to challenge him, to suggest purchases and donations, and to worship Manet with a passion verging on the unsound. They visited artists' studios alongside my father and decided which paintings to buy before they were finished and which finished paintings to buy, in order to ensure that the dross never reached the market. Apprentices learned to keep a silken scrim between the Berenzon Gallery and its clients. A buyer eager for a painting was not cause enough to sell it; rather, Father placed the paintings with owners who could add luster to the artist's reputation.

At my side that evening in January, my father resumed his ritual of recitation. "Sisley, 1926," he said. I stood and began to walk around the room, pointing to the place on the wall where each painting had hung when I was six.

"*Watering Place at Marly in the Snow*, *Banks of the Seine in Snow*, *The Bridge of Auvers-sur-Oise*." My brain seized up. I couldn't remember the rest. Father listed them quickly.

He accused me, on that occasion and others, of possessing the ardor of an aristocratic art lover—once something was mine, I planned to keep it forever. Indeed, because I had to be removed from the gallery whenever my father sold a painting, I spent most of my childhood elsewhere, usually with Bertrand and Fanny Reinach, the grandchildren of the Count Moïses de Camondo and my favorite playmates. So that night, when, as I often had in the past, I asked why Father could not take *me* on as his assistant, he reminded me of my childhood temper. "All that wailing whenever we sold something, throwing a tantrum, pulling at your mother's dress. We had to clear you out on the days the owners came to fetch their new paintings." I began to speak, but he stopped me with a raised hand. "Don't worry yourself so. Time for sleep, my boy. Check that the main entrance is locked." He gestured toward it with his chin. I was dismissed.

I wanted to pace the gallery's green floor in my own tuxedo. I wanted to have a near-photographic memory like my father. But as I did not, I needed the gallery there to guide me. I raised my fist to strike the glass door. Yet because my father was not a man of violence, of sharp words or brutish action, I lowered my hand.

THAT NEXT DAY, IN EXPECTATION OF MY ENEMY'S arrival, I dawdled in the living room with its convenient heating vent. When she came, Mademoiselle Clément's heels clicked a double staccato down the hallway. I peered into the gallery and glimpsed one slender leg, a high-arched foot, and the black shoe dangling from it.

"Shall we discuss the influence of Spanish artists on French painters?" my father said.

"In Spanish or French?" Mademoiselle Clément asked.

"French will be fine."

The girl talked and talked. I imagined that she had a large gold key sticking out from between her shoulder blades like a pair of wings and that an attendant continually wound it. Father stifled a yawn. She instructed him on the details of Manet's single visit to Spain in 1865. She informed my father of facts he already knew in a voice that did not take this into consideration. My irritation turned to curiosity.

"My fascination lies primarily in Goya's influence on Manet. Manet adopts the composition of Goya's history paintings in order to layer his own critique of Napoleon's regime with Goya's condemnation of French barbarism in Spain. I'm thinking of the connection between *The Execution of the Emperor Maximilian of Mexico* and Goya's *3 May 1808*."

Through the chute came Manet's interest in eliminating the

halftones of the palette and his lasting friendship with the painter Berthe Morisot, who was also his sister-in-law. Rose cited Baudelaire's essay, "The Painter of Modern Life," and Zola's defense of *Olympia*.

"Bravo," I whispered. I could not compete with the mind that belonged to the woman with the beautiful instep. I felt awe and envy, one of which registered in my ribs and the other in my stomach. Her voice reminded me of the flute solo in *Daphnis and Chloé*, the sound of waving scarves, diaphanous colors, a changeful pitch unwilling to rest on any note but returning often to the same theme. I think I must have fallen in love then.

Lucie entered the room with a tray. The room was quiet, and I could hear the sounds of sipping and blowing across the hot tea. I leaned back from the heating vent, tropically warm. I opened the window on the hour and let the peal of bells drift in.

While my father talked, I thought about the operating theater of the medical faculty. A female cadaver with its head shrouded lay greenly sweating formaldehyde on a table with a wobbly leg. The day's discussion was on reproductive diseases, and as the surgeon pointed to the woman's ovaries, I considered how my father's artists must have attended lectures such as these.

Down below, I heard my name.

"Hard work, medicine," Rose said.

"Oh-ho, not for Max. Things come easily to that boy," Father lied. I fished my heavy textbook out from underneath the sofa where I had thrown it, blew the dust off its cover, and tried to study for the next day's class. The names of the bones in the skull slid around on the page each time I looked away, trying to re-create the picture in my mind.

When I heard my father's chair scrape back from his desk, I looked through the heating vent again. "Shall I speak with your son?" Rose asked.

"No, no," Father sang. "Valves, veins, tendons, hospitals, and moaning invalids, those are his passions. He prefers the morgue to the museum."

I stood at the top of the stairs while my father and Mademoiselle

Clément commented on the rain outside. Rose said she was unprepared for this weather. Thinking of Humphrey Bogart, I descended the stairs and offered to accompany the young woman to her destination.

"My gallant son, Max." Father's mustache twitched. "May I introduce to you the lovely Mademoiselle Rose Clément." I took her hand in mine and she looked at the floor through a fan of black lashes. She was a woman as Ingres would have painted her: luminous skin, impossibly long limbs, and hair so fine it never stayed in its combs but found its maddening way to the sticky corners of her mouth. Her blouse revealed the bracket shape of her collarbone, and I imagined the white, lacy brassiere, with all its complicated hooks and straps, beneath.

"You could walk me as far as the Métro," Rose offered. "I've some distance to go underground after that."

She shook hands with my father, bending slightly at the waist. I plucked an umbrella from its stand and jabbed the tip out onto the street. It opened with the sound of a sail catching wind. Rose stepped under. As we walked the ten paces to the corner, rain ran down my collar.

"So you're the infamous son," Rose said.

Unsure how to respond, I lit a cigarette. She took one as well. The smoke hung low under the umbrella.

"What is amiss here? I don't mean to offend you when we've only just met. I like you instinctively. I have a good sense about people. Like a collie. It's rather clear there's a family *situation*, and even though I'd give anything to work with your father—to work with a legend—it seems like it could be a minefield, too. I don't need any job that badly. I could keep working at the Louvre and eating my two tins of beans for supper."

"Only beans?" I asked, trying to steer the conversation from my father.

"Unless I've been asked to dinner or I visit my aunt, who feeds me like I'm going into hibernation. Well, sometimes it's a can of beans and a can of soup with the cheese that I keep out on the windowsill. It's a dream come true. A freezing garret on Île Saint-Louis with a bathroom down the hall that I share with a constipated waiter and a nymphomaniac. I don't have an oven, and it wouldn't be much good if I did. It's a struggle to convince myself to heat the beans."

Our shoulders jostled against each other as we tried to avoid colliding with a mother pushing a pram. Rose shifted her body so that it was directly in front of mine under the expanse of the umbrella. I could have kissed the curve of her neck.

"Truly," Rose continued, "why would anyone not want to inherit his gallery? It's breathtaking. And lucrative beyond my wildest dreams. A goose that lays golden eggs."

"No idea," I said. She looked skeptical.

"He doesn't think I'm cut out for it. I don't have the eye, the taste, the memory, the savoir faire." I ticked each trait off on a finger. The way Rose fixed her eyes on me made it hard to fit words together. "They corralled me into medical school. They want me to be a pediatrician, but I've failed at least one exam every semester, and I would have been expelled long ago if there weren't so few pupils left. We'll be halfway through this century by the time I'm finished. I'm not much of a student and don't try to be one."

"That," Rose said, "is a tired cliché, and surely there is some nice dark psychological explanation for your deliberate failure." Although I was slightly uncomfortable with my psychological state as the topic of conversation, I was happy for anything that would keep her attention. "You know Ivan Benezet?" she asked. I nodded and pictured the back of the Breton student's neck, his reddish hair and gingery freckles, the broad shoulders, and his shirt stretched across them. "He's in your medical class."

Despite his size, or perhaps due to it, Benezet was a mild-mannered fellow. Though he did not know my name, he had invited me to several student outings. I never attended any.

I could guess his importance by the way she mentioned him. "Is he your boyfriend?" I asked. Rose nodded. "Lucky chap," I said.

She shook her head and colored. "You could tell him that."

"I would," I said, "but then I'd have to start going to Basics of Surgery again. I don't have the stomach for it."

"Ivan loves that class," Rose said. We laughed for no reason and then fell quiet, surprised by our loud voices under the humid umbrella. A trolley rolled by, bell clanging.

Rose leaned toward me. "Do you like to dance?" she asked. I tried to say yes but did not succeed in touching wooden tongue to cottony palate. "You look like you would be a fine dancer. Fox-trot, Charleston, the dances they're doing at Bal de la Musette?"

"I haven't been there in a long time," I lied. On my last visit there, my companion and I spent the whole evening kissing in the corner, not dancing. She was of Czech extraction, and I had done my best to help her forget the sorrows of her homeland.

"You seem like you would be a good dancer. Lanky, not a string bean but not a muscleman, either."

"Thank you—I think," I said.

"No, it's a compliment," Rose said. "I love to dance, but men are always afraid to ask me because chances are I'm taller than they are. And a girl's legs look nicer in high heels, so what am I to do?"

We walked west onto the Champs-Élysées, toward the Métro at Georges V.

"Would you like to have some lunch?" I asked. "There's an excellent place around the corner. Fast, first-rate pepper steak, and a dozen times better than anything they're serving on white tablecloths around here."

"Sorry," Rose said, and she did sound as if she meant it. "I'm helping Ivan review for an exam on the skull."

"So he's in my Anatomy class as well," I said.

"Then you should get to work, too." She had a small birthmark above her mouth that moved when she smiled. "Though the word *steak* does make me hungry. Good-bye, Max."

She raised her hand to her ear, touched it to make sure the earring was in place, then smoothed her hair behind it. I wasn't sure whether to kiss her cheeks or shake her hand. I felt my head and torso jerk in separate directions from each other. She leaned toward me, and I didn't so much kiss her as press my cheek against hers.

I watched the men on the street watch Rose descend into the

Métro, shaking their heads at the way her hips swung as she shifted down each step in her black-heeled shoes. I felt an undeserved pride—they must have thought she was with me.

By the time I returned home, the rain had stopped and the old women of the neighborhood had reappeared, walking their dogs. The old women wore winter coats, though the day was not cold, and muttered to their pets. A terrier scratched helplessly at the pavement.

From behind his desk, my father called out, "So?" I sat down across from him.

"She's unusual," I said. "Strident. An eccentric. Intent on the job. As am I." Father pretended not to hear me. "Lovely to look at," I added.

"I didn't notice," Father said. He finished addressing an envelope—its second line read Élysée Palace—and pushed the bill away from him. "Max, the Berenzon Gallery needs to be ahead of the times, not with them." He gestured with his pen in the air. "Women will have the vote any day now. Miss Clément is part of a new breed, the hungry, independent, middle-class, educated elite. You and I will be out of touch and stale without the likes of her. I'm canceling the rest of the interviews." He punctuated this with a single clap. The crooked eyes of a Picasso nude stared at me piteously. "She knows her Goya, by God! Now there is only a single but significant obstacle in our path, Max."

Mother streamed across the gallery floor in her kimono, her face porcelain white without its paints, her eyes flashing and ready for one of her cherished fights with my father. Mother dressed only when she was satisfied with her practicing. It was then two o'clock in the afternoon. She played piano from eleven to two, and again from three to six, though some days she sat at the piano bench for barely an hour. She was fond of saying, "I practiced enough even as a child to last a lifetime."

"Auguste has told me all about your plan, Daniel," Mother began. Our chauffeur was her special confidant. "A woman does not go to shul without a hat." Father rolled his eyes at her Yiddish. "She does not go to the theater without a companion. She does not engage in commerce without her gloves. And she certainly does not move into the house of a strange art dealer if she is a decent lady. She's unchaperoned. No proper parents would send their unmarried daughter into such a situation. If they cannot save her from disgrace, I will."

"*Ma puce,*" Father said. "For a woman to enter this field, she'd have to be plainer than a librarian. This is a curator, Eva, not a cancan dancer." He poured a scotch and swirled it in his glass.

"This business of yours, it does not have a kosher reputation. And what would people say about my son?" I cracked my knuckles and she slapped at my hands. "Not good for fingers," she said. "Or my husband! Nikhil was perfection. Why not another young man like Nikhil?"

"Of all the assistants, your mother only likes royals from the subcontinent," Father said, and dabbed at my mother's mouth with his napkin.

"Or why not Max, for goodness' sake, Daniel? You choose a *girl* over your own son."

Father gripped his glass as if he might throw it. Instead, he drained the liquor in a swallow. "You know why, Eva," he said. From outside, the two-pitched whine of an ambulance covered his words.

"Why?" I cried, standing up.

"This is not the business for you, Max, any more than you are prepared to fly an airplane or perform surgery with your left hand." The edge in his voice sounded like a knife touching its grindstone. "You're a rich man's son—"

"Your son," Mother said.

"—and though it's no fault of your own, you lack the hunger, the desire to hunt and chase." I tried to protest, but Father drowned out my stammering. "Your morose face would depress the clients, make them feel all the sadness they've come here to escape."

My mother reached for my hand, but I snatched it away and walked up the stairs while my parents fought in whispers.

LATER THAT EVENING, I RANG BERTRAND REINACH, WHO said he could meet me in Pigalle, though not until ten o'clock. I looked at my watch, which told me I would have to wait three hours.

I wandered around the city, eating a stale egg sandwich by the quay until it was time to walk to the Eighteenth. Bertrand never appeared at our meeting place. Later he explained that he had been experimenting with the sexual pleasures of self-strangulation and had fainted. As usual, I was neither sure what to believe nor what was stranger, his extravagant stories or the joy he took in telling them.

I went into a brasserie and began talking to two nurses in white uniforms. I said I worked in a munitions factory. They had been raised in adjacent homes in Toulon and were hurt when I said I had never been there. "But I would love to visit," I added. "Please tell me all about Toulon. What should I see when I go there?" While they reminisced about the miners' museum, the maritime museum, the prison that Hugo described in *Les Misérables*, and the cafés along the waterfront, I procured them each several more drinks.

When the bartender wiped down the counter and announced he was closing, I bought a bottle of wine and paid him what he asked. I tried to convince the two nurses to hurdle the wall of Père Lachaise with me, though only the less pretty one agreed. I figured out that she was Annette when her friend said, "Don't make me say 'I told you so,' Annette." However, Annette scraped her leg and tore her uniform on her descent from the wall and began to cry and insisted I take her home. It was much harder to get out of the cemetery than to get in it, we discovered, and the girl was sullen and weeping quietly and we were both sober and unhappy.

I felt bad because of the ruined uniform. As we walked, I fished some money out of my wallet and offered to pay for a new one. Annette held the crumpled notes in her hand and shook the small stack twice. I could tell she wanted to take it, but since a monetary exchange with a man would have smacked of something else, she gave it back. We felt more kindly toward each other after that.

Eventually, we found a ladder leaning against a crypt and used it to climb over a low point in the cemetery's wall. It was four in the morning, and I hailed a taxicab and bought her daffodils from a merchant setting up his stand in Les Halles, near Annette's apartment. This seemed to cheer the girl and she gave me a kiss at her doorstep and said she would invite me upstairs if her roommate didn't snore so loudly. I said I wouldn't pay any attention to it, but Annette said no so vigorously that her curls bobbed against her cheeks. She shut the door and locked it quickly behind her. I knocked twice but she had, I supposed, already trotted upstairs.

I walked toward home, crossed the Seine and back for good measure because the morning light was beautiful, smoked a cigarette with the policeman who patrolled our neighborhood, and drank a coffee in the café by our house. I arrived at school in time to stare briefly at my exam on the bones of the skull before falling asleep.

Chapter Three

I saw little of Rose Clément, even after she moved her two upholstered valises into the Nurse's Room on Valentine's Day of 1939. She did not allow Auguste to drive her to and from the Louvre. She did not pause to converse with me when I lingered in the gallery wearing a new shirt. Nor did she take her meals with our family, as my father's other assistants had done.

Sometimes, this was for the best. At the dinner table, my parents argued. Father had been unsuccessful in keeping the newspapers from Mother. She practiced less and less but sat at the piano bench with the instrument's keys covered, listening to the wireless.

"Germany isn't Poland," my father said when she panicked about the news. "There are no Cossacks in Berlin."

"Hitler is a crazy man. When I hear him on the radio," Mother said, pressing her temples, "I can barely understand this German he is speaking, his mouth is so full with spittle. And he is an Austrian? But his accent is fake, Bavarian. That Goebbels, he speaks beautifully. Like Satan, but his articulation is perfection. He must be the envy of singers everywhere."

My father reached across his dinner plate and laid a hand on hers. She snatched it away.

"You know nothing," she hissed. "You've lived in such comfort here. Now you've got butter on your sleeve." The pitch of her voice dropped. "I heard them arrive, on horseback." Father met my gaze, looking for a conspirator.

We mentioned neither our absent guest nor the empty chair awaiting her, except on one occasion. Father reported that Mademoiselle Clément had inadvertently insulted the Princess Noailles by calling a certain Gauguin a "good deal." The princess never spoke of money herself and bought paintings without inquiring about their price; she left those details to her lawyer. "Snobby old cow" was what my father liked to call the princess. Still, I felt sorry for Rose. With Father, it was so easy to make a mistake and not know it. You could sense his punishment later but could not identify the crime.

After the second week of Rose's apprenticeship, the empty fourth chair disappeared and we returned to our regular table configuration.

"Thank God you've stopped wearing that wretched cologne," Mother said to me before dinner. "All my food tasted like musk."

"Pity the Poles," Father said to her, turning on the radio. "They lost you, their national treasure."

On the radio, the announcer speculated about German territorial demands, rendering my father's joke inappropriate.

"Pity the Poles," my mother said, somber now.

We ate in silence.

THAT WINTER, I GATHERED THAT MADEMOISELLE Clément took long hot showers because I often heard water rushing in the pipes and, when I turned on my own spigot, found the water cold. After dark, the lamp in her room made a yellow square in the courtyard until well into the night. I watched it for a shadow or a shape. My most prurient attempts to rig up an old motorcycle mirror on a string and dangle it like a fishing lure failed. I could never get the mirror to lie flat or reflect from the right angle. Rose's private quarters remained so. I took to skulking in the hallway between the gallery and the street, hoping to catch her there. But I only frightened my father, who struck out at the shadowy figure in his corridor.

"*Verboten!*" he shouted, when he realized it was me. We had begun to speak German to each other as a nervous joke. I went back to tinkering with the motorcycle mirror. I started lifting barbells.

For a month, Mother talked only of the German refugee question and whether it was better for Jews to go to the Philippines or the Dominican Republic. Mrs. Roosevelt backed a move to accept twenty thousand exiles and then christened the Yankee Air Clipper America's first Queen of the Skies, baptized with water from the seven seas. The Italians issued a call to arms to three hundred thousand men, all war babies and those previously deemed physically infirm. In France, I joined the lines of other young men seeking to enlist. The prospect of war seemed to offer a more exciting alternative to school, and the constant reminders of my own failures at home. I was aware, too, I am sure, that my father had never had the chance to serve.

When I visited the draft board, the flatness of my feet was the cause of much attention. I noticed that my card was filed with a crease at its corner. I visited a doctor who recommended a series of painful exercises and sold me a pair of "reshaping shoes." When I told my father, I could not tell if his laughter was out of relief or at the humor of the situation. He had his own preoccupations. Some clients who decided to buy had their paintings shipped directly to houses in the country. Lucie hid bags of sugar in the closet where I kept my tennis racket. To Mother, Father repeated, "Don't worry." She replied, "I do." I wondered if they remembered that they had had a son at all.

The heat clanked at the same pace it had my entire life, and yet that month seemed to pass more slowly than others. Rose's presence was fleeting. On one occasion, I passed by Father's office as she sat at the typewriter, in a green sweater with a hole at its elbow. Notes in a looping hand were torn in two in the garbage. I found her in the hallway bathroom once, with a black tongue, as a pen had burst when she licked its nib. I handed her a white towel and said, "Ruin the cloth," and she looked grateful and closed the door on me as I stood there, staring stupidly at her stained mouth. To the light in the courtyard, I sang along with my new American record, *There's an oh-such-a-hungry yearning burning inside of me*, and I felt every word in the marrow of my bones. Eventually, Auguste said, "I hate this Cole Porter," so I only played the album at a low volume and closed the window when doing so.

STILL, AS ABSURD AS THIS MAY SEEM IN RETROSPECT, I thought mostly of Rose. When my curiosity about her overwhelmed my common sense, I decided to investigate her living quarters. I would find her diary and learn the secrets of her heart. Anything important in the house not on a canvas was hidden in the kitchen. Searching in the spice cabinet, behind the teapot Lucie kept filled with whisky, I found a key attached to a paper disk on which was written *Nurse's Room* in my mother's hand. I planned my invasion for that afternoon, when Rose was at the Louvre, as she was most days when I returned from my medical classes.

A few hours later, I crept down the three stairs that led to the hallway off of Rose's suite. I could not recall the last time I had been in the Nurse's Room. I imagined it had housed my own caretaker at some point, though I never recollected having anyone look after me aside from Lucie and Auguste. The hallway had two doors. I passed the first, which held a shuddering, rusting furnace. The second door opened, with a jangle of bells, into Rose's room.

I had expected a jewelry box, and I stumbled into a riot. A stack of comics—Belphegor, Tintin, and Spirou and Fantasio—spilled to the floor and would not be coaxed into a pile. In the process, I knocked a pair of muddy roller skates off their pedestal (the Paris telephone directory) and into the dinner plate Rose had used as an ashtray. I cursed aloud.

On her desk sat a typewriter with a single jammed key pointing accusingly. Beside the typewriter was the secret to her solitary meals: a portable burner and a can of beans with a punctured lid.

I considered examining the contents of her dresser drawers (that haunting flash of white lace, once, at the waist of her skirt) but heard a tread in the hall and ran out, past the furnace and directly into Rose.

"Snooping about?"

"No," I denied. "The hot water—Father said I—"

She raised her eyebrows. "I should have left the door open for you. Saved you the trouble of picking that lock. I tried it myself once, just to make sure it could be done."

"I had a key," I said.

"Finger my underthings, did you? Did you find my diary? No? Well, that's because I don't keep one. For exactly this reason."

She swept past me into her room. The door remained open.

"What a mess you've made," she said, and examined me, hand on hip. "Enough already! We have business to discuss."

Rose pushed aside the clothes and the damp towel on her desk chair and threw the things in a heap on the floor. She perched at the foot of her bed, rolling an unopened can of beans on the carpet back and forth with her stockinged foot.

"How are your studies?" she asked.

"Fine," I replied, my throat dry.

"You should assert yourself more," she said. "I think you have a fine mind."

"Thank you," I said. She took out a cigarette and waited for me to light it, which I did.

"Tell me, what did I do wrong?" She picked a flake of tobacco from her tongue. "I know from that Swede that your father takes his assistants to visit the artists in their studios. I bought a new dress the week he had the appointment with Braque." She blinked forcefully and looked out the window. "I was planning to wear it and return it with the pockets sewn. But I'm never invited. I've waited four weeks, and I know he's visited at least that many studios. It's past Easter; soon the high season will be over. I need to know what the artists are working on to stay current and useful."

"I don't know what you did wrong," I said, both wanting and not wanting to leave.

"Then find out," she said, "or I cry about you sneaking around my room and getting your grubby fingers into my things."

"I didn't do that."

"But you thought about it. Tell me what you know."

I inhaled. "You talked about money," I said. "That was your mistake. You told the Princess Noailles the Gauguin was a good deal."

"That woman is a princess?" Rose stabbed her cigarette onto the dinner plate. "Why does she dress like that, with her horrid lipstick smeared on her teeth? She kept spitting in my eyes while she talked. What an awful woman!" Rose put her hands over her face.

"Don't take offense," I said, "because I think you will."

"I promise. Give me something to swear on." The can of beans rolled under the bed. "*Zut,*" she said. I stretched out my leg to find it and our knees touched. My foot located the can, and I sent it back in her direction.

"It's a custom. The princess, on the one hand, expects everyone to know she's filthy rich. How rich, and how she spends her money, on the other hand, is a private matter. So she can dress in a fur that's been dead fifty years and have her chauffeur drive her around town in a rusty old box. 'To live happy, live hidden.' She never *ever* talks about money. I doubt she knows how much she pays for anything. Her solicitor handles it and makes a heap for himself."

"I was just making conversation. What can one say to those people?"

I shook my head. "Don't ever mention a price unless someone asks you. Pretend you hadn't even considered that money was involved. Turn to my father, as if you're saying, Mr. Berenzon, you handle this mystery."

Rose chewed her lip. "How long until I can visit a studio?"

I shrugged. "I have no idea. You know Father won't speak with me about his business."

"You had heard about the princess."

"That was said in passing to my mother, who also despises her."

"Why?"

"She's an anti-Semite. She makes a show of leaving the orchestra early when they play Mendelssohn or Offenbach."

"Yet she still buys paintings from your father."

"True, but he is not the artist, nor is he her dinner guest."

I waited for Rose to comment on the injustice of it, but she only looked pleased with understanding the puzzle and its pieces.

FATHER HAD BEEN TO VISIT MATISSE IN HIS MEDITERranean sanctuary on Cimiez Hill, with its cages of doves, Moroccan tapestries, and views of the Roman ruins. Father loved the South in the winter, without its hordes. He was childlike and gay after a few hours spent in the presence of his artists, and this was both infectious and infuriating to me.

Tanned, sitting at our dinner table, he said, "Last time, I chose one set of paintings and when I had a leg over the threshold, the old Buddha said, 'Wait, Daniel, those ones I have decided to keep!' He's got a right to sell them on his own, of course. He suffers for them, says painting his delectable models and vases is more like slitting an abscess with a penknife or kicking down a door. Today Henri told me he begins to paint when he has the urge to strangle a man! I just nod. The paintings are so lovely. What a batty old Buddha! This time I chose all the ugly paintings and he switched his dotty mind and would only give me these marvelous still lifes and pink nudes. You could squeeze the lemons on the canvas, they're so bright. We're lucky we live across from Pablo and not Henri."

"Henri has fewer legal problems," Mother said.

"Only because he's too old to chase skirts. Now they all just work for him. And divorce suits Picasso."

"Does it?" Mother asked. Her right hand played sixteenth notes against the tablecloth.

Father had helped Picasso negotiate the separation from his ballerina wife. (Before Rose, the thought that the world possessed a woman more beautiful than Olga Khokhlova had been inconceivable.) Picasso had worried that his beleaguered former bride would wrest half his paintings from him in the settlement. For three days, Father had sat over Monsieur Picasso's bankbooks, unwilling to trust anyone else to the task, and the two men drew up long lists of his assets. Somehow, Father had convinced Olga to part from Picasso without either money or art.

"Now that he has the Russian off his mind, he has five new paintings ready for me. I'll see them this afternoon. I've been dreaming of these, painting my own Picassos in my mind." Father snatched up my mother's hand and kissed the curled fingers. "Can you feel it, the current running through us? We've grasped the cord that ties Manet's generation of French painting to ours."

"Picasso is not French," I said.

"He's French now," Father replied.

"As French as Mother," I said, and she laughed.

MATISSE'S AND PICASSO'S NEWEST PAINTINGS MUST have pleased Father indeed, as the next morning he announced that he had set aside ten thousand francs—roughly the price of a new automobile—for me to invest in a painting. I took his blank check with a whoop and without a question ran for my coat and hat. It was eleven o'clock: auction hour. Mother went to her piano smiling. Father spoke to me tenderly, as if I were a young child. "This will be a grand occasion for you, Max. Take it all in at first. Don't act rashly." I laughed and told him not to worry. I flew from the house, eager to spend the bounty I had earned but not deserved.

Drouot's appeared as a mirage amid the soot-stained facades of the city's apartment buildings. Though I had passed by the old mansion many times before, leaving my father here to buy treasures for his gallery, I did not enter it until that Monday, March 20, 1939.

I joined the crowd streaming inside and inhaled the smell of damp wool, face powder, and Macassar mustache oil. A woman with a nimbus of white hair led her spaniel amid a trio of Italians, holding their lit cigarettes above the crowd. The Italians debated which way to go and split in three different directions. The crowd slowed, swerved, and merged. It was thrilling to be there instead of in the lecture hall of the medical faculty, watching my surgery professor slice the skin of some jaundiced cadaver.

The rooms at Drouot's were not numbered in any discernible order. From Room Three by the entrance, at a sale of mid-eighteenth-century medical equipment, as if to remind me of my dereliction of duty, an auctioneer bellowed, "A perfectly preserved scalpel!" Room Five, next door, was a sea of Oriental carpets. I could not locate Room Six, where the auction of nineteenth- and twentieth-century European painting would be held. I finally found it upstairs, next to Room Twelve, where a sale of fur coats attended solely by women already wearing fur coats was under way.

Room Six was the largest at Drouot's, with red velvet walls and carpeting and its white number six dangling loosely above the door. At the front of the long room was a platform, not unlike the ones I saw photographed at the Olympic ceremonies in Berlin, with two level tiers divided by a raised third plank; the auctioneer stood on this center plank, tapping a gavel into his palm. He resembled a painting of a cherub, with wide-spaced eyes and a pink mouth. He took a breath, touched his blond hair, and began the auction.

The auctioneer sold five paintings in less than five minutes. Five times he had cried, *"C'est vous? Adjugé!"* and yet, as much as I craned my neck and twisted in my seat, I could not fathom who had bought the painting. There was almost no detectable movement in the sea of overcoats. Everyone's nose was buried in the Sajan Auction Company catalog with a Sisley winter scene on its cover. I leaned over a few shoulders and saw that the auction goers marked down the starting price over the final bid for each painting like a fraction.

"*Psst.*" A man leaning against the wall hissed at me and beckoned with a fat finger. He had a leonine head and a sailor's complexion. "You're in the wrong section, young man," he said, in a rolling Greek accent. "Sit up front only if you can remember Waterloo. Any man who can still chew his own food stands in the back or on the sides. That way you see who else is bidding. Understood?"

"No one seems to be bidding at all," I whispered.

"Yes, they are. Stand here with me." He yawned. "Not that you should buy anything. It's strictly professionals today. They have their own tricks." I craned my neck but recognized only my father's friend René Huyghe, paintings and sculpture curator at the Louvre, looking mole-eyed and funereal in his gray suit.

Lots 31 through 42 sped by in a blur of Dufy watercolors as

Drouot's employees in bellboy jackets barely had time to lift the paintings to the podium before they were whisked away.

By Lot 45, I had begun to recognize familiar faces. There were four young curators who had once come to our gallery to authenticate a Tiepolo; there was Madame Bernheim in the back, reading Proust; Alain de Leonardis had one arm in a sling and the other round the shoulders of a blond American model; the Wildensteins' oldest son was present, in need of a shave. To my surprise, I saw Rose, who nodded but did not smile before turning back to her catalog. Auguste winked at me from his seat at the end of the row. Ludovic Delanoë, my father's former secretary, was there also, back from his two-year tour of South America and biting his nails.

The auctioneer described Lot 50 in fantastic words that did not match his flat voice: "A classic example of Sisley's finest winter scenes, almost a symphony in white, ladies and gentlemen. Similar examples are in the Jeu de Paume. Bidding will begin at five thousand. Do I hear five thousand three, Monsieur Berenzon?" Upon hearing my name, I looked up with a start, but no, the auctioneer addressed my father, who now stood in the doorway, barely in the room at all. Father's eyes skimmed over me and his mustache twitched. A lily pinned to his breast had dusted his lapel with gold pollen, which shimmered in the light as if Father himself were gilt.

After ten thousand francs, my father indicated he would raise the bidding by five hundred, holding up five fingers. The gesture was so cool and knowing that my hand automatically tried it. "Eleven thousand from the young man to my left," the auctioneer crowed. Father did not glance my way, and raised to eleven thousand five. The auctioneer fixed me with his electric stare and asked for another five hundred. "No," I whispered, shaking my head, and an old woman with a yellow hat and veil took my place to do battle with my expressionless father.

Father stood with his arms folded. The hands that flashed in and out of the crook of his jacket were so pale he could have been wearing white gloves. At forty thousand francs, he was victorious.

"Forty thousand," the auctioneer announced, "to Monsieur

Berenzon in the back." A Drouot worker with brass buttons on his jacket parted the crowds and delivered a bid slip to my father. Father turned on his heel and, for a moment, the black lapels of his coat lifted off his chest and floated. He must relish, I imagined, how the bottoms of his fine shoes spun on the carpet. Then he left and did not look my way.

In turn, Rose, Auguste, and Ludovic all also bid on Sisleys and—whereas my father had won the most beautiful one—his three employees paid only a fraction of my father's grand sum. Each paid in crisp bills, so their funds were not recognizably the Berenzon Gallery's. My father wanted the whole lot of Sisleys—a sale of so many must have been unusual—but did not buy them all himself because the auctioneer knew him, sped the bidding along, and swelled the price. My throat tightened as I thought, Look, Father, I have learned just by watching you. You needn't have even explained to me these gears and their timing. It would have been enough just to have let me stand by while you played. But did you have to call upon Auguste and Ludovic for this favor? Why not your son?

I reached into the pocket of my second-best suit and crushed the smug blank check into a ball. Father had already purchased anything he could have wanted from this auction.

I understood then that this boon—the auction, the ten thousand francs—had not been my father's idea at all. It would have been my mother's, extracted from behind the bedroom door.

"Sorry you didn't win that Sisley," the Greek said to me and patted my arm. "You won't go home empty-handed today, young man. I have a good intuition for you."

"We will pause here at Lot Fifty-seven for an exceptional occasion," the auctioneer trilled.

"Such a peacock," the Greek said. "Nothing but professionals here," he complained again.

"A remarkable masterpiece, ladies and gentleman: the *Ham*, by Edouard Manet, a work from 1875, nearing the end of the artist's life, heretofore in a private collection." The room rustled to life like the sound of a cloud of bees sweeping in.

"Somewhere a rich man is burning his furniture to heat the mansion," the Greek said with a laugh. I slid him a sideways glance because my mind was racing in the other direction: Surely the Manet was a last-minute addition. Father would not have left if he had known it was for sale. This happens once in a lifetime, I thought. Rose and Auguste and Ludovic had spent my father's bills, but with my blank check I could buy it. For Father. Or for myself—I could build a collection around a Manet.

"We'll begin bidding at seven thousand francs," the auctioneer sang. As I raised my hand, René Huyghe's haggard face leaned into my field of vision. *No,* he mouthed at me. *Fake.* I shook my head; I didn't believe him. He would have a proxy there. He wanted this painting for his museum.

Father had allotted me ten thousand francs and bidding quickly raced past this mark. The colors in the room grew brilliant and bright, and I felt as if I were hovering half a meter above the floor. What luck fate had brought me, just to be there! I hardly heard the amounts I agreed to, I only nodded, raised five fingers, and felt the auctioneer hook his eyes into mine.

Manet's *Ham* hulked in the center of the canvas and was humble in its scale; if it was a life-size portrait of a ham, then it was a ham for an old man without a wife. The knife in the foreground had a worn handle and a dull bent blade. It was not the great quivering pink meat I had seen on the Sunday tables of my father's friends whose names I often read in the newspapers, houses in which everyone watched to see if we would eat their roast.

Rose had the palm of her hand pressed to her forehead. René thrashed in his seat, drew his finger across his neck, then stood to leave. "I won't watch you do this," he said. I turned my face back to the painting and raised my hand to shade my eyes. The auction room's lights glared off the surface of the canvas. My father often said, "A beautiful painting makes me want to shield my eyes. I buy when I have to look away."

A man with the posture of a gendarme bid a few meters from me. He wore the rosette of the Legion of Honor on his coat, and I watched his jaw muscles clench and grind between each bid. He had bought several other paintings already—he would start thinking about the money soon, wouldn't he, the vast sum, with the auctioneer's fees on top of it? When he bowed his head and reached out to hold the hand of the woman standing beside him, I knew I'd won. "No more," he said. His wife looked downcast. *My boy! My boy!* I could hear my father say, as he rose from his desk chair, beaming. Finally, I thought. Now it can all begin!

The Drouot assistant strode toward me, arm outstretched, as if he would just hand off the sales slip that was my everything.

"Your name?" he asked, eyeing a blonde in a thin blouse. When I told him, he said, "Of course," and laughed when I withdrew the creased check from my pocket. I had to ask him for the amount, and when he said seventy thousand francs I felt my knees give. My hand shook as I wrote.

I waited through the next six auctions. My mouth tasted of metal. Rose followed me out the door, where René lay in wait, talking to himself and making small angry gestures. He grabbed me by the wrist, sputtering.

"Hello, René," I said.

"From ten rows away, it's a suspect object."

"We're at Drouot's."

"There are plenty in this business who are crooked. Like the Galerie Zola scandal." I hardly heard René speak. "Think about Manet," the curator pleaded. "He wanted to build up paint on the canvas in three dimensions. For the paint to emphasize that it is *material.* Gauguin mixed wax into his to dull it. Your *Ham* shines like a Dutch master."

Rose looked away and my lungs constricted. She agreed with René, then.

"Varnished," Rose said. "Licked."

René kept one hand over his forehead, as if when he let go of it his skull might fall apart into its bones. "Your father—" he faltered. "We have to see Arthur."

"Arthur?" I asked.

"At the cash register," Rose said.

We hurried to keep pace with René, who had gone galumphing down the stairs, as much falling down them as running. "He's worried what your father will think," Rose whispered, "knowing that René was present when you bought the painting. Your father supplements his salary, just like he does with mine and the director at the Jeu de Paume."

A gnomish man with a full beard and pointed ears greeted René from behind a pane of glass. CAISSE, read a gold plaque beside a sliding window, which the gnome raised. "René," he said in a tetchy voice. "You never come to visit anymore."

"Arthur." René was short of breath. "Sajan put a fake Manet on the block upstairs, and Daniel Berenzon's boy here bought it. You have to nullify the auction. The son's name isn't on the account, so to buy it in the father's name is the same as a stranger doing it. It's an illegal transaction through and through."

The gnome hummed while René spoke. "Now, now. The young man here seems perfectly calm. He is Daniel Berenzon's son, after all. Remember, we too are a family business. We welcome Berenzon's heir here as Ulysses was hailed by the Phaeacians. And we happily waive any paper-signing claptrap under such exciting circumstances." The gnome turned his lamplike eyes on me. "In fact, we've all been wondering why he's hidden you from us." He extended his hand. "Welcome into our family, young Berenzon. I heard it was quite an auction. I might have flown upstairs to marvel, but you see, it was over so quickly I hadn't the time."

René pulled my hand from the gnome's damp grasp. "Exactly!" he shouted. Rose looked pained. "No Manet is going to sell in four minutes. Seventy thousand francs is a fortune, to be sure, but the last Manet the Jeu de Paume bought five years ago was three times that. The cost alone is an argument against its authenticity. Don't you agree?"

"These are difficult times, René. Many are leaving Paris, selling their artwork for whatever it will fetch. The world is not a stable place. Our currency is fickle. Art! Art is the only solid investment. Art and bullion." The gnome smiled, revealing his gold teeth. "When the Luftwaffe first appear in the sky over Paris, will you have time to rush to Crédit Lyonnais and wait in line with all its other weeping clients, or will you pluck your fortune off the wall and make for the countryside?"

"I shouldn't go to the bank at all," said Rose. "I'd find a pistol and—"

"This is a waste of time," René said. "I'd like to speak with Mr. Drouot."

"Don't," I begged.

René already stood on the second step of the stairs. "Why?"

Must he ask? Because I wanted to appear strong in front of Rose. Because my father would detest any public acknowledgment of a mistake. The voices in my mind began to roar.

"Max?" René asked. I shook my head, took leave of them, and returned to Room Six. I handed one of the uniformed men my claim slip, gave him delivery instructions, and took the back staircase to the foyer. I touched the pocket where the check had been. I did not know how much seventy thousand francs was worth, but the thought of the number made me wince.

"Max?" Rose called, but I did not stop. I pushed past the knot of people lingering before the door and into the whipping March wind.

A flock of seagulls swooped low over the street, crying bitterly. The round portal windows of Drouot's and the dampness of the air heightened my sensation of being near the ocean during a storm. I recalled leaving my father on this corner when I was a young boy, though at the time I did not think to ask why he separated from us here. With the romance of an eight-year-old, I was more preoccupied with the journey that Mother and I would continue on without him. Auguste had driven us up the rue des Martyrs, past the cobblestones glittering with scales from the fish dealers and the dusty windows of the antique booksellers, to the foot of Sacré-Cœur, which I told Mother was made of chalk, and she said *No, plaster of Paris, that's how the stuff got its name.* At the church, we fed two centimes into the binoculars and Mother lifted me up to look through them. I told her what I saw: the long steely roofs of the Comédie Française, the flags of a military parade, a windmill ("It's a dance hall," she said), the Eiffel Tower, and an invalid girl carried up the stairs in a chair.

I made Mother recount the story of how Saint Denis walked for hours after having his head cut off, and how he finally laid it down where we stood and declared a church should be built there, at the apex of the hill. We strolled to a small plaza behind the church where a dozen men in suspenders and berets had set up their wooden easels. They called out to us, and Mother chose one with an Italian accent to sketch my portrait on a piece of butcher's paper.

We rode the funicular down to the plaza of Saint-Pierre. Strong gusts made the cable car swing and jounce. Father met us in front of Drouot's, a wooden crate under his arm. He had disliked the butcher-paper portrait. "Ten francs for *that*! But it's not even our son! They must have given you some ugly boy's picture by mistake."

"Until Pablo paints his portrait," my mother had said, "you leave me no other choice than to patronize the fine artists of the place du Sacré-Cœur." Her voice had been strained.

"Berenzons don't have their portraits painted anymore," my father had replied, as if he knew that would make her cry. At the time, I had disregarded the strangeness of this and only considered it one of the many inexplicable interactions of childhood. I had assumed my parents spoke of the foreign world that existed before I came into this one.

Outside Drouot's, I raised my head at the clattering of bells from the campanile of Notre-Dame-de-Lorette. I could hear the *tap-tap* of a woman's shoes hurrying behind me. The blanched dome of Sacré-Cœur loomed above and I walked toward it. The rest of the heavens darkened for rain, but somehow Sacré-Cœur remained light and flickering. I pictured the amateur portraitists in the square beyond the church, how they would run for cover when the angry rains began and how they would call out from beneath striped restaurant awnings to sketch the faces of those who hurried by. I resolved to walk until it began to rain. By then, Father would know of my mistake and I could return home.

WHEN AT LAST I WAS ON RUE DE LA BOÉTIE, I FOUND MY father, much to my surprise, sitting in the gallery, wearing his coat and gloves, with the Manet fake unwrapped on an easel before him. The canvas was no bigger than the cover of a dictionary. A magnifying glass rested on the table beside him, and a full ashtray.

"Good, you're home," he said. "I was worried you were going to do something clever like throw yourself in the Seine." He clapped me on the shoulder. "I spoke with Robert de Rothschild while you were out. He said if it was a fake, then it would be the work of this fellow who poses as a Hungarian noble, Baron von Horty. Rothschild has had some dealings with him as well, though I think the false pedigree was the part that irked Robert most. I don't know why Robert's being so kind to us, but he sent his lawyer over to the Conciergerie, and von Horty confirmed that our Manet is part of his forged œuvre. Von Horty's as strange a fellow as you can imagine. He's blackmailed some senator to keep him in the fashion to which he has grown accustomed. He has a beautiful harpsichord right there in the jail with him, which requires tuning every week since it's so damp." When a matter interested Father, he moved at lightning speed.

That night, during our silent dinner, amid the loud clanking of silverware against plate, my mind churned. I was responsible for several losses of varying sizes. I had made a fool of myself before my father and Rose. I had begged my father to draw me into his business dealings, yet when given a test I had failed. I pushed myself away from the table and gathered the painting from my father's office in the gallery.

"Where are you going with that?" Father said. "Don't destroy it! Fakes are excellent instruction! They teach us lessons!" he shouted to my back, as I hurried upstairs.

I dragged a suitcase from the recesses of the storage alcove in my bedroom. I opened it, and a cockroach scuttled away, leaving his dead comrades behind. When I swept them out, their dried wings and shells crackled. I stowed the painting in one of the valise's inner pouches. The parcel made it sag. I closed the case with a thud and clicked its latches shut.

It was as if a key had turned inside me. I had wanted to twin the stupid, sullen *Ham* with my father's *Almonds*. Each mute still life needed its mate; each was too bleak without the other. I felt nearly drunk when I bought the *Ham.* Father's joy at my triumph would have outrun his surprise at the price. I had let my mind close down on my doubts like a steel door. I did not consider that my father regarded my mistake as a rite of passage—that any collector who says he has never made a questionable purchase is a liar.

I sat atop the suitcase with my head in my hands, for how long I did not know.

Then my father was before me. "Why are you sitting there in the dark?" he asked, and kept his hand around mine until he opened the door into the hallway.

When we stepped out into the light I became a man again, and we both let go.

Chapter Four

THE NEXT DAY, I LISTENED TO THE RADIO WITH Mother. A Russian diplomat explained the importance of Finnish territorial concessions lest the Germans invade the Hanko peninsula or use Karelia or Lapland as the bridgehead from which to attack Leningrad. It seemed to me that they were talking about Mars. Mother turned off the radio and played a few bars of music.

"When I hear Finland, I think of Sibelius," she said. I looked out the window at the haze around the winter sun. "My teacher heard Sibelius give a lecture on the overtones one hears in a meadow."

"You hear those, too," I said.

"Not a meadow," Mother said. "At least, not usually. We don't spend much time in meadows. Yet." Mother repeated daily her desire to leave Paris. All cities, she thought, were at risk. She played a few more bars of music. "Here's someone else," she said.

"It sounds the same."

"It's not." She played one phrase, and then another. "That's Sibelius." More notes. "And that's Mussorgsky, who came first. But I can't blame the Finn." She played some more. Finally, she said, "One can hardly blame a copyist." I realized then what she was trying to say. This was her own oblique, nearly opaque forgiveness, then, for my transgression.

In my youth, it had come as a revelation to consider that some of my mother's strangeness was a result of her speaking to me in a language that was not her native tongue. With the crisis in Europe, though, as Mother grew ever more unusual, I decided that she would have been perplexing in any language. Or rather, that language for her was a necessity but not her preferred means of communication. Thus, during an explanation such as this, it was best to sit quietly. I had not the training to discuss Sibelius or Mussorgsky. At times I wished I had continued the music lessons of my childhood. As an adolescent, this same kind of wish had led me to study Polish, secretly, for a few months in hopes that one day I would speak to my mother in a proud declarative sentence and she would answer me with joy and clarity. Sadly, perhaps because gifts of music and language are often linked, I possessed neither one.

She was now playing a new piece. "*Pictures at an Exhibition*. Mussorgsky wrote this for the painter Victor Hartmann, who died young. They had an exhibition of his watercolors, and Mussorgsky went and composed a piece for each of the paintings. A composition that accompanied him throughout the exhibit. This, the *Promenade* that I am playing, means Mussorgsky was walking between paintings. Movement One. And the first painting he saw was *The Gnome*, and that's Movement Two." She played the *Promenade* theme again. "Listen to how dignified and precise the rhythm is. Then he sees another painting"—I could hear a key change— "and that's *The Old Castle*. This is the closest you can ever get to that exhibition. They say all of Hartmann's paintings have been lost, so there is only the music. And Mussorgsky drank himself to death."

THAT SAME MARCH, MOTHER DEVELOPED A NERVOUS cramp in her right hand that gripped her four fingers into a claw, leaving only the thumb mobile. It appeared spasmodically, and no doctor could treat or diagnose it. Her performing schedule was curtailed. No longer tied to the symphony season, she clamored for a move south. There was a known specialist in Nice and a hypnotist in Bordeaux. The humid climate might be good for her clenched muscles. Father delayed. Mother practiced Ravel's *Concerto for Left Hand*.

March of that year also beheld the last great exhibition at the Berenzon Gallery—though of course we did not know this at the time—with works by Degas and Cézanne. Mother insisted on attending the opening, though she gave guests her left hand and retired earlier than usual. Somehow, Father must have warned the company of her condition: there were no requests for a performance, no coterie of tipsy favorites afterward, upstairs, leaning against the piano and singing.

When the pyramids of cakes and champagne glasses had been cleared away, my father and I sat on the divan, shoulders touching.

I anticipated the ritual with painful pleasure. Father could be cruel and dismissive of me during the day, before my mother or Rose, but when it was evening and the green carpet turned the gallery into a forest glade, my father was a different man from the one others saw during daylight.

With my eyes shut, I recited the paintings and he listed their dimensions.

"*At the Milliner's*," I said. "A woman trying on a hat. This is more muted than later works, because Degas is not going blind yet so there's no need to paint in those iridescents."

We heard a glass break upstairs. "These fits!" Father stood and stamped his foot. "Whatever pills that quack gave your mother aren't doing anything but making her hair fall out." I heard Mother wail. We both started.

Still, I did not want Father to go to her yet. I needed to ask him *something*. A thought gnawed at me. Father made to leave, then paused. "You're too old to recite paintings every night with your father, aren't you?" Before I could reply, he closed the door, and I heard him take the stairs to the apartments two at a time.

I lit a cigarette and continued to mutter the names of the paintings.

Someone entered the room behind me. "They say talking to yourself is a sign of money in the bank." Rose's voice was throaty, and she wore an orange silk dress I recognized as one of my mother's castoffs.

The ceiling above us creaked and groaned. Water rushed through the pipes. Father drew Mother a bath. There was splashing and murmuring voices. First Mother laughed, then Father.

Still standing, Rose made one full turn, as if she were seeing the gallery for the first time. "Imagine growing up with a father who discussed fine art—his fine art—with you every night."

"He won't talk about much else with me," I said.

"Still," she said, "consider the alternative."

I nodded, unsure of what to say.

To my surprise, Rose sat beside me and shut her eyes. "Where shall we begin?" she asked.

I paused, hoping to avoid the Degas ballerina statue thrusting her bronzed chin and narrow rib cage in our direction. She was eerie, too childlike and too suggestive.

But Rose pointed to the Degas. "*Little Dancer Aged Fourteen.* Not beautiful, yet inviting, and likely a prostitute." Rose tilted her head like a bird.

"They were in an impossible situation," I said.

"Call it what you will. The original was wax, with real human hair and a tutu, and it made the crowds furious."

Upstairs, my mother turned on her radio. Music this time, not the news.

"*Le nozze di Figaro,*" Rose whispered. Mother had taken her to the opera some weeks earlier, when the orange dress must have been exchanged. I had a sudden vision of Rose pinning the syllables of Mozart's title like a banner on a clothesline. "*Non so più.* My heart hurts, it is so beautiful." She touched her fingers there.

"Bertrand brought a dancer from Pigalle back here once," I began, aware that my brain was not permitting me to fix ideas (dancer, prostitute, Bertrand, painting, the humming feeling in my blood) together in a sensible way. "She kept asking how much each painting was worth and was disappointed that I didn't know. I made up a figure and she said, 'Oh, that's not a lot of money.' "

"Why didn't you know?" Rose asked. "Why did you bring her to the gallery?"

"It was Bertrand. They left after ten minutes."

The knuckles on her hand touched my own. We were both exhausted from the party. Her soft speech made me want to lean in and listen to the small intake of her breath. I flushed. I could not think. What would my father have done? I pictured him in my place, a young man, holding her, threading her hair between his fingers, looking at *Almonds* while he kissed her.

So I drew her face to mine. I could smell the familiar honeysuckle scent behind her ears and on her neck. Upstairs, I heard the radio turn on and off, then on again, then off. It was my parents, fighting over the dial and its stream of bad news. The orange silk skirt of Rose's dress pooled around her legs. I thought of the poem where the woman says, *I am half sick of shadows.* The bells outside rang midnight, then the first hour of the day.

Rose whispered, between our breaths, "Your father paid three hundred thousand francs for the Degas in 1931 and did not exhibit it for five years. Then Alain de Leonardis bought it for a million francs." She let me unhook her brassiere. "The Cézanne sold for sixty thousand at auction and your father has reserved it for the Mariotti collection for eight hundred thousand francs."

I put my hands under the hem of her dress and lifted it to her waist. Rose gasped. I grew dizzy and single-minded. She pushed me away when I tried, with what I thought was considerable charm, to remove another article of clothing. "The Picasso was part of a lot: three paintings for three hundred seventy-five thousand francs. The nude alone will sell for three hundred fifty thousand." The church told us it was half-past two. We began to fall asleep kissing. Soon dawn hovered outside the diamond-paned skylight, a gray cat pressing its back against the glass. "The almonds seem to glow, don't they?" she said.

"It's strange that my father has never been able to sell it," I said, and tried to kiss her some more. She drew away.

"Max, I file his correspondence. He gets letters every week asking after that one—from São Paulo, New York, Peking—and he just tells me to throw them out. *Almonds* is not for sale. He bought it for thirty thousand francs in 1918 from—"

"Yes, I know," I said. I didn't.

The diamond-paned glass grew light. I gathered up Rose's shawl. Holding her shoes, Rose made her way toward her apartment, and I could swear the paintings turned to look.

As we crossed from the gallery to the hallway leading up to the Nurse's Room, Rose put her hand back to stop me. My father stood before Rose's door, still dressed in his tuxedo. Twice he lifted his hand to knock, then dropped it to his side. Shaking his head, he thrust his fists in his pockets and walked back to the kitchen.

"What . . ." I began.

Rose shook her head. "I don't know."

I left her. It was nearly 5 a.m. I heard the cook moving about and the hiss of gas and the clank of a cabinet sprung open. A pot rattled against its shelf and then against the stove.

WHEN MADRID CAPITULATED AND VALENCIA CLOSELY followed, my Anatomy professor Negrín, whom I had never really thought of as Spanish, stepped in front of a train at Abbesses. According to the newspapers, Negrín had shouted, "Death to the Fifth Column!" I suspected the paper embroidered the details of his suicide. He had been a soft-spoken man.

Our exam was therefore postponed. I had attended the class in only a desultory fashion, it was true, yet I could not believe that Professor Negrín had died, and thus for once I reviewed for the test. Rose offered to help. We studied in the Jardin Labouré, which was garishly sunny and blooming.

"Did you go to the lecture today?" Rose asked, her voice odd.

"No," I replied. I did not want to see Negrín's substitute at the front of the hall, pretending that nothing had happened.

"Will you get the notes?"

"No intention of it."

"Ivan said the lecture was interesting—"

"He's a brute."

"—on the birth ailments of children."

"You shouldn't talk to him."

"He came to the Louvre to tell me about a case study from your class."

"I have enough case studies here at home," I said.

"I'll say," said Rose.

Though the sun remained bright overhead, we heard a gathering storm of tapping, like the sound of a rain shower coming in.

"I left my umbrella at home," Rose said.

I lifted my gaze to the parted garden gate, and we watched a stream of blind children pass by, walking quickly and ticking their canes, laughing and calling out to one another. "Cailleux has three new Matisses in his gallery," Rose said, after the children were gone from the street. "And your father has an exclusive contract with Henri for *première vue*. You understand what that means. Henri can choose what he might want to sell privately or keep in his own collection, but after that your father is the only dealer who can sell the paintings when they first go on the market."

I nodded. "So tell him. He'll be hopping mad."

"No," Rose said, closing my anatomy book with a clap, "you are going to pay the Cailleux Gallery a visit. I have my own suspicions, but I want to hear what you think before I tell you." She walked ahead of me out of the garden. "Go and beguile whatever imbecile is working there. Pretend you're interested in buying and ask all the naive questions you're afraid to ask your father—or me—about the paintings. He'll fall right into your lap." I grabbed her by the waist, and she let me kiss her, briefly, and then appeared to change her mind.

AT THE CAILLEUX GALLERY ON RUE WASHINGTON, A GIRL with a pink sweater and a vacant stare followed behind me as I circled the room, where three Matisses were displayed. I asked her when they had been painted, if Cailleux had others, what they cost, and if I could take the photographic plates home with me (as was standard practice when one considered investing thousands in a painting). The assistant's name was Mademoiselle Clothilde, and I told her I only liked pretty paintings and pretty girls.

"They're Matisse's most recent work." Mademoiselle Clothilde smiled weakly. "And these are the only ones we have, though more are expected. Of course, the master's genius is hard to predict." She adjusted the kerchief at her neck.

I paid a small deposit for the photographic plates and left, puzzled as to why Rose had sent me.

Later, Rose and I were in the gallery.

She was looking at the Morisot on the wall, the *Woman in White.*

"Why did you send me to Cailleux's?"

"Think of it as a gift."

I did not understand. Rose sighed. "Max, you're too kind, too full of humility. I seem to share more with your father in this regard. We both doubt, calculate. What do you think of Cailleux's Matisses?"

"Not as nice as ours," I said.

"And why not?"

"They lack motion, fluidity," I said.

"That is your first thought—can you guess mine?" I shook my head. "They're forgeries."

"Not more fakes," I said.

Rose lowered her voice. "Your father will want to lose his mind and explode at Henri, and then he will have risked his contract altogether. Tell him to approach by telephoning Matisse and saying that Cailleux is selling fakes and that Daniel knows Henri isn't paid for them. That way, even if your father is wrong, he still looks like he's acting on the side of his artistic client, and he only confirms what all the artists think anyway: that dealers don't understand their art, they're just moneymen. No more."

I took this in unhappily, but followed Rose's scheme the next day. By April, her theory of the fakes was vindicated, and I had never seen my father so pleased with me.

INCREASINGLY ROSE LET ME VISIT HER IN HER ROOM AT night. I tried to tell myself she acted out of desire, though I had come to suspect that Rose never possessed motives so simple. Sometimes we drew so close to each other that she would push me away with both hands, turn on the light, and pick up a comic—as if the levity of the material could soften her rejection. Worst of all, she might turn on the radio. Two foreign ministers, von Ribbentrop and Mussolini's son-in-law, made their alliance, and we all said the Italians were dirty and weak. May and June passed in this way. But I could think of nothing but Rose and the heat that radiated from her skin without my hand even touching it.

"Why not?" I begged, one night in July.

"It's reckless," Rose said. "Everything could happen too fast."

"You make me feel like being reckless," I said. Her face below me was so close her features blurred.

"It's easy for a man to say that. I'm the one with something to lose." A kiss on the forehead, maternal, without heat.

My intentions were otherwise—that she would not lose, that I could save her from whatever strangeness she might have felt as employee, as sweetheart, as houseguest, as apprentice, and so on. We could run the gallery together.

I had in my possession a family ring, its diamond modeled on the Dresden White.

"For whom?" Mother had asked when I requested the jewel.

"Rose, of course."

"I find it bad practice to give people what they do not want and then expect something in return," she said.

A RINGING TELEPHONE WOKE THE HOUSEHOLD AT FIVE-thirty the next morning. Mother, convinced it was news from Warsaw, answered in Polish. The caller hung up and rang back a moment later. I groaned, rolled over, and returned to my dream of playing tennis knee-deep in a field of mud.

I heard a tap at the door and felt a cold touch against my cheek. There was Rose, pale and shaking in her dressing gown, sitting at the foot of the bed. In the town of Saint Etienne de Saint Geoirs, some 560 kilometers away in the Isère, her mother had suffered a stroke. She had been rushed to the hospital, where her life hung by a thread.

"I have not spoken to my father in five years," she said, "and there was his awful voice on the telephone. The train to Grenoble leaves tonight at ten and does not arrive until the next morning. I can't delay sixteen hours. Mother may not wait."

"We can drive the Delage," I said, and she looked at me with a mix of fatigue and gratefulness. We left at quarter past six. It would be a twelve-hour drive if the tires held out.

ROSE WAS SILENT FOR MOST OF THE TRIP. I NATTERED on about my dream from the night before; about my friend Bertrand, who always called me "old man," and his mournful sister, Fanny; about a bullfight I had attended as a child; and so on.

"Do you want me to be quiet?" I asked her, somewhere in the hills near Dijon.

"God, no," she said. "You're a wonderful radio that switches frequencies without me having to change the dial." In another sixty kilometers, we did listen to the radio, but the news was nothing but reports of executions in Spain and whether the death toll was ten thousand or ten times that. Eventually, we switched back to my babbling and then, once it grew dark and my eyes tired of staring at the road, we were quiet. It seemed as if we were driving away from history and the talk of war.

Once, I ventured, "You have never spoken of your father."

"He disapproves completely of my life. He didn't think I should even go to university. He did not go himself. One of those men perpetually resentful for not having had a son. Art, to him, is only an indulgence."

"That hardly seems a cause for such a falling out."

"It is my single true joy," she said, and I felt a sadness at hearing this.

The tires finally capitulated when we skidded over a cattle break on the outskirts of Saint Etienne de Saint Geoirs. We left the car, right side sagging, on the rutted road, and went the rest of the way by foot. Rose clung to my hand.

We tiptoed on the strip of high ground between the muddy path and the farmer's fence to our left. We passed a stand of poplar trees, then a makeshift camp. A single child's shoe, without laces, waited by the road.

A cobblestone square with a concrete fountain appeared before us. A café and a restaurant, both with grimy windows and tattered awnings, showed signs of life at either end of the plaza. One emitted tinny music. A dog trotted out of the other, pissed against the building's facade, and hurried back into its bar. A monk in a cassock, with a rope around his middle, shuffled by.

The hospital was only a few paces beyond the town square, behind a high wall. The first nun we met cried out with joy at seeing Rose. "You've grown so slender and chic! What a beautiful coat." She caressed its sleeve in her childlike fingers. "Look at what Paris has done to you!" She herself wore the extraordinary habit typical of those days, her starched wimple like a winged ship.

"Catherine, do you know where my mother is?" Rose asked.

The young nun colored and her hand dropped to her rosary. "Look at me, going on about your coat. It's past the regular visiting hours, but I know she'll want to see you. I go in there and sing to her, and she watches me but doesn't say a thing. Your father hasn't come once. She's had no visitors but me, poor Madame Clément!"

Rose inhaled sharply and I thought it a dangerous sound.

We followed the young nun down a dim hallway. Her skirts streamed out over the varnished floor.

"I'll go in first to tell her you're here," the young nun said. "On account of her heart."

Once Catherine disappeared, Rose said, "I thought she might have died already." I wiped her eyes with my handkerchief and she took it from me. "Will you stay outside when I see Mother, Max?" she asked. "She knows very little about my situation in Paris, and I want to explain it to her." I agreed. After Catherine emerged and Rose replaced her, the novice offered to take me on a tour of the hospital grounds and gardens. Even though it was dark, some of the oldest buildings were still lit at night and, the young nun said, even prettier that way.

She was twittery and gay as we strolled between the rows of herbs and vegetables in the kitchen orchards, gesturing with her hands so that the wide sleeves of her habit fell back to reveal plump, hairless arms. She reminded me of an uncooked biscuit. We returned to

Madame Clément's ward in three-quarters of an hour and found Rose outside, shaking the hand of a young doctor who had also been her classmate. He shook mine, too, heartily but with some disappointment. This hospital was unlike the ones I was used to in Paris. There were no patients in sight and no news on the radio, only Maurice Chevalier.

We walked back through the shabby plaza, through a series of unlit side streets, to Rose's childhood home. Rose smoked as we walked, coughing while she inhaled. We arrived at a two-level house with a slanted roof. A window on the second floor emitted a sooty yellow light. It began to drizzle. Rose pressed the buzzer and waited. We heard a movement inside.

"I swore I would never sleep in this house again," Rose said.

I pulled her away from the door, tugging her alongside me through the mist, through a maze of alleys with low-hanging clotheslines. "There must be a hotel then, somewhere, even if we have to sleep in its parlor."

Inquisitive lights lit our footsteps as we passed.

"The only hotel is in the plaza," she said. "The proprietress is the aunt of the doctor you met in the hallway. We'll be the gossip of the town."

I had begun to envision Rose still sleeping next to me in the morning and the pleasures of waking her up.

"We could let two rooms," I said halfheartedly. Her face lifted.

"You would do that?" she asked, and added, "And pay?"

I said I would and she kissed me. Someone inside the dingy café hooted. We entered, and Rose spoke with the white-haired woman behind the bar, who took down two keys from their hooks below the liquor bottles and led us to our rooms.

Mine had evidently not been used in some time, as a layer of dust covered its surfaces. A newspaper waited in the trash bin, as did a bloodied bandage and a rusty razor. I was nearly drunk with fatigue. When I pulled the musty blankets to my chin, a sleep as heavy as sand settled over me.

When I awoke the next morning, I took my breakfast alone.

"Mademoiselle Clément is already at the hospital," my hostess told me. Somehow the whole town knew of her mother's illness. I went out in search of Rose.

It was Bastille Day, and the infirmary managed to have a quietly festive air. The doctors wore carnations in their buttonholes. Several people greeted me by name. I could only smile, confused.

Rose appeared at my elbow as I walked through the hospital herb nursery, which was robust and tidy in daylight. "Mother's not well enough to see you," she said. "They say she's out of danger but too tired to spend more than a few minutes, even with me. Still, I'm to send her regards and her thanks." She slipped her hand into mine. "I've a surprise for you," she said, brightening.

Despite the holiday, Rose had procured a picnic. To my relief and chagrin, the young doctor and his father had fixed the Delage overnight. We drove the car for thirty minutes along uneven roads, past another small farming village and its fields of alfalfa and artichokes and up into the mountains to a meadow.

"This is beautiful," I said.

"No," Rose said. "You've saved me from this place."

"How?" I asked. "I'd love to say I did, but you're the more capable one of our duo, don't you think?"

"It's the promise of you," she said, and my heart swelled so much I could ignore her next words. "You're a good boy, Max. Better than I deserve." I was nearly twenty, and I was no longer a boy, except in one regard.

The tarte tatin and the wine made me giddy and drunk. Bees and flies buzzed above us and even the sun seemed honeyed. Eventually, Rose fell asleep, and I must have, too. When I awoke it was the gray of a midsummer's night. Rose was rattling a box of firecrackers.

"Let's go to the quarry," she said.

Ahead, the torch in her hand lit the way. I followed down the sloping meadow and over a path in the woods. In Rose's voice, I sensed a certain deliberation, as I often did, though usually it was with regard to art, not affection. I sensed that she was trying on a role: that of a normal young woman in love. Where I stood in relation to this role, I did not know. I thought of Manet's women, and of the nude in his *Luncheon on the Grass*. The scattered picnic at the sitters' feet and the men's relaxed poses are meant to suggest spontaneity, and yet the role of the central figure, the naked woman, was always uncertain and unsettling. I, at least, no matter how long I looked, could never read it. Like Rose. Like all of Manet's women—on balconies, in Argenteuil beside a *canotier*, tending bar, at a picnic, lying in bed—all places where one's purposes become obscure and the women, for matters of self-protection or modernity—could I ever understand?—became unreadable.

At best, I wondered, I would be asked to play the lover. I consoled myself with the hope that Rose would find the role fitting and that in real life she would follow.

We stopped abruptly at a rock ledge. The water beneath us was as still and silver as mercury. Rose began lighting the firecrackers, which burst into showers of red and white over the water, and I saw the night clouds reflected in the surface while the firecrackers burned. Our laughter echoed back at us from the rocks.

"I want to go swimming," Rose said.

"Down there?" I said. Sheer rock encircled the quarry. "It's like jumping out of an airplane." I blew out the torch and waited for my eyes to adjust. "You won't dare."

"I won't?" she asked, taunting me. She sounded girlish, even mean. The night regained its contours, with the pale woman beside me in the half darkness, knees bent to her chest, as mine were, our corresponding limbs touching. Her skirt fell back from her knees. I slid my hand across them, urgent now. Rose shifted, settled with her back against my ribs. I ran my hand over the buttons and frills of her blouse, then under it. "May I?" I asked her and she nodded, her head against her knees, and I kissed the ridges of her spine that stood out against her neck. My hands felt along the backs of her legs. Rose pushed them away.

"Max," her voice was tender, even apologetic.

She stood, turned, and found the box of matches. The firecracker she lit did not sparkle but was a steady flame, as bright blue-white as a flashbulb, a flare, the kind the enemy would use, in less than a year's time, to drop from hot air balloons over Allied lines at night. She held the flare above her, and in the bright light, in the second before she leaped, I thought of all the paintings of women who transform to escape the lust bearing down on them, Syrinx to a flute, Daphne to a laurel, and Rose now like a comet. The flare extinguished. She came up, laughing at the water's cold.

ROSE'S MOTHER GREW STEADILY STRONGER DURING THE time we spent in Saint Etienne de Saint Geoirs. We left on the afternoon of the third day. What I had not told Rose was that I had desired, were her mother well enough, to ask her for her daughter's hand. But despite my earnest intentions, uncertainty overcame me. And Rose, as always, was a step ahead. She must have seen the velvet box with my mother's ring. In the car ride, after two hundred kilometers of silence, she said, "I have never expected to marry. Perhaps I am ill suited for it. Or, perhaps there are things that occupy me more."

I, not listening, understood this as a temporary state.

Chapter Five

WHEN ROSE AND I RETURNED FROM THE ISÈRE, Lucie reported that my parents had left the day before, setting out early for their annual pilgrimage to the South. Father was concerned over Matisse's ill health. The painter suffered from terrible stomach pains that were, he believed, the result of a botched appendectomy years before. Matisse could not stand up to paint but was comforted with sketching, he said. He sent Father a note, which was left out on his desk (and which I read), saying, *A colorist makes his presence known even in a single charcoal drawing.* Father, who was unable to receive a consensus on which Parisian doctor treated stomach ailments most successfully, took two down with him. Lucie followed my parents that evening. I was glad to be in the house unobserved.

I sent Bertrand an urgent message, asking him to meet me at La Palette. My friend arrived an hour late, wearing a gray cashmere suit coat with some war medals from the 1870s pinned to it. When I commented on his attire, Bertrand said, "I'm prepared for battle, as always," and saluted. We sat at an outside table. He hailed the waiter, and two cups of coffee appeared.

Bertrand withdrew a notebook and scribbled into it. "I've a new idea for a play, about my uncle Nissim, the famous Camondo. I'll interview veterans from the war. It will have a Greek chorus, except the chorus is all wounded beggars, and they're telling the story of my uncle and how it seems—at least it seems to me—that he had to die, like Icarus in a monoplane." His uncle Nissim, family darling, equestrian, and airman, had been lost over the Atlantic in the Great War. When his aircraft disappeared, Bertrand's grandfather gave his house—and in it, the largest collection of seventeenth- and eighteenth-century French furniture and art outside of the Louvre—to the French state. I always thought this strange, though I never spoke of it to Bertrand—this Turkish Jew's obsession with French art at its most frivolous. And then the grandfather donated his museum, as if it were his self, to the country that had killed his son. Though of course the Count de Camondo did not see it this way. His sacrifice was supreme, nationalistic, a sign of how French his family had become in less than a generation, as if by collecting art, he had arrived. As he told my father, "I am a banking man so my children can collect art and theirs may paint."

An artist next to me sketched Bertrand as he wrote, shadowing his hollowed cheeks, arched nose, furry brows, and big ears. It was too good.

Bertrand filched the unopened sugar cube from the side of my saucer and bit into it.

"Well? News?" he asked.

I told him about the quarry on Bastille Day, my mother's ring, and the silent car ride.

The artist smirked. Bertrand said, "Well, then," and looked away. "You've found such poetry in heartbreak."

My eyes must have been brimming. This had an effect on Bertrand.

"Oh, no, Max," he said. He jerked his hands around helplessly. "You don't want a woman that stupid." He pointed a threatening finger at me. "Don't say you do. You choose the wrong women to love. Like Romeo and Rosalind. At the end of the play, his heartsickness over her seems minor. Someday, yours will, too."

"I don't read English plays," I said.

"If you only love a thing for the chase of it, you don't question if you love the thing itself because you never get close enough to see. You love to yearn, Max, you love to desire. But desire is simpler than love. Here's what your mother would tell you if she were able to string more than seven words together that don't involve Brahms: You're a handsome fellow, smart though you don't try, kind to old ladies, and not greedy like your friend Bertrand. Your motives are simple and pure—"

"Don't treat me like some house pet. I'm leaving," I said. Bertrand ignored me. I stayed.

"You love her, so you want to marry her. Therefore you're a good man! Not that there was ever any question of that. I know you're friends with me out of great charity of spirit, since we have nothing in common other than our caste and race and our formidable mothers. So why, Berenzon, in your old age, why would you continually want to waltz yourself into an arrangement in which you can only and continually fail?"

"I haven't failed," I said, unsure.

"No? Well, then, be disappointed."

We did not look at each other.

"This discussion of love is unmanly," I said.

Bertrand made a disgusted face and said to no one, "Berenzon is like a brother to you, so you will forgive him when he gets mad at you instead of at the floozy who has stamped on his heart with her pretty foot." He stood and threw a few coins on our table. Three bright brassy coins, the circles of the saucers, the white cups, the black irises of coffee grounds at their centers, all circles and eyes.

As I fumbled, I knocked into the art student's table and spilled his coffee onto his sketch pad. It was an accident, though I was not unpleased. His portrait was looking more and more like an anti-Semitic rag. We pantomimed reproach and apology. I tried to give him some money, he acted insulted, and someone muttered about Jews. I looked at Bertrand. Neither of us was in the mood for a fight.

"Stay out of this," I said to the speaker, who wore the blue overalls of a street cleaner.

Outside, Bertrand said, "Really, old man, you think I can't tolerate a picture, a drawing of me as I really am? Hook-nosed and with ears built for flying? I thought it was a good portrait." He looked into the windows of a building across the street. They faced east, and the sun winked off them like a lighthouse's warning. "If you hadn't ruined it, I was going to go back there after you left and buy it from him. But I was too embarrassed with you around."

I jingled the coins in my pocket.

"Give me some of those," he said.

We stood a few meters from a blind man. He had the words GASSED AT YPRES scrawled on a piece of cardboard and hung by a string around his neck. "You go on," Bertrand said, moving toward the beggar. "I want to talk to him. Imagine, being blind." He shook his head in disbelief. I thought my friend might be lying in wait for the street cleaner with the blue overalls. We said good-bye, and I continued along rue de Seine for a way and then turned back.

My friend squatted on his haunches beside the blind man, who sat on the sidewalk. Bertrand gesticulated with his hands, then caught himself and put them under his armpits. The veteran held the piece of cardboard in his pink hand while he spoke, and shook it three times, violently. With his other hand, he made the gesture a magician might make when releasing a dove.

I could not imagine what the two men had in common, and yet when I turned the corner, Bertrand was still at the blind man's side.

NEARLY AN HOUR LATER, AS I WALKED ALONG THE SEINE, I heard a tinkling and felt a tap at my shoulder. It was Bertrand and his medals.

"Let's go sailing," he said. It was blustery and beginning to rain.

"No."

"I promise, thou shalt not think about that contemptible girl for at least sixty minutes. *Vale la pena, hombre*," he added. I did not know how he knew Spanish. "It's worth the risk."

The risk Bertrand was referring to was that, in fact, to go sailing required us to steal a boat. Which we did, which Bertrand often did, somehow with me in tow.

This one was named *Madame de Pompadour*, with a flimsy lock that Bertrand broke against the moorings. We tacked through the green-gray water of the Seine and sped under the bridge at the quai de Grenelle while the Métro rattled the trestle overhead. A roar rose from the crowds at the Vélodrome d'Hiver and drifted above us like a cloud. We turned our collars up against the wind, ducked under the swinging boom when we changed course at Garigliano, and floated between the bridge's pilings, as sturdy as giant's legs. *Madame de Pompadour* was a sleek skiff. Her hull was painted blue and her brass railing shone. Below deck, Bertrand found a melted box of chocolates and three bottles of beer, of which I drank two and Bertrand the other. The sail back to the dock near Austerlitz was more difficult. The wind had switched directions, and we were sailing into it once again.

When the quay was within sight, the breeze dropped off. On the shore, a man gestured angrily to two policemen.

"This is the best part," Bertrand announced. My nerves jangled. "Nice and easy," he said, landing the boat with extravagant finesse. "Hello," Bertrand called out in English.

The two policemen rushed over, nearly tackled us, and shoved us against the wall of the embankment. We had been through this routine before. I did not know why Bertrand would not purchase, or at least rent, a boat like any other Parisian who loved to sail. The owner of the *Madame de Pompadour* looked on with satisfaction. Shackled, we were prodded along, up the stairs to the roadway and the police wagons. The younger officer pushed down on Bertrand's head and hustled him into the car. The other checked over his shoulder and watched the owner of the *Pompadour* float out of sight.

"Easy there," the older cop told his partner. "It's Patrice Le Tarnec's nephew. We've got to let him go." Le Tarnec was the assistant chief of police and Bertrand's uncle by marriage. The Camondo-Reinachs believed he granted them universal immunity, like some Swiss diplomat might have.

Grinning, Bertrand held out his wrists. Once unchained, he fished in his pocket for a few bills. It made it all a game, a pantomime.

"Gentlemen, thank you," he said, and we ran to the Métro station at Cardinal Lemoine. The wind that had abated earlier picked up again and licked at my face and hands. It began to rain, a sweet-smelling summer shower.

"Wasn't I correct?" Bertrand asked.

"About what, fool?"

"You haven't thought about the girl in an hour." He checked his watch. "Or more."

I admitted he was right.

Bertrand slipped past the gate, I paid my ticket, and we boarded the train.

FOR THREE MONTHS AFTER MY UNFORTUNATE VACAtion in the Isère, I remained in love with Rose, though not as before. She let me creep into the Nurse's Room at night, and sometimes she came to my door and we clung together until the sound of Lucie waking up the kitchen pots roused us from bed. We stayed clothed, like children. At first she permitted me to kiss her, and then just to press my face into her cheek or the curve of her neck. She advised me on gallery matters and, when the bill for her mother's hospital care came to the house, I opened the envelope of my own accord and paid it. For her saint's day, I gave her a gold chain with a gray pearl pendant. On the last day of my medical examinations in Surgery, Anatomy, and Pathology, I found an eighteenth-century treatise on Cuvier that must have cost her a month's salary propped up on my desk. I saw few friends other than Rose. My studies improved as my misery deepened.

To my mother, I had long ago returned the diamond ring modeled on the Dresden White. She extended her left hand and took back the velvet box and placed it directly into her suitcase, which was already full of clothes and musical scores. Mother worried that Poland would fall any day.

When it did, on September 1, 1939, Rose said, "This arrangement is not good for either of us. Plus, the beds are too small. I'm not sleeping well. My presence is required at the Louvre."

I protested. She opened the door to the Nurse's Room. I left and flung it shut. But Rose must have put forth her hand, because I heard her cry out. Then I stood in the hallway, and she wept on the other side of the door but would not open it again.

A sweater I had left in her room was returned, neatly folded outside my door, along with my spare bicycle lock. It stunned me that these stupid, mute objects outlasted love. No square of yellow light illuminated the courtyard. The bathwater scalded, I cracked my Cole Porter record in two, and France declared war.

Chapter Six

When the third day of the war brought an air-raid alarm, Father transferred two hundred and fifty paintings to the vaults at Chase Bank. Mother played Chopin as Warsaw was bombed. Father asked Auguste to make inquiries at the embassy as to the whereabouts of the aunt who had raised her, and he returned empty-handed. On the radio, General Commissioner for Information Giraudoux announced that our news would be as complete as was "compatible with safety," and the next day he bought six Matisse charcoal sketches from Father and asked for a discount. "Even if the Germans were to step on French soil," he told Father, "it's impossible to imagine them advancing. We learned our lessons in the last war. Their defeat would take no more than eight days, maximum."

I was called up once more for the draft, assigned to searchlight training, and issued an overcoat with civvy bone buttons that, the officer told me, was lucky because I would be excused from button-cleaning duty. But then, my conscription was reversed. Somehow my flat feet, miraculously overlooked, had been rediscovered. Father did not look me in the eye. Auguste said, "It might have been good for him," to my mother, when neither thought I was within earshot. I felt the glares of women in the street, asking *Why aren't you there?* at the Maginot line, where French troops stood staring dumbly across at the Siegfried line, where a smaller group of Germans stood staring dumbly at us. The British children evacuated from London returned home. RAF planes dropped leaflets, not bombs, over Berlin. A CONFETTI WAR, the newspaper called it.

Before dawn one October morning, I awoke to the sound of a handful of gravel thrown against my windowpane. I kicked off the covers. My mouth tasted like stale cigarettes and beer and I had taken to falling asleep in my clothes now that I no longer slept beside Rose.

I pulled aside the curtains and saw, in the gray light of the courtyard, my friend Bertrand.

"How did you get in?" I asked.

"Magical powers," he said. "Abracadabra. Now, hurry."

Although Bertrand was also one of the few young men left in the city, I had not seen my closest friend in two months. He would not speak of his draft board meeting, beyond saying that the examiners had found him "psychologically unfit." He cursed them. "You cannot imagine what a shame this is in my family. I was the first man at the commissioning officer's door."

I met Bertrand on the street a few moments later. He wore a green Tyrolean hat and was feeding a baguette to a stray dog that had rested a paw on each of Bertrand's knees. Bertrand spoke to the animal. She tilted her head to one side, tongue lolling, and barked, as if in reply.

"She doesn't like the Germans either," he said, rising. He hooked his arm through mine. "We must walk with alacrity. There's something you've just got to see. And on the way you must pour out your heart's contents to little Bertrand, as I am full of selfishness and spite for our fellow man."

THERE WAS SOMETHING UNREAL ABOUT MY TIME WITH Bertrand, as it was often late at night when we saw each other. We sped down damp sidewalks, past the quiet black bridges and their watchful statues. Childhood friendship initiates comfortable silence, too—a boyhood intent on toy trains, sand, rocks, insects, and a desire not to draw the adults' attention.

Bertrand stopped abruptly, across the street from an unidentifiable middle section of the Louvre along the rue de Rivoli. "Here we are," he said.

He pointed to eight white trucks parked in a line. Beside them, tense and unspeaking, stood the vehicles' drivers, burly in shirtsleeves and suspenders, with shadowed faces and prodigious mustaches. A trail of excelsior led from the trucks to the Denon gate entrance.

"They're evacuating the Louvre," I said. "If they're in Poland today, they're over Paris tomorrow."

"Look at those legs," Bertrand murmured, and tipped his hat in the direction of the legs in question. "They can't bomb Paris. Our women are too beautiful."

"That's Rose," I said, surprised. She held a sheaf of papers, and her face was hidden by a red hat.

She saw us and approached. "You shouldn't be here," Rose said.

"Max is *in* on the ins-and-outs of the city," Bertrand drawled. He spread his hand before him, as if brushing aside a curtain. "He is Baudelaire's flâneur of 1939, the cataloger of the city's thousand beauties and tragedies, unsolved mysteries, and unspeakable crimes—"

"You must be Bertrand." Rose interrupted him. Somehow, I had kept one from the other.

"Mademoiselle." He bowed and kissed her hand. Rose blushed.

"What's happened here?" I asked.

"It's what hasn't happened that everyone fears."

She explained it thus: Her British counterparts had delayed emptying their museums, as such an act would crush the public's fragile morale. But with the threat of the Soviet-German alliance, King George, it was said, realized his mistake and gave orders to evacuate the Tate and the national galleries, overseeing himself the departure of the royal train, which moved at a speed of only fifteen kilometers per hour so as to reduce the effect of the vibrations on the artwork inside. The Louvre, then, had feverishly followed suit. Only such an emergency merited recalling all its employees (and others too, packers from the Samaritaine department store and the Bazar de l'Hôtel de Ville, dressed in their striped uniforms) from their holidays.

Most paintings were taken off their stretchers and carefully rolled. Those too fragile were fitted with giant wooden cases and moved in scenery trucks from the Comédie Française.

There had already been a debacle with the van carrying the *Raft of the Medusa.* All the trucks were driving at night, without lights, on unlit roads. First, the trolley wires in Versailles were lower than in Paris and, amid a terrifying tangle of sparks, the truck had nearly caught fire. Gingerly extricated, its roof singed but undamaged, the truck set off again with postal workers in tow who used insulated poles to lift up any dangerous trolley lines. The van of Watteau's works had also been lost for several hours. Its driver, like many others, had never been more than a few kilometers outside of Paris, let alone to the château in Chambord. The driver mistook a bicycle's light for a signal from the caravan and followed the wrong road for hours until he stopped, by chance, on the crest of a riverbank.

Bertrand and I followed alongside Rose as she spoke. She was warm and vague at the same time. I knew better than to take her hand.

We walked steadily east through the museum. Dust-covered men reeled past us like dazed ghosts. "We have been here three days and nights," Rose said. "The châteaux are all ready now. They've sand on their floors, fire teams standing by, and the hygrometers are working."

"Father just sold a Boucher to build a steel and concrete hut along the Maginot line," Bertrand said. "The *ouvrage* will have an eclipsing turret, and they'll name it after Uncle Nissim. Then my sister will go there to plant rosebushes around the bunkers, because the front is ugly and the soldiers are bored." This sounded like a Bertrand concoction, but from other sources I knew it to be true.

The Louvre's galleries all led, like spokes to the center of a wheel, to the *Winged Victory of Samothrace.* We had arrived there, on the museum's first floor, looking up to the score of steps that led to its third, over which a wooden ramp had been constructed. Scaffolding sufficient for a house surrounded *Winged Victory.* The famous bosom was covered by a heavy piece of leather and encircled with rope. A second box of slatted wood was built around the statue, this one with wheels at its corners. The wings of solid marble still looked ready to take flight. A noose cinched where the head had been a thousand years before.

"There is Monsieur Michon," Rose said, "the curator of Greek and Roman antiquities." The hall grew silent. The bespectacled curator must have given a signal. The statue was hoisted a millimeter, then rocked forward. Four men, two on each side, strained against the ropes that controlled her descent. The wings quivered under their own weight as she rolled down the incline. When the wooden cart reached the ground floor, no one spoke.

Someone called Rose's name, she took her leave, and a guard showed us to the exit. When Bertrand turned his face to me, it was ashen. His eye twitched.

"Get some sleep," I said to him. "If you could see yourself!" We were walking along the Seine.

"Max, I have two secrets to tell you. Something makes me think I should say them now."

"All right," I said, unwillingly.

We paused midway across the Pont des Arts. The metallic bridge creaked in the wind that rose off the water.

"I've been keeping these secrets for years. Practically decades." We leaned over the hand railing on the bridge, overlooking the Île de la Cité. I did not face him as he spoke. "I promised Léon"—this was his father—"I wouldn't tell you until you were twenty."

"That's in five months. And a promise to the patriarch, that's biblical."

"Or that fathers betray their sons. That's biblical, too."

Bertrand gave a shrill laugh and spun his cap out over the river like a discus. We watched it float away on the green water.

"What was that for?" I asked.

"Why not?" he said. "Some impulses we give in to, others we do not. I have just resisted my impulse to tell you my two secrets, but I gave in to my curiosity about how my favorite hat would look twirling over the water. It's all a balance."

"Let's go to La Palette," I said. "Maybe the flamenco dancer you like will be there."

He shook his head and began to walk backward, away from me. "I'll wait till you turn twenty," he shouted as he receded. "Now I've given you something to look forward to. It's my early birthday gift."

He flashed me the V-for-Victory hand sign, turned on his heel, and descended the stairs that led to the embankment of the Seine, where derelicts from the Great War lived in tents and burned rubbish and their hungry dogs barked. If I had remembered my hat, I too would have thrown it into the river.

WHEN I SAW BERTRAND AGAIN, WE HAD PASSED INTO A new decade. Two million Britons had been conscripted. French soldiers ambushed their first detachment of Germans near the Vosges. And while there were rumors of mental patients killed en masse in Germany, in France it was merely illegal to sell beef, mutton, or veal on Monday or Tuesday. Friday remained meatless. On rue de La Boétie, we ate well. Winston Churchill warned the neutrals, "Each one hopes that if he feeds the crocodile enough, the crocodile will eat him last," which our French papers reported widely, as it was such a fine quote. Bertrand and I went to a strip club in Pigalle. It was my twentieth birthday.

Inside Le Chat Noir voices murmured, a woman sang onstage, and another laughed behind a closed door. The cash register sprang open with a cheerful ring as we threaded our way to our seats between waitresses towering on high heels. I took it all in: the shapely ankles, polished toenails, jewels, and, in close proximity, the feathers and the breasts. I wondered if any of the dancers were secret German agents. Bertrand and I ordered two whiskies from a waitress with cleavage like a ravine.

One dancer, a brunette, wore her hair curled in two Cs against her cheeks. This made my pulse race, to see a hairstyle like Rose's when she first came to rue de La Boétie. Her nipples were dark red and the size of twenty-franc pieces. Soon I was very thirsty. Bertrand muttered something unintelligible and left the table. I finished my whisky and, a while later, Bertrand's. I ordered another round of drinks. The waitress recommended a new American cocktail. I ordered two and enjoyed one after the other. The women danced to Mistinguette, Josephine Baker, and Fréhel. Peacock feathers floated in the air. When Bertrand hadn't returned by the waitress's third visit, I stood unsteadily and went in search of him.

He was not in the WC or by the bar but sitting at a far table, half-lit by a bulb from the hallway, hunched over a notebook.

"I've had an idea," he said, "for a play."

"That's fine," I said. "I have better company than you, Molière." From the corner of my eye, I saw that the brunette with the pageboy like Rose's had returned to the stage.

Bertrand shook his head. "Like Rose?" he said. I must have spoken out loud. "Whom your father has his way with every night? Oh, no, old man."

My pulse was like the snare drum accompanying the striptease unpeeling onstage. I reasoned drunkenly that I had never been in a fistfight but that my twentieth birthday was as good a time as any. As my fingers curled and my hand swung of its own accord, I marveled with a feeling like grief that desire could switch so quickly to rage. Bertrand deflected my punch. "You fool," he said. I lost my footing, fell backward, and helped myself to unconsciousness.

I AWOKE IN AN UNFAMILIAR BED WITH A WOMAN NEXT to me. I touched my forehead, which felt like a bruised melon. One of my eyes refused to open.

"Good morning, Max," she whispered, leaning over me.

In the half-light, I could barely make her out. Long black hair falling around her face. Cheekbones like the balconies in a church. Lipstick, perfume, and powder. A face more interesting than pretty. Ghostly limbs moving as if in a dance. A kimono embroidered with dragons fell back from her arms. Then I remembered where I was, and who she must be.

"Hello, Fanny," I said to Bertrand's sister. "I like your robe." I recalled a day, years before, when Fanny was a pallid thirteen-year-old in mourning, wearing her customary black, passing a nargileh to the other children who had come with their parents to mourn her grandfather's death. "It's not black," I added.

She counted on her fingers. "That was seven years ago, almost to this day."

Fanny slid the kimono from one shoulder, and then the other. She had small breasts and a narrow waist with almost no hips. She lifted her hands over her head so that her breasts rose and her stomach stretched taut.

"Good Lord, what happened last night?" I asked.

"Bertrand brought you home after a fall. He said the hospitals were all already full of drunken soldiers. Anyway, you're not that hurt. But it was enough to make you pretty amorous."

"Did we—?" I asked.

She smiled. "You're still clothed."

"You're very beautiful," I said, trying to cover my tracks with this gallantry. As I kissed her, I was aware that I was also still drunk, as I sometimes forgot who she was and could only think of what I touched. I never said her name, certain I would say someone else's.

Outside, wind pushed against the house and the windows shuddered with rain. A dog whined and scratched at Fanny's door, then set to howling. We froze. There was the squeak of bedsprings, the rumble of feet, and a whispered command to the dog, which continued to growl.

Man and beast left the hallway, and the bedsprings creaked first under the returning weight of owner and then—a light leap—hound.

We waited for the house to become silent again.

Fanny sighed. "Bertrand will be jealous of me," she whispered. I was not thinking of Bertrand. I pressed my thumbs into the parentheses of her hips. Fanny kissed me between my brows.

"What?" I asked.

"He wouldn't mind being in my place right now."

I sat up in bed. My head ached cruelly.

"What?" I said again. I tried not to shout.

"I can't believe you didn't know," she said. "Why do you think they didn't let him into the army? What do you think 'psychologically unfit' means? We've all suspected it forever, though no one dared breathe a word until the last of Grandfather's generation died. It's not something we tell everyone, but it's 1940, for goodness' sake. Don't look so shocked. It's no different from our kind of love."

"Bertrand hasn't said anything to me," I said. "If he had wanted to, he would have mentioned it." Fanny shrank away. "Maybe this wasn't your secret to tell after all. You're ruining a friendship with your big mouth," I said. "Telling lies."

"I'm not telling lies," she said. She threw back the bedclothes and put on her robe. "He sent me here to tell you." A single sob escaped from her, capable of waking every one of the house's many sleepers. Fanny ran from the room with one bare foot—she had not waited to retrieve her other slipper.

WHEN I LOOK BACK ON THAT NIGHT IN JANUARY OF 1940, I shout at my adolescent apparition, "Run after her! Apologize! Take poor Fanny in your arms!"

And then I wonder. If Fanny and I had been tied to each other, if I had loved her rather than shamed her, would she, or even her whole family, have followed my own through what happened next? I often dream that I am standing, silver-haired and stooped—true to my present age—with Fanny's satin bedroom slipper in my hand.

That dawn, however, I dressed hurriedly. An army of servants patrolled the halls at all hours, so an invisible exit, even at six in the morning, was impossible. I pulled the heavy drapes aside, threw open the window sash, stood on the sill, and—final proof of my inebriated state—dropped two floors down to the ground below. I registered a shout behind me as I fell. My knees buckled, and I pitched forward, tearing my palms against the stones of the terrace.

I rose, gingerly. Behind me, Bertrand stood in his bedroom window. He gestured with his cigarette toward the balcony from which I had leaped. I turned away from him, and the front gate opened automatically, at a hidden command from inside the house.

Only later would I realize that Bertrand had sworn to tell me two secrets on my twentieth birthday. One, Fanny had revealed to me: in fact, on the day Bertrand had promised to tell me himself. By the time I ascertained the second, it was 1945 and I had not so much as spoken to or seen Bertrand or any member of his family in that half of a decade. No one had considered that France could fall.

PART THREE

AUGUST 27, 1944

COURTESY OF THE NATIONAL ARCHIVES

Salle des Martyrs, Jeu de Paume Museum, circa 1940–1944

Chapter Seven

THE SILENCE OF THE CITY AT HALF-PAST FIVE IN the morning felt supernatural. The sky was gray and low, as if someone had stirred ash into milk. From the passenger's window, I watched petals, confetti, ticker tape, a woman's glove, and a handkerchief spin past, lifted and twirled by an invisible presence that still celebrated yesterday's rout of the *Boches* from Paris. We drove a wood-burning car resurrected from a bygone era and bought from a butcher. The tires of the *gazogène* thudded softly as they rolled over upturned cobblestones, broken bottles, and bullet shells. They had lost much of their air in the fifteen-hour drive from Le Puy. From behind where my father and I sat in the truck's cab, the old butcher's meat hooks rocked against each other and the engine gave off a drowsy smell. The auto made a wide arc onto rue de La Boétie, and Father pumped its brakes. The rhythmic crunching and clanking noises slowed, and I heard the celebratory pop of rifles to the southeast, in the direction of the place de la Concorde. Then all was quiet again, save for the knocking from the meat hooks and the crackle and drop of a piece of wood burning in half and breaking into the fire.

Up and down rue de La Boétie, our neighbors' windows were darkened by blackout paper, and at first glance I thought our home was no different. With a grinding of gears, the vehicle came to a halt.

Another piece of wood broke and settled in the combustion box. We were home at last, and neither of us moved. I had not seen my street in four years and three months.

Father thumped the steering wheel with his hands. When he turned to me in the murky light, his eyes looked bruised. "Shall we?" he asked.

The familiar flooded my senses: the bronze post, the depression in the curb from trucks driving up to the gallery door, the tile facade of the bakery, and the gold address integers—*2* and *1*. By the time my years numbered the same, we were living in Nice at the Palais de la Méditerranée, which my mother referred to as "the dog pound." Other hotels held ten or fifteen people to a room. We were three when we should have been a hundred.

I inventoried impressions I had not known I might ever lose. This was the sidewalk where I had caught Rose's hand, her coat open though the day was brisk, and said, *Mother insists we leave*, and she said, *Your father gave me the key to the vault*. As if he already knew that she would refuse to come with us.

I told myself, that day in August 1944, that it was unreasonable to expect Rose to be at the gallery, standing on the sidewalk, awaiting us, her beauty shimmering like the heat on the road. Yet if she had been there, I would not have been surprised, as if the force of wishing could have made it so.

I took two strides away from the car and pressed my face to the gallery window. The blackness inside was granular and quivering. I could make out the white marble mantelpiece, gray in the dawn.

"What do you see?" Father asked. He stood next to the car, rubbing his hands above the brazier.

"The mantel," I said.

"What, the shades aren't down?"

In five broad steps, he was over the curb and at the gate. His ring of keys jingled and the metal-barred door to the foyer opened, leading to a second door. Rust blossomed over its lock, as if it had been in a flood and the waters had withdrawn. Father stepped aside, and with a shove from my shoulder, it gave.

We took in the smell of burned things. There had been a fire.

The carpet had been seared away in large swaths. Holes were gouged in the walls where the fire had spread. The skylight had shattered, scattering glass. The spandrels clung like metal spiderwebs. Father jerked forward and the floor stuttered beneath our steps.

We entered the second room of the gallery. The fire seemed not to have stretched here, though the room was coated with a light ash. We passed into Father's office, with the vault beneath the false floor, where we had hidden the last ninety-seven paintings in the hours before we fled Paris for the South. We had hauled sacks of lime, each as big as a boxer's punching bag, into the corners of the storage room to protect the paintings from the damp for the months we expected to be away. Another 250 paintings—awaiting Father's next exhibitions or sale at a later year—were already in the depository of the Chase Bank.

We descended into the vault on steps that sprang out automatically when the floor slid back, with a mechanism like a cuckoo clock. There were no paintings, only exploded sacks of lime, sodden and gummy, and a cigarette stub on the stairs. Father rested with his hand against the wall. We stayed there only a moment—there was nothing to look at or for. I helped him up the stairs, out of the vault, my hand at his elbow. We were stricken and silent. There were no barriers between this moment (Father, moaning softly) and another one that I could not quite grasp, in which I also wandered around that second gallery room and wept and there was the smell of something burned, and the paintings on the walls were covered with black, and an identical great loneliness reached up a paw and knocked me aside so that I felt askew and utterly at a loss.

Father and I gathered papers from the floor. Communist propaganda, pamphlets with mangled spelling, copies of a Fascist newspaper that had been, it appeared, published in our house before the liberation, denunciation letters from neighbors I knew. In one, a veteran from the Great War demanded the government issue him a new pair of shoes since his cobbler had, much to the veteran's irritation, disappeared. We were archaeologists in our own tomb.

I looked toward my father and watched him grow pale. I thought, *My father has begun to die.*

Yet when I reached to take his hand, he snatched it back as if I had bitten him.

"This is no time for the sentimental," Father said, and instantly I felt ashamed. "Someone's here."

"I feel it, too."

"Not that. There is a noise in the hallway."

The voices belonged to two figures, one in a stockinged cap sewn with a red star. He opened his palm to show us his brass knuckles and then swiped his fist through the air. The other had a pistol and said, "Don't make me use this." We ran.

Outside, Father stumbled over the doorstep, hurtled forward, and fell to the ground. His hands went to his mouth. For a moment, I thought he was uninjured. Then he parted his lips and blood burbled forth with specks of broken teeth in its stream.

At the hospital, while Father waited to be fitted with a bridge for his gums that would make all his food taste like tin, we listened as a nurse admitted a man who had shot himself while celebrating in the streets. Our victory had already become stupid.

Chapter Eight

IT WAS THEN THAT WE LEARNED. FATHER SAW TWO skeletal men at the Hôpital de la Charité. The Soviets liberated a camp named Majdanek, which sounded like a bone stuck in my throat. We staggered into and out of a newsreel in which we saw the horror of the Jews in the extermination centers of the East. There was open weeping in the theater, and also a few who called out "propaganda," "lies," and "unbelievable." Then, posted on a wall near the Métro, printed on broadsheets of newspaper, were pictures of bulldozers pushing heaps of bodies. Soon these photographs were replaced by pictures of everyday German citizens led through the camps, in fur coats, with their handkerchiefs pressed to their mouths. Father went to the Red Cross agency with a list of friends we had not heard from, but they turned us back, saying it was too soon.

Father grew weak and listless. Distracted by this unfamiliar version of my once-gleaming father, thinking only of him, I went on a walk and was struck by a blowsy old man piloting a bicycle too small for his fat. A crowd knotted around, asking if I was injured. I said I was fine, that I had just had a bit of a shock. I wandered down the street, feeling shattered, trying not to stumble, repeating, "A bit of a shock, a bit of a shock," like a children's nursery song.

One, two, three days passed. I felt half mad with my desire to search for Father's paintings, but some plan of his always held us back, as if he were afraid of what we would find, and then another newsreel would be released and we would again be delayed.

On the first day that the Bureau des étrangers announced it would hear cases—we qualified, unbelievably, as foreigners—I stood in line three hours before it opened and my father joined me four hours later.

"Stop scowling, please," Father said. "You shouldn't scowl around these people."

Rose haunted me ever more strongly. Perhaps, finding the news from the reels incomprehensible, my mind sought a familiar sorrow. I ran into the street once, sure that I could feel her presence. And yet she, too, was invisible.

Through the mire of bureaucracy for which my country is so famous, I pursued my father's paintings. One agency required a form from a second, which necessitated a stamp from the third, which had to be filed by a date that had already passed in order to make an appointment with an officer at the first, who would soon leave his post and be replaced by a younger uniformed man who demanded a whole new set of papers. None of my father's records from before the war could be found. We presumed that most of them had been burned, though that did not explain why his accounting file at Chase Bank, which dated back to 1933, had also disappeared. Neither Matisse nor Picasso kept careful books; they relied on my father and his assiduous assistants. Hence we had no documentation for any painting Father had acquired or, just as importantly, sold, in the seven years before the invasion. The works he had bought through the auction houses would be accounted for, but those were often lesser ones; masterpieces were purchased directly from the master. Since my father had had no written contracts with either Matisse or Picasso, we learned (through a newspaper article) that both had adopted new art dealers in his absence. War stopped neither production nor commerce. Picasso went to Kahnweiler, his dealer from before the Great War, and Matisse, so we heard, betrayed my father with an American.

If Father was crushed, he hid it behind the soliloquies he delivered, maddeningly, in a raised voice, to the tailors, cobblers, upholsterers, and grocers in line with us at the different refugee agencies: "The act of painting is munificent, and yet the artist himself is rarely generous. When his artwork is lauded and he is enriched, it is because of his genius. When his paintings are ignored and he has to tighten his belt a notch, it is the fault of the art dealer. And yet he can exist without me, whereas I cannot exist without him." The agency had closed before we reached its door. We walked down to the boulevard Saint-Michel. Father shrugged and ducked into a four o'clock newsreel.

From there, I passed the Luxembourg Gardens, where, I had read, one of the final battles for the city had taken place. The dirt was churned up as if it had been chewed, and the remains of a German six-pounder gun were buried in a trench that zigzagged the length of the avenue. The bars of the park's gate stuttered alongside me. Before the war, on a rare snowfall, this section of the Luxembourg would have been closed off, so that passersby could admire how snow draped its fountains and grassy hillocks. In springtime, girls chased hoops and boys proudly carried their toy boats, still wet from the fountain, in solemn outstretched arms. Now it was unrecognizable, except for the gate.

I descended into the train station and rose again at Les Halles, intending to return to our hotel on the boulevard Sébastopol. As I climbed to the top of the Métro stairs, I had a sudden feeling of the vast tunnel behind me and the locomotive whisking away with swaying, stupefied bodies inside. A black van idled at a stoplight. It was the only car on the street, which struck me as uniquely sinister. We had heard that there were mobile vans in which deported Jews were poisoned, a story that we had dismissed at the time as too ghastly to be true. The black car sped forward, its tailpipe streaming fumes, and I had again the sense that I had ascended from the Métro into the wrong city and in a body that could not quite contain me.

At the hotel, the concierge told stories of girls who had once consorted with the enemy left with shaved heads and an O branded on their brows, a vengeance carried out unchecked because everyone was afraid of being called a collaborator, and, in those days, we heard that many such accused were shot. One late night, I thought I heard

Rose's name bounced over the concierge's counter (though I also heard it while listening to water drop from the faucet into the sink, in the jingle of money on the bus turnstile, in the straining of the violins in a Rossini broadcast), but when I asked the speaker to repeat himself, he eyed me strangely and said, "I'd stay away from politics if I were you, young man."

AS IF I COULD NOT ACCEPT THE WORLD I HAD EMERGED in, during those first days in Paris, I awoke persistently expecting to find the dark rooms in which we had spent the war: those of Monsieur Bickart's farmhouse in Le Puy, and its odor of the chicken coop, the dray's stamp and whinny, the earthy smell of the green lentils, and the fond way our protector rubbed their stalks between his fingers. The relative simplicity of that time now seemed like a luxury. I worked in the fields alongside Monsieur Bickart. The soil was black and rich from the volcanoes that had spread themselves over Le Puy a millennium before. Above the distant town stood a bronze Virgin, who blazed when the morning sun found her hillside.

Monsieur Bickart called me Jacques, the name of his nephew who had worked a summer on his uncle's farm in 1931, after the Depression. Jacques's boots, which I wore, were a size too big, and I stuffed their toes with newspaper. If any of the citizens of Le Puy believed I was Jacques, they were either very young or so old they had become young again. My parents were required to remain hidden in the house and, often for long stretches, in the root cellar. We supposed Monsieur Bickart did not want to test his neighbors' tolerance as, to begin with, he was a Protestant and so already under suspicion.

Bickart possessed an accordion, of which both he and my mother were jealously fond. Each waited impatiently for the other to finish playing. One day, in passing, a neighbor complimented Monsieur Bickart on his astounding progress on the instrument. That evening, the accordion broke, which was nearly a crisis in the household, as our host decided it was best not to fix it. Mother sulked until Monsieur Bickart gave her the lace-making kit that had once belonged to his grandmother. Following a manual printed in the 1860s, Mother taught herself to make guipure, the kind of filet lace for which the Massif Central is known throughout the world.

We paid Monsieur Bickart for our protection and care, a single enormous sum, the total of which I never learned, that had been withdrawn from my father's safe before we left Paris. Withdrawn from the safe because, by the time we fled, access to our accounts at the Chase Bank was already compromised. It took my father and Auguste days to realize no bank teller would let them do anything other than make a deposit, and so they left empty-handed. Those accounts, though, in the weeks after our return to Paris, in the dingy hotel by the markets of Les Halles, were my one comfort. It was said that the presidents of the Banque de France, Crédit Agricole, and Crédit Lyonnais all kept their money and treasure at the Chase Bank. Surely, these would have been untouchable.

IDLY, ONE SEPTEMBER AFTERNOON, WHILE TRYING TO engage my father in something other than reading the newspaper, I asked him if, while I looked for the paintings, he should purchase anew the works of his former artists.

Father replied, "I bought paintings in the twenties and thirties, expecting to sell them in the forties. I can no longer afford what I once owned."

I did not know what to say and left the room. As I stalked about outside, my thoughts returned to Rose. She, of all people, seemed to offer a solution. We had been in Paris for eighteen days and I had not yet seen her. The thought struck me as nearly inconceivable. The Louvre remained a locked fortress. I had even been to the lycée she attended as a prize scholarship student before she entered university. I haunted 21, rue de La Boétie, too: the first time, I saw a young man sleeping on the floor with a rifle beside him. When I returned that day, the gate was locked with a chain as thick as my wrist.

At our hotel I asked the concierge to ring the museum once more for me. As he did, I studied his face with its florid skin and webbing of blood vessels. His hands shook when he held the telephone, as mine did when he passed me its receiver. I gave my name and asked the switchboard operator to connect me to Rose Clément. She said, "Who?" I repeated Rose's name. I knew then that she was married. The concierge smiled at the crossword in his lap and clucked his tongue, while I waited and blinked at the ceiling.

The operator returned and requested that I not contact this person again. I sputtered to the dead line. I wondered what my crime had been. The concierge gazed at me unsteadily when I handed him the telephone. His nose was red and resembled a potato. "Hope is the devil wearing a new coat," he said, after a long pause, and returned to his puzzles.

I climbed the stairs to our empty rented room and stood by its window. The trucks rumbled by and belched their fumes into the dim space. There was the bell of the knife grinder, with his grindstone attached to his motorcycle by a rickety cart. Housewives, maids, and cooks streamed outside, their hands thick with knife handles, the blades pointing down like mechanical fingers. I too wanted to make my dull self sharp.

MY MOTHER COULD NOT PLAY AN OUT-OF-TUNE PIANO, but I could, so I walked down to the Seine, past plane trees and their bark flecked as if a thousand boys with pocket knives had been at them, to the *antiquaires* on the quay.

I looked in several shop windows before I found my vendor. His wares were not prints of great value, but were on quality paper with clear colors and lines. From the stoop, I examined the engravings: a map of Versailles and its emerald gardens and fountains impossibly blue, an eighteenth-century curricle, and a preening cockatoo with a stiff red comb. The shop's owner had displayed his prints in frames of good taste—in fact, the frames were finer than the prints themselves, so as to trick the untrained eye. I felt my father's presence.

As I walked into the shop, my eyes adjusted to the smoke-dimmed haze. I ducked to avoid a low-hanging chandelier. A figure in a black coat with a hairless head hunched over a desk, studying a paper he held close to his face. I planned to stride toward the man at the front of the store—I was a newly sharpened knife, after all. Instead, the long sleeves and swinging hem of my jacket, sized in the years before the war, threatened towers of teacups with every step.

The shopkeeper lowered his paper. He had a glass eye. The marble fixed on me, while the other jerked up and down. He took in my person—the fray at my sleeve, the wrinkles in my pants, the muddy specks on my shoes.

"You look familiar," the Cyclops said, in a voice like a radio actor.

"I have a familiar-looking face," I said. Perhaps my father had been in this store after all? I had his eyes, I supposed, and the nose, long and round at its end.

"You were here once before."

"Yes." The eye slid toward the door as a couple paused in the store window. The woman wore a cape with long white gloves. After a moment, her escort pulled her along by the crook of her arm.

"Now that the old guard is gone, you've all grown so young," he said. I tried to tell where his eye was focused. "Would you like to see my acquisitions since your last visit?"

"Very much so."

"I'm a family man," he said. "I wouldn't keep this kind of a collection. But how else is one to stay in business?" He opened a drawer marked ARCHITECTURAL DRAWINGS and took out a box covered in leather.

I was shown one pornographic photograph after another. They were all of children, little boys and girls. The legs and hair-covered hands of grown men hulked in the background, or to the side of the frame. The lips of the girls shone with lipstick. I winced inside as each page sliced to the bottom of the pile and another sliced to the top.

"You don't like them," he said. "I can tell. The collection is picked over, I admit it. I'll have new ones by next Thursday. You can leave just a small payment and I'll lay aside the very best. I have an eye for a gentleman's favorites."

I saw that there were drawings underneath the photos. "I've considered starting a collection," I said. "Nudes from the middle or so of the last century." He set down the box. "I can't pay much. But every man deserves his own treasure trove of beauty."

He gazed at me with great feeling. "It is true, young man; they can take many things away, but never that." I studied his face. There were nicks from where he had cut himself shaving, short scratches as if a cat had leaped at his cheek and tried to cling to it. I looked down.

And there she was, an early Manet, fluttering on the top of the pile of sketches from another scaly box labeled NUDES, XIXÈME. My Cyclops could not know, otherwise his hands would have trembled as mine did, now wadded and clammy in the pockets of my coat. Olympia was not yet the proud whore trying to pose as a grand woman. Here she looked half-witted, with a blond pompadour and a ribbon tied comically around her neck, as if she were a Christmas gift.

I thought of my father and Matisse.

I first showed interest in several lesser prints.

"A real Degas, monsieur," the Cyclops assured me of another picture. "A pastel, a *café concert.* Any man would be proud to start his collection with such a masterpiece."

I asked for a magnifying glass to admire the counterfeit Degas's faulty monotype. "Isn't this a beauty, monsieur. Yet surely it's too rich for me." I inquired about two more cheap imitations and, gathering my grease-stained gloves, said, "Let me see that top sketch again. The nude with the red bow—that looks hastily done." I hoped my voice did not quiver. They say those with poor vision have keen hearing.

"I've had trouble pricing this one," the Cyclops said.

"Why?" I asked.

"A young man brought it to me after he'd bought the lot from someone in the government who was transferred to the colonies. You know how that went, those last few months." He named a price, I hesitated, he lowered it, I frowned, he lowered it, and I bought a Manet for what Bertrand said he paid for a girl at Chez Suzy in Pigalle. I handed the man his bills, and I stepped out into the street—how could it still be daylight?—my face was wet and my Manet was in a wax envelope. It cannot rain, I thought.

I crossed the street to the Seine side. The black windows looked like missing teeth in the white apartments on Île Saint-Louis, and in the distance the spire of the Palais de Justice pricked the sky.

My new sketch would not have lingered, unpurchased, on a legitimate market. The last honest owner of this Manet could only have been a connoisseur. Who he was, I would never know.

Chapter Nine

I RETURNED TO BOULEVARD SÉBASTOPOL. SÉBASTOPOL, I thought, another battle from another time. The trees that lined the street were beautiful, heavy with early autumn leaves. I followed the gated remains of the arcades, remnants of the older tangled Paris, and held the Manet close to me. The print could take us from this place.

I opened the door to our hotel room with a bang and had flung my hat down on the chair before I realized that my father was in bed, fully clothed and with his shoes still tied.

"Are you sick?" I asked. Father shook his head. "Didn't you go to the government offices today?" My father nodded. "And?" He held his palm out, to indicate *nothing*.

"Don't you see, all the paintings are gone. They were taken, systematically or piecemeal, but there are none left."

"We're not looking in the right places yet," I said. I sat on the edge of his sagging bed and, with trembling fingers, withdrew the Manet.

He sat upright at the sound of the wax paper. "What's this?" he asked, in the old pleased voice.

I handed him the sketch. "From a shop along the quay. A talisman, sent to us from the past."

"Nonsense," he said. His face was gaunt and frightened.

"Look at it."

Father ran his finger along the margin of the page, which was bent. He hesitated. "The damage to the picture is fresh and very minor," he began. He spoke as if in a trance, as if I were not in the room at all. "The creases here are not yellowed. This was well cared for until recently." He drew the room's single chair toward him, cleared it of its clothing, and rested the drawing on the seat. "I see no fading of the paper, so one presumes that it was not kept in a frame, on display, but was guarded as part of a collection. Hence its owner had others, larger, more beautiful oil paintings, for his walls."

"It's stolen," I said.

He looked at me with disgust. "No, looted."

"I don't understand the difference," I said.

"This is useless." Father turned the sketch over to see if there were markings on it. There were none.

"How much did you pay for it?" he asked. I told him and he drew his breath in. "There's no question. You must give it back."

"To whom?"

"Exactly!" Father shouted. "Don't you see how they made this happen?"

"No," I said. My head felt leaden.

"Our paintings have disappeared, yes, you understand that."

"For God's sake."

"No proper owner who had so many paintings that he did not even desire to display this would have sold his Manet to whatever fraud you found hawking his wares down by that filthy river.

"This painting speaks to us, can't you hear it? It explains that the *Boches* stole paintings and, unaware of their values, sold them to third-rate shams, who also were dumb to their value, so that now you can buy it for next to nothing, still knowing it is four times as much as the picture-vendor paid. It would have come from a private collection, because it would have been protected in a museum, and if it were from an art gallery, the *Boches* would have had a better sense of the worth of the merchandise they were looting. But they didn't dare touch the national collections, only the private ones.

"It is not a Manet I have ever cared about," Father said. He put the magnificent sketch back in its wax sleeve, rose from the bed, and threw open the window. In came the sound of a colicky child, wailing. In a room across the boulevard stood a pale woman with her breast bare, trying to offer it to her infant. The child turned his face from the nipple, crying inconsolably.

"Our missing artwork falls under the ludicrous jurisdiction of the Bureau des étrangers. We must return the Manet, Max. If not to them, then via the Louvre. You may regret this later, but I will not."

"Consider it an investment," I argued. "For the short term, even. If our other accounts are closed, then we have money in this."

"Impossible," my father said, and lit a cigarette. "The painting is unsellable on the legitimate market. Any fine painting brings its provenance with it. No respectable dealer would buy this Manet from you."

He paused and tapped his lip while his cigarette burned and smoked.

"We'll return to Le Puy soon enough."

"And stop looking?" I asked.

"Throw Death off your scent, Max. Give it all away. And when it is taken from you, say it is God's will." He blinked. "Take this to the Louvre," he said. "It will be your skeleton key to her shut door."

I had hoped, in the long car ride from Le Puy, that this time with Father would allow me to know him better, so as to avoid angering him, so as to burnish his love. I could have one hundred years, I thought now, and still that would not be enough.

That night, with the Manet in a drawer so neither of us would look at it or begin our argument anew, Father said, "On my honeymoon with your mother in Capri, on our first day there, we took a sail. Floating out at sea, I saw an abandoned life vest. I did not draw your mother's attention to it because it seemed an ill omen. When our boat ride was over, as we walked along the beach, Mother found a pair of eyeglasses, unbeknownst to me. Before dinner, I said I planned to take a stroll. Mother said she would rest. We met at the police station, each with his evidence. The next morning, the schoolmaster's body washed up on the shore." I thought Father had fallen asleep when he added, "I cannot stand to be in Paris much longer."

I took the Manet to the Louvre several days later, along with a letter to Rose, of which I had written a dozen versions. When I asked for Madame née Clément, two guards appeared and again, with an increasing degree of hostility, I was instructed to leave her in peace. A secretary took the wax paper package from me and stood at her desk, waiting for me to depart. Surely my unimposing presence did not unsettle them. Therefore, it was something about Rose, and I did not know what that was, other than that she too had unsettled me.

THE MONTH OF OCTOBER PASSED IN A STUPOR, AS IT often does, though the Soviets were marching through Yugoslavia, then Hungary, and Czechoslovakia. Amsterdam was without electricity. The vigorous Americans liberated the Philippines. The German they called the Desert Fox was dead, supposedly by his own hand. And then it was November and the rains began. By December, there were bitter slanting storms, leading to a winter season at which historians and meteorologists would later marvel as the coldest in France since the Prussian siege of 1870–71 forced Parisians to eat the animals in the zoo. (I still remember reading that the first to go were two elephants, Castor and Pollux, known as the "pride of Paris." The tiger and a pair of lions were spared because a neat kill would have been too dangerous to execute. The primates starved to death because of the belief that to eat them would have been, as I recalled reading, "akin to cannibalism." Those were different times. Perhaps.) The offensive in the Ardennes began, and rumors were that casualties were high.

My head still throbbed faintly at night, on the spot where I had fallen against the curb, and when my blood pressure rose, it bothered me then, too, as when I went from gallery to gallery, asking the dealers if they had any Vlaminck or Laurencin sketches for sale, since such modern artwork would betray the invisible fingerprints of wartime acquisitions. Few Frenchmen were buying in those days, so my presence was enough to rouse suspicion, if not alarm, and more than once I was asked to leave. There were times when I was simply overwhelmed by outside news. In January, after the liberation of Auschwitz-Birkenau, I found myself almost shouting in a gallery on rue Bonaparte, and had to stop searching for days.

Then it was February. Dresden smoldered. I returned to our hotel in midafternoon, though it was already dusk outside, as if the clouds of ash had drifted west and darkened our skies, too. The key to our room hung on its peg like a ripe fruit and, for once, the concierge lifted his nose from his book of puzzles to peer at me with boozy interest. He raised his eyebrows and muttered *"Hein?"* This alarmed me, and I took the stairs three at a time.

I arrived on the fourth floor and saw a wedge of light from our room in the darkness of the corridor. I looked through the door before pushing it open. Two men in American uniforms stood facing my father, who sat on a chair in the farthest corner of the room, atop my clothing from the previous day. Father stared at something outside my line of vision. I thought I detected a third presence in the room, which, when I pushed open the door, I understood was not human.

The two soldiers turned and one slapped his massive hand to the pistol at his side. My father saw me and said, "Thank God." The soldiers parted and I stepped between them into the center of the room, by the foot of the bed.

Three paintings tilted against its chipped headboard. Two I recognized and one I did not: the familiar pair were from Father's last Cézanne exhibition before the war. In one, blocks of color—reds, pulsating greens, and browns—gave way to rooftops, mountains, and walls. The second painting was sky and tree branch, with the sky's blue straining, ready to push out in three dimensions between the reedy trees. The third frame held a Cézanne portrait—an earlier work, I guessed—of the artist gazing sidelong at his mirror.

I looked at my father and then at the Americans. "You must be Max," the taller of the two said. He addressed me as *tu*. American informality never ceased to irritate me. His French was assured and quick, but spoken in the heavy accent of those who, I would come to learn, lived in the Midwest. His spectacles reflected the lamplight, as if they were mirrors. Both men had removed the name patches from their uniforms.

"They found your paintings," I said to my father.

"Tell them," the second soldier said in English, "that if we say how we got them, it'll cost extra." He was fair-haired with a wrestler's neck.

Father stood. "Get out," he told the soldiers.

I gave my father a furious look. "How much?" I asked him under my breath.

"Five hundred thousand francs," the tall soldier said. "And that's a deal."

"You said four hundred thousand, right?" the wrestler mumbled. The other shook his head once.

"We'll get more from someone else," the tall soldier said. "But we thought it was only polite to offer them to you first."

"Let me look at the paintings one last time," I said, in a voice thick with melancholia. I was deciding which one to destroy. I chose the Cézanne landscape. How many valleys of houses had he painted? A Cézanne face, and his own at that, was a rarity. In the second painting, I loved the way the sky seemed to burst through the sapling trees as if it was a form, an organ, or alive and sentient, and pressing against the canvas.

With a gesture, I asked to examine the portrait.

"Sure." The wrestler replied in English. Even with the two khaki-colored Americans crowding our room, the pictures seemed to breathe space into it, to shift the distances and depths as if all along these had been mutable. On the back of the Cézanne portrait was a family crest, a crown with five arrows gathered behind it, and then a stamp in Fraktur script. I could make out the letters A-B-E-T-Z. Now I knew where it came from; this was Rothschild booty. The palace of the Jews, turned over from one conqueror to another. I had a flash of envy, too. The Rothschild painting was the rarest, the most precious of the three.

Father leaned over my shoulder and breathed in my ear, "Don't you dare." He had guessed my intentions. I let go of the painting.

"We don't bargain with thieves," Father said. "Once you give these back to me, I will be happy to sell them to you for their market price." The wrestler laughed and gathered up the frames roughly and shoved them into a limp rucksack.

"Too bad," said the taller one.

"You'll regret it," said the other.

"In exchange, then, I have something for you." Father's English was halting. "I have a curse for you to take back to America and give to your wife and daughter and son."

"Please." The taller one laughed, snatching the rucksack from his friend.

"Hush, Bub," the wrestler said.

"Your firstborn will die, maybe before she walks, maybe when you are an old man, but you will live to see the funeral and hold dirt in your hands and—how do you say"—he made a scattering gesture—"over a grave. I give one curse, since, after it, everything decays."

The tall man grinned but twisted his wedding ring. The wrestler patted his pocket to check that his wallet was still there, then crossed himself on our threshold.

"Kikes," the wrestler said, and they closed the door with a bang.

I started into the hallway. "Stop," Father said. My hand was on the doorknob. I turned it. "Please don't," Father pleaded. Since I was moved by his curse—that the worst fate Father could imagine was the loss of a child as precious as I—I did not go after the American soldiers.

FATHER SET OUT FOR LE PUY IN EARLY MARCH AND returned to Paris a week later. He told me only that Mother had rented a cottage and begun to give free piano lessons to the neighbors. He spoke as if he were continuing a conversation with himself. "Eventually, my other paintings will rise. They will float to the surface, as the bodies of the drowned do. But not in my lifetime. Perhaps in yours. Which explains your zeal." His speech was uninflected, an accusation lying flat, almost a threat: *You will outlive me.* Then, lock-jawed, "Now we must go home together."

"Home to where?"

"To Le Puy." Mother refused to return to Paris until the Germans and the Japanese surrendered. "I spoke with Auguste today," Father said, not looking at me. "He was kept on in the house up until the fire."

"How did you find him?" I asked.

"I had a flash of brilliance." He snapped his fingers and grew animated as if turned on by a switch. "It came to me while I was waiting in the bread line. I remembered his sister's name, and that she lived near Chartres and worked at the candle factory for the cathedral. When I rang her up, Auguste answered." Father pulled the blanket over his feet and leaned back against the bed pillows.

"How is he?"

"We were both overcome when we realized we were speaking to each other after five years."

"And Lucie?" I asked.

"Still in Paris. And married, for the first time. And at her age." Lucie would have turned fifty-five or so, I imagined, though she had not seemed to change at all in the twenty years I knew her—not her jet-black hair, or her pinched face, or her fat man's laugh. "Her surname is Zbrewski or something difficult to pronounce. I have it written down." He gestured toward the leather address book on the bedside table.

The conversation with Auguste had mainly concerned my father's library of photographic plates. Before the war, Father used the plates to show collectors paintings he thought they might buy, as well as to keep documentation of the hundreds of works that had passed through 21, rue de La Boétie. The plates occupied seven cabinets, each three drawers tall, in a storeroom in our basement. Father would have preferred to keep them closer to his office, but Mother was afraid that the film would catch fire.

The Germans emptied the cabinets into paper sacks and labeled each with a painter's name. Then they put an announcement in the dailies that there would be a sale in two days' time. Picasso arrived four hours before the sale was to begin, and Auguste let him into the gallery. He purchased the complete collection of his own works, and those of Georges Braque, and filled the seats of a taxicab with the paper sacks.

"The plates sold for very little—each bag cost thirty francs," my father said. "I did not ask Auguste if he considered acquiring any. Who knows? Maybe he thought it fruitless to buy only thirty or forty plates when there were hundreds. Maybe any cost was more than he could spare. Perhaps he worried that we would not return to Paris to repay him."

"Picasso could have bought all the plates, ten times over," I said.

"You see, Max"—Father's fist came down on the bedside table and the lamplight quivered—"this is why we do poorly when we affix ourselves to objects. They lead to longing and to speculation. This makes a man sick." Father coughed. The curtains billowed, although the window sashes were closed.

"Like Goethe," I said, with hollow cheer. "*Let the observer look steadfastly on a small colored object and let it be taken away after a time while his eyes remain unmoved. The spectrum of another color will then be visible on the white plane. It arises from an image which now belongs to the eye.*"

Father rolled onto his side and slid both hands, their palms pressed together, beneath his cheek. I slept the same way, body curled like a fiddlehead, hands almost in prayer. So this had been coded in my blood. Not his prodigious memory and not his artistic clairvoyance. Neither his ease, nor confidence, nor grace.

"You're right, son," Father said, after a pause so long that once again I thought he had dropped off to sleep. "If Goethe is our guide, then we leave Paris tomorrow morning." His words came in a rush. "We've been dipped in the hatred. It's making my mind feel a little—" He shook the box of matches on the table. "I've been dreaming of my own father. Of shelling and gas. My mind plays movie reels of the Great War, though of course I have no actual personal true memory of the battlefields. So if I am dreaming of the war, I must in fact be dreaming of something else altogether."

I did not know how to respond. Father sat upright, opened the small black notebook he kept with him always, and withdrew from it a folded SNCF timetable.

"There's a ten o'clock train. If it's still running. That's a civilized hour. We'll be home after dinner. We shall surprise your mother."

I do not recall if I protested, though I must have, or, as I fell asleep that night in March of 1945, if it was my decided intention to flee from my father while he slept. I know only that when I awoke, I thought, I have to give him up. The idea seized upon me with the tenacity of a spasm and I leaped from bed. I could hardly keep my hands from making a clatter as I unhooked my coat, removed Father's billfold from the drawer, and took half his money. I lifted his black address book off the table and patted my pocket for our map of the city. I took Father's hat because it was nicer than my own, bundled up my suit and two shirts, and held my shoes in my hand. I opened the door and slipped my valise, heavier than I remembered, into the hallway.

"Where are you going?" Father asked, his voice thick.

"Just to the toilet," I said. "Go back to sleep."

"Won't you check on the baby?"

I hesitated in the doorway, halted by the strange question, which surely came from some dream—one parent's request that the other check on their sleeping child as if, with darkness each night, came death. I closed the door behind me.

I changed in the WC and made my way in damp stockinged feet to the foyer, where the concierge was eating a piece of buttered toast.

"I'm a creature of habit," he said, asking with narrowed eyes if I was going to turn him in for buying, or more likely selling, butter on the black market. We called those profiteers by the acronym of their goods: a BOF, for *bœuf, œuf, fromage*. "I was raised by nuns, you know. No one to call Mummy."

I nodded as if I understood. "New hat?" he asked brightly.

"Just today," I said.

"Yesterday," he corrected. "Good for you. I could use a new one as well." He touched his cap, a pillbox like an organ grinder's monkey might wear. We both gave a hushed laugh and I strolled out into the night.

Chapter Ten

I FOUND MYSELF IN A BAR IN THE MARAIS, WHERE the late-night drunks were leaving as the morning drunks arrived. I hoped a warm beer would calm my nerves. I told myself that it was Father who had forsaken me first. I only wanted to keep looking for the paintings because I was convinced they were close at hand and the time was right to find them. I could not acknowledge that I searched out of an incomprehensible compulsion, or that whenever a strange sadness crept upon me, my first thought, like a drunk to his drink, was of the gallery and my father's collection.

I must have drifted to sleep, for when I awoke, I had no recollection of the hours between five and seven. I read a newspaper (the date was March 10, the headline AMERICANS FIREBOMB TOKYO) and talked with a municipal worker who kept one finger hooked on the strap of his overalls and told tall tales of bare knuckle fights in the merchant marine. At ten o'clock, I staggered out onto the street.

A notice, with a six-sided star in one corner and a French flag in the other, flapped against the carousel by Métro Saint-Paul. It read:

> *Les absents* from the East are boarded at the Hôtel Lutetia. Friends and family are advised to visit the central information desk between seven and four o'clock, Sunday through Friday.

I thought of Bertrand. Yes, he was "absent." The word struck me uncomfortably. But I wasn't sure what they should be called, the Jews who had been deported, who walked like skeletons on the newsreel.

No, I could not accept that Bertrand had been arrested at all. He was too clever, too bright, too quick and foxlike, too charming to have been swept into the same trap. His absence made me sick with panic. They had the museum in their family's name, for God's sake. I tried to calm myself. I decided to go to the Hôtel Lutetia.

On the stroke of ten-thirty, I rose out of the Sèvres-Babylone Métro at the eastern corner of a park with a low gate and high hedge. Children shrieked from behind the bushes and, through a gap in the shrubbery, I watched them chase after one another, raising clouds of golden dust with their feet. One child stood off to the side, a boy in a blue jumper, scratching at the dirt with a knobby stick. Every few moments he paused and leaned on the branch, as if it were a cane, and watched the other children. On the swings, girls pumped their legs: skirt hems fluttered, curls bobbed, and shoes flashed. The creaky chains brayed like donkeys. The boy returned to his solitary digging with the point of the stick.

The hotel loomed before me. Its dun-colored exterior coiled around the corners of two grand avenues. The word LVTETIA burned in red electric lights over the thrusting central facade. It was a fortress, a cement arch of Art Deco design. I smelled the dust from the park and the coal-burning cars that one still saw frequently in those days following the war.

I waited for the light to change over the boulevard Raspail so I could cross to the hotel and join the knot of people clustered before the open doors of its central lobby. That crowd parted, for a moment, into a horseshoe shape, as if it were a stage for those of us waiting on the curb on the other side of the boulevard. A man with green army pants and strange yellow shoes leaned over a woman in a spring coat who wept so forcefully that he struggled to keep her standing. He had been carrying a burlap sack, which he dropped. Beans spilled out onto the street and the audience, in the horseshoe, bent to gather them.

I noticed other faces, lurking just inside the shadows of the rooms in the Lutetia, watching the tableau as I did. Traffic raced by. I wondered if the signal system was broken. The light did not change. A woman beside me pointed at one of the windows and shouted, "Lilianne Rossi!" and ran into the oncoming stream of cars as if they were phantoms. A horn blared. Brakes squealed. The woman was struck and her body made a dull sound and then flopped to the pavement. She wore a dress the color of lilacs. I had gone to the hotel expecting horrors, but not this one. For a moment, I thought she was dead. Then she rose, miraculously able to walk.

Something made me glance away, and in a flash I saw that my father was seated at the café outside the Lutetia. He heralded the waiter (also held rapt by the scene of the man in yellow shoes and the weeping woman) twice, unsuccessfully. Then the waiter stood in front of my father's table and blocked him from view.

I felt a small presence brush by me. It was the boy from the park, still holding the dusty stick in his hand. He picked his way around the accident without glancing its way and walked into the lobby of the hotel. In the distance a siren started its two-pitched wail.

I fled the scene, ran down into the Métro, and boarded the first train that appeared on the platform. My father must also have seen the advertisements for the central information center at the Lutetia. He too sought news of Bertrand's family. I told myself that I was not ready to see my father yet. I would return to him in a few days' time, once I had word of the paintings.

I WENT ONCE MORE TO THE LUTETIA THAT SPRING, IN the very early morning, as the street cleaners sprayed down the pavement and the water jumped into the air in a fine chromatic mist. It smelled rank because it came from the Seine, which was the color of a rotted lime.

I stood in the vestibule of the grand hotel, my eyes adjusting from the bright morning outside. Before me shifted a wall shingled with hundreds of pieces of paper on which were written names in block letters, then addresses, phone numbers, dates, and places: Sobibor,

Majdanek, Płaszów, and Auschwitz-Birkenau. There were codes that at the time I did not understand, their digits often preceded by the letter *A:* A-8019, A-500, A-7087. Many were written by parents looking for the children they'd left behind with neighbors and nuns.

I waited by the information desk, behind an old man who whispered in Yiddish to a volunteer. When he was sent away, disappointed, the volunteer greeted me.

"Good morning, sir." He spoke with exaggerated slowness.

"I'm here to see Bertrand Reinach," I enunciated deliberately, so he would recognize that I was calmer than the others.

"Very good," he said, and withdrew a slim book with gold leaf pages and a leather binding that read HOTEL LEDGER. He traced a tobacco-stained finger across a floor plan. His foot tapped as he looked.

From a hallway to my right, I heard a child wailing and, above us, the patter of feet. "Monsieur Reinach is not here," the man said. "I'm happy to show you the list of our current residents—"

I shook my head.

He glanced at the snaking line of people behind me. There were lines everywhere and always. "I truly am sorry." He spoke with an eastern accent. I pictured a map from a newsreel before the invasion of France, of streaming lines covering Poland, Lithuania, Hungary, and felt a wash of shame.

"You can contact the Red Cross displaced persons bureau," he said, the forms already in his hand, "and also UNRRA. It's all written here. Remember to consider all the different possible spellings of a name when you submit this to them. That may speed the process.

"We are glad to see you here," he said, as if I had been a guest at the hotel. I walked away.

In an unseen room, someone played piano, a Chopin étude my mother loved. I followed the sound. Twin girls, with identical blond braids, sat beside each other on the piano bench. One played only with her right hand, the other only with her left. They swayed in time with the music, which then abruptly stopped. One twin scolded the other in an unrecognizable language and pulled her hair. The second girl climbed down from the bench and ran to the volunteer to complain, chattering to him in the same bizarre speech. He left his podium and came to where I stood by the piano.

"Twins," he said to me. "There are several of them here, and these two speak only their own language. They invented it in the camp. I can usually guess what they're telling me, so I respond as best I can. They've begun to speak French. They'll forget their made-up tongue soon enough."

"Chopin," I said to the girl who remained on the bench, and I smiled at her as warmly as I could.

"Chopin." She beamed at me and began to play a different étude, though only the right hand. Her sister pushed past me and clambered to the bench, and the rumbling base joined the trilling treble.

"Bertrand Reinach?" I asked the girls. They twittered and kept playing.

I FOUND MYSELF AGAIN AT THE LOUVRE, AT THE ENTRYway to Rose's office, where I had time only to repeat my desire to see Madame Clément before a security guard built like the strongman from the circus hustled me out of the building, gripping my arm as if deciding whether or not to break it. Outside, released, I looked up at the guard and recognized him as a classmate from fourth form.

"Théo," I said.

"Max Berenzon? How did you get here? Sorry for the rough welcome." I remembered that Théo had also been a bully in school. I could still picture him wearing the dunce cap. During tests, his neck craned over my shoulder. After one, he had asked me, *When you read, how do you keep the letters from moving around?* I was surprisingly glad to see him.

"Everyone's very protective about Miss Clément," he said. "Some of the Résistants wanted to bang-bang-bang her." He made a pistol with his hand and fired it, making his finger, the muzzle, jump with each shot. "They came to the Louvre with their straight razors and the branding iron. She had to change her name, and they relocated her to a new apartment."

Rose, then, was unmarried, as I had sensed all along. As she had promised me.

Théo sized me up and down. "Never thought you and me'd fall for the same gal, Berenzon. Oh, it's clear from your face." He gave me a motherly pat on the shoulder. "I can tell you where Rose lives. No use in you wasting your time around this museum. All snobs, they are. They're about to send her on a trip to Switzerland or Zurich or some other place where there are caves with paintings in them?" He squinted at me.

"Lascaux?"

"No, different caves, with real paintings. Like, by What'shisname." He shook his head. "She lives at thirty-one, rue de Sévigné, fifth floor. Judging from her window, I'd say her door'd be the last one on the right. No point in me standing out in the street anymore, now that I've scared her, too."

"Thirty-one, rue de Sévigné?" I repeated. "Fifth floor, on the right."

"That's it," Théo said. I thanked him and received a bone-crushing embrace, which I tried to return.

"There's some muscle on you," he said, then called "Good luck!" after me as I ran. I could have lifted a house off its foundations.

Rue de Sévigné was not so far. I caught the door to the courtyard just as it was swinging shut and leaped up the stairs of the building. As I rounded the corner to the fourth floor, I recalled a teacher who had told our classroom of boys that there were a limited number of locks in Paris, and the chance that your house key could open another man's home was one in twenty-seven. On my father's key ring jangled a dozen keys or more.

After one more flight of stairs, I was at her doorway. I frantically tried to open Rose Clément's lock. On the sixth key, the door was opened from within and I stumbled forward into the arms of a slender boy. He pushed me away. "No one is here!" he shouted. I clutched the banister to keep from falling down the stairs.

"I'm lost, my mistake," I said.

He snarled and slammed the door. Undeterred, I tried the neighbor's, but none of the keys fit.

I left. It was growing dark and I did not know where I would spend the night. I had been staying in a fleabag hotel by the Gare de l'Est. After four days, the patroness let it be known that there was a five-day maximum. I understood that the limit did not apply to her regular clientele, only those she considered refugees. I wandered down rue de Sévigné, past the walled gardens of the great letter writer for whom the street was named. I rang the tired bells at the counters of six hotels. The only ones with rooms to let asked for more than I could pay.

Back out on the street, I heard singing, followed it, and found an open basement door. There were Jews inside—I was still in the Marais, after all—a dozen men in black, scattered like musical notes across the rows of benches. They swayed and bobbed and murmured and burst into song and then stood still, and then sat. I stood in the doorway, unwilling to enter.

"*Juif?*" A man hurried over, brandishing an ear trumpet. "Where is your tallis? Do you have teffilin?" I had none, I gestured. I took off my hat. "Leave it on!" I crept farther into the chilly room and stood in the fourth row.

At first I held the prayer book open and turned its pages when the men around me did. After an hour, I folded the book closed and held it against my chest.

I wished Bertrand were with me. At various times in his life, he had taken up Torah study, never staying with it for long and yet always returning to it.

I felt as if I were falling down a stairwell in a dream. Around me, the scraps of voices rushed forward and together like birds rejoining formation. The men covered their heads with their white prayer shawls and put their hands over their eyes. Each time I was left alone, staring out over this sea of ghosts. On the third time, a gnarled hand grabbed me on the shoulder and pulled me under the tent of his prayer shawl while the men sang words that made them cover their eyes in awe. The man kept his grip. His armpit reeked like a woolen coat in the rain.

Still, in this double enclosure—arm holding me close, white silken tent—the intimacy was overwhelming and I had to shut my eyes.

When the prayer was over, I turned to thank my protector. Three identical men, all my father's age, stood before me. They could have been brothers or prophets and were all immersed in prayer. Until one Hasid looked up and, with an eye as bright as a bird's, winked at me.

The men around us broke apart, finished praying at a signal I did not recognize. I looked down at the floor, unsure of what to do. My valise sat at my feet.

"So?" the friendly Hasid asked and made a hangdog expression, which I took to be my own. Behind him was shuffling, the stacking of prayer books into an uneven tower, and the minor chords of Yiddish.

"Are you lost?" He folded his prayer shawl into a worn velvet pouch that closed with a zipper.

"I'm not," I said.

"Lost in the spiritual sense," he replied.

"I won't be converted."

"Oy, I don't mean that either." He had an accent like my mother's. "Let me tell you a story. Two Chelmites went for a walk. The first one said, 'Look! Bear tracks!' The second one disagreed. 'No, those are deer tracks!' They were still arguing about it when they were hit by a train." He paused. "Well, you've lost your sense of humor," he said.

I did not know who Chelmites were. I looked down at his feet. He wore the same yellow shoes of the man I had seen at the Lutetia, holding up the weeping woman. Then I too got the joke and laughed once, loudly.

"But *nu*, what's so bad? You're young, you're not unpleasant to look at, you even had parents who took you for braces on your teeth."

"I don't know where I'll sleep tonight," I said, without having intended to tell him.

"No place to stay, is it? Not such a tragedy."

Chapter Eleven

CHAIM TENENWURZEIL SHOWED ME MY ROOM without any comment. I was to sleep in a narrow, short bed. With little else to unpack, I hung my father's coat in a closet with a splintery floor, next to a suit shrouded in tissue paper. A silken strip on the sleeve, the kind one usually removes, told me that Chaim had made the boy-sized set of clothes himself.

That night, as I lay awake, I thought of the strange series of events that had led me to this place. I rolled to my side and fumbled in my wallet for the scrap of paper on which I had written Rose's address. "Thirty-one, rue de Sévigné," Théo had told me. But Théo had never really learned to read. Théo had asked me how to keep the letters from sliding around on the page.

I dressed quickly and crept across the parlor. Picture frames glinted and the wind rustled the pages of the songbook open at the piano. Though Chaim had retired some hours ago, light still shone under his bedroom door.

I was in the hallway, on the stairs, and then the street. I sprinted toward 13, rue de Sévigné, not 31, the high stone wall of the Musée Carnavalet running alongside me, its long halls filled with imperceptibly swinging signs from old taverns and cobblers and apothecaries. I lit a match to read the list of names by the doorbell. One was unassigned, so I pressed it and leaned back between the lengthening rings to see if the noise made a hand reach. I rang and rang, but the rooms on the fifth floor remained dark. The church on rue de Rivoli chimed eleven o'clock.

With a squeak, a window on the ground floor swung outward onto the street. It revealed a woman in a nightdress with an infant in her arms.

"That's enough," she said. "Are you looking for her, too?"

"I'm Max Berenzon. I'm sorry to disturb you. Mademoiselle Clément is a family friend. I've just returned to Paris—from the camps," I lied, to my surprise. "I live with another *absent* at forty-five, rue de Sévigné. Forty-five, like this year we've been given. Isn't that odd, to come back from the war, and move to the same street as one's dear friend?" I babbled on, as if my mind were rattled.

The woman's pinched expression flickered. She was close. Her wan hand parted the darkness and touched my cheek.

"What we have done—what France has done—it will take generations to atone, to recover." The baby in her arms whimpered and curled his fists in his eyes. "Tired boy, tired boy," she murmured, kissing the child but looking at me. "You could come in here," the woman offered. "Since your friend left for Switzerland tonight. Working for the government. Or a Swiss museum. Or was it a bank?"

My mind bent around the word *Switzerland.*

"Tonight?" I repeated.

"Tonight, yes, tonight, tonight," she sang, rocking the infant from side to side. His bald head was like a pale egg.

"Won't you come in here, young man? Baby's tired, he'll be sound asleep." Her finger twirled around my earlobe. "Or we could even leave him downstairs and creep into your friend's apartment. I have the keys—I clean it on Wednesdays. She'll never guess."

"No!" I backed away from her and began to run in the opposite direction. A phonograph chided me from its open window. *"Tu? Tu? Tu! Piccolo iddio!"* the soprano sang, above the gathering waves of violins.

"I know what they did to you," she rasped. "Give me a chance to repay the debt. My name is Marianne," she said, in a loud, clear voice. "Look at me, look at me! My God, will someone look at me?"

Around us, the street stirred to life. I stared at Marianne, who held aside her dressing gown to reveal her nipple like a target and her bare breast, as if she were Marianne in the Delacroix painting.

I turned down rue de Sévigné and cut through the narrow, smaller streets. The city's old fortress walls were visible above me, silent and runic. Here was the place du Marché Sainte-Catherine.

I did not believe that Rose had left Paris.

I sat at a café table in the western corner of the plaza. I could tell the night was a pleasant one.

A wiry man with tawny skin and matted hair appeared in the plaza, wheeling a bicycle strapped with bundles of rags. A German shepherd trotted behind him. The vagabond set about displaying his collection on the plaza's cobblestones: an army canteen, a jug of liquid, matches, a flak helmet, a broken straw hat, and three metal stakes, each with a rag bound at its tip.

"Fools and fishermen," he shouted, running in a circle in the center of the plaza. "You sit there licking your fingers while my dog chews her tail until it is nothing but raw flesh and bloody fur!" The bitch lifted her head, and her ears rose to two points. Her tail, intact, curled like a question mark behind her.

The vagabond darted to the teahouse across from where I sat and squatted down so that his face was level with the sitters'. *"I'm like the king of a rain country, rich but sterile, young but with an old wolf's itch!"* he bellowed. A man with an eye patch drew his arm around his companion. In the spotlight of the teahouse, the vagabond pulled his tattered shirt over his head and threw it to the ground. He had ropes of muscles and a starved look. The square of sky above the plaza was blue-black, and I strained my eyes to follow his movements.

"Do you have gold in your veins," he asked, "or milk from a witch's teat?" He lit a torch and held it in his right hand, then took a long draft from his jug. He spit, and the air around him exploded in flame. The crowd gasped and sighed. He danced around the square in leaping steps, rhythmically spitting out the kerosene in great bursts. Then the fire-breather approached the café tables and demanded money in an outstretched, oil-spattered hand. His arms and chest were hairless and coppery.

There was the scent of kerosene in the air, as when I had come across the wreckage of a fallen RAF plane in Le Puy near the end of the war. The British bombed at night, accurately, and the Americans during the day, from a higher altitude and with less precision. Monsieur Bickart lost his cousin this way. We grew to hate the American pilots. "Cowards!" He would shake his fist at them, running out into the yard while the rest of us dashed for the root cellar.

"One pays to look at everything!" the fire-swallower shouted. "City snobs! Bastards! You look, you pay! Hurry up now, slow-wits! Just a centime. Mulattos! Impotents and eunuchs!" He thrust his head back, and a fountain of sparks burst from his mouth. It was as if a pail of flame had been thrown against the walls of the plaza and in it, a tall woman stood beside a man holding a suitcase. They had stopped to examine the spectacle. Rose? I was far from certain. In the next burst of flame, I stood and called to her, upsetting the table.

And then, with an audible buzz, the spotlight in the teahouse exploded, and the windows around the square disappeared, as if black paint had been poured into the empty column of the plaza. A few people cried out in surprise; most groaned. Women trilled as men made their advances under the cover of darkness. The waiters cried, "Bills, please, ladies and gentleman, pay your bills, please," and there was the sound of chairs scraping back from tables.

I ran across the square, colliding with others, jostled by them. "Stop! Stop! Pay your bills!" the waiters wailed. Couples locked hands and I crashed into their joined arms, as in a schoolyard game.

The place du Marché Sainte-Catherine was open at three corners, and I pushed through the blinded bodies toward the edge that led down to rue de Rivoli, repeating Rose's name until it ceased to make any sense to me.

Chapter Twelve

AT THE END OF MARCH, I RECEIVED A BATTERED envelope with its foreign postage stamps already torn off. Chaim handed me the letter, puzzled. I took it to my room, which we now called Daniel's room, as that was the name of Chaim's son, in whose bed I slept. I tore open the envelope and tried to read the familiar script. Rose. Her letter began abruptly:

> I've heard now from several different sources that you are looking for me, though each one describes an unfamiliar man: at the Louvre, you were an art thief with a guilty conscience and an early Manet. An Oriental asked my neighbor on Île Saint-Louis for my whereabouts. The museum security guard couldn't recall your last name. The concierge of my former residence fell in love with an *absent* from the East and remembered your address. (By the way, I have met a girl here—an American translator!—whom I think you would adore.) Is this a permanent address for you or not? I will think not and continue to take precautions: I am the intended target of a group of vigilantes who believe I was a collaborator.
>
> I was last in Austria, where the American Monuments men have uncovered the Ghent Altarpiece. A German professor led us to it, then killed himself, his wife, and their child. One of the Americans stole the bedspread from Goering's house.

If you have come this close, M., then you will find me. Which I would like. I will be in Paris again in May. I would write some code into this letter, some secret meeting place, but know little about my return, nor what Huyghe and Jaujard will determine of my security. Are you looking for your paintings? Don't. Do you know why?

By a circuitous route, the following document came into my hands and I thought I would pass it along to you. Perhaps it has some legal use, which I doubt, given the outcome of this war. More likely, it will merely serve as a curio.

RC

Clipped to Rose's letter was a revocation of my family's citizenship. She did not even write my name. I cast Rose's letter on the floor.

Chaim appeared in the doorway of Daniel's room. "Look out the window, quickly," he ordered. I obeyed, still in my dream state.

"Her there, with the limp," he said.

"She works in the bakery."

"Yes, and her husband is a policeman. My wife Sorole went to her bakery twice a day. The bread woman told Sorole every morning when there was going to be a roundup so we could hide at our neighbor's house, because their door was stronger than ours. When the police knocked, we didn't answer, and they didn't break the door down. We held pillows over the mouths of the children so they wouldn't give us away. Sorole and I always debated her, the bread woman. I said she acted in defiance of her husband, out of discomfort with what he did. Sorole thought she worked with him because the policeman could not speak out and used his wife as his mouthpiece. Two different views on marriage, I suppose. The bread woman did not warn Sorole of the *rafle* in which I was arrested. Maybe she was sworn to secrecy by her husband. Or her child was sick and she did not go to work that day."

Chaim stepped back from the window and grabbed my chin in his hand.

"You are young and full of promise," he said. "You have ten fingers and ten toes. This is important to keep in mind when one receives a letter bearing bad news."

THAT NIGHT WAS A SLEEPLESS ONE. MY THOUGHTS hovered and darted around the room. At four o'clock, my thoughts turned from Chaim. I was gripped with the belief that, despite my father's and Rose's discouragement, that from their separate corners of the Continent they were both urging me on, as a rider with his whip. Both said they wanted me to stop, and yet I did not believe them. Was it the lover's delusion, where he rejects his beloved's refusals and thinks only that she wants more certain confirmation of his affection? This was not impossible. Yet I could not shake the feeling that each wanted me to find something in my search for Father's paintings that was different from what I in fact was seeking.

THE NEXT DAY, CHAIM INSISTED I VISIT THE LOCAL police station with him. "All Jews should know how the police operate," he said. Standing before the jailhouse, in his wide-brimmed hat and black coat with the pleated tail, he looked like an emissary from a bygone century.

Before us opened a long rectangular room with a checkerboard floor. Tobacco smoke stained the walls and ceilings. Rows of wooden chairs faced two desks, which were each occupied by policemen, one redheaded and the other bleach pale.

We took a number, eighteen, and a pair of seats. Chaim crinkled with the sound of cellophane wrappers as he leaned over me, and his breath smelled like the caramel that clicked between his cheek and teeth. His beard tickled my ear.

"I wouldn't have obeyed a German officer, Max. I wouldn't have reported to the police station if I had known the *Boches* would be waiting for me there. But it was the French police, here in *Paris*, in their blue and white uniforms, who knocked on our doors." He rapped once against his chair. "So I went, as obedient as my own child."

We sat in silence. A breeze blew in from the street and sent the stacks of documents on the albino policeman's desk flying through the air.

"Ludovic!" shouted the redhead. "Use your pistol to hold those down. What a mess!" Numbers sixteen and seventeen rose and disappeared.

"Number eighteen," a baritone voice sang out. The junior policemen fell silent and began scribbling.

The police chief stood in the doorway, tall and lean, his breast glistening with ribbons and badges. At the center of his lapel was the double-barred cross of the Resistance. He reminded me of an American actor.

I did not pay attention to the initial round of questions the chief asked and Chaim answered: name, place of birth, parents' names. Instead, I admired General de Gaulle's slogans on the wall: *Paris résistant*, *Paris martyrisé* and *Paris libéré par lui-même*, *libéré par son peuple*.

"Year of birth?" the chief asked.

"Nineteen hundred and five," Chaim answered, taking ten years off of his age. I feigned disinterest.

"Address?"

"Four, rue Pavée." This must have been the synagogue where I met him.

"Business?"

"I run a shop that repairs parts for automobiles."

"So you own a garage?"

"It is more specialized. The work is skilled and complicated. Most of my employees were trained as clockmakers." I would learn later that this lie was a reflex from the camp, where, Chaim told me, those with mechanical skills had a better chance of surviving.

The chief paused with his pen over the form, then wrote *mechanic*.

"Will you keep your last name?" the policeman asked. Chaim stared hard at him. The chief took a cigarette out and offered the pack to us, a generous gesture. Chaim took off his hat and looked inside its crown. Its label bore the name of the tailor's shop he had owned before the war. He replaced the hat on his head.

"Tenet. I shall change it to Tenet," he said. "And, sir, you have no cigarettes left."

"How strange," the chief said. "Excuse me." He took another pack from the desk. "How did you return to France, via Odessa and Le Bourget"—an airport outside of Paris—"or the Gare de l'Est?"

"Gare de l'Est," Chaim said.

"How many months were you in convalescence?"

"Three."

"At the Lutetia?" Chaim nodded. "Lovely hotel." The chief looked down at his papers. "You are entitled to six more months of double rations, as all people absent from France during the war are given nine months' total of double rations."

"Fine," said Chaim.

"And a monthly sum of five thousand francs."

Five thousand francs did not guarantee Chaim would be well fed, let alone me. Chaim searched for the fringes of his prayer shawl to twirl around his fingers but did not find them. He had tucked them into his waistband before entering the police station.

Next, the chief wrote out a bank draft for Chaim and laid it on his blotter. He took a wide-handled stamp, pressed it against the ink pad and then to the identification card. When he lifted the stamp and saw that the word *Déporté* had come out clearly, the chief said, "Ah, good," and pushed the card toward Chaim, who rose, white-faced. I stood, too. "I will not have this printed on my card," Chaim said.

"All the other *absents* have the same stamp. Without it, you cannot have your double rations, your free visits to the doctor, your five thousand francs," the chief replied.

"Then I shan't have them."

"*What?*" I said. I had been thinking about food the whole meeting. Potatoes, chicken, cheese. I had heard that all *absents* were given three jars of marmalade. I had dreamed of jam. "Chaim, this is a mistake—" I tried to say, pulling on the hem of his sleeve. He snatched his arm away.

"Stay while he completes a new card properly," Chaim ordered me. He got up to leave.

A gust of wind blew the door shut behind him and I heard the officers in the waiting room curse. One hollered at the other again about keeping his pistol atop the stack of papers.

"I don't know where it went," the policeman moaned.

"The war has unsettled your uncle's mind," the chief said to me, after Chaim had left.

"He's saner than I am," I replied.

CHAIM WAS NOT IN THE COURTYARD OF THE COMMISSARIAT or waiting on the benches across the way. With the new papers under my arm, I turned toward home and saw his scarecrow figure stalking down the street, his coat fanning out behind him.

I called out, "Surely you've lost your senses."

Chaim pressed against the wall as a girl with stocking seams painted on her legs passed us. He would not touch any woman.

"I could not have that word printed on my identification card, Max," Chaim said. I nearly held out my wrist for him to grab, as I knew he would. "That police chief—"

"Yes?"

"—wearing the *Croix de la Reine* on his lapel—"

"I noticed it."

"—the glorious sign of the Resistance?"

"I know what it is." I struggled to keep up with him.

"In 1942 I was arrested by the same, the exact same, police chief."

"Are you sure?" I asked.

Chaim winced. "How could I forget?"

I blushed with shame. "You could have denounced him right there. He should be hanged. The Resistance should kill him on the street."

"He's not my concern now. And if I turn him in, he's probably protected. Perhaps his boss also collaborated. I don't want to be pulled up before a judge and relive what happened in 'forty-two. Besides," Chaim said, "I got something from him as well."

When we returned to Chaim's flat, my companion drew from his overcoat a pistol, the bank draft for five thousand francs, and a full box of Gitanes. "We had to learn to steal," he said.

"You'll never be able to cash the bank draft. The police chief will realize it's missing—"

"—and keep my rations for himself. He's gotten a good deal. Why would he make trouble for us? He and I have a silent pact. He knows that some, though only a very few, of the men he sent away in 1942 have returned. He will know, then, that I may have met him before, back in the days when his office had a picture of Pétain on the wall instead of slogans by de Gaulle. That will be enough to keep him away. And I've had enough of them. 'Paris liberated by her people?' On the contrary."

As I laid out our food for lunch—a baguette, some cheese, a jar of olives, a bruised apple—Chaim asked me, "And where is your family?" I said Le Puy and explained the paintings and the rift with my father.

"The first dilemma is not one I can comment on," Chaim said. "For me, I would want the paintings in a museum, so my poor kin could go and gawk at them. Yet I have sympathy for your plight. These are not family portraits; those I would want to save. Surely those are destroyed because they are of value only to those who had them painted. Is each painting of your father's a token for a thousand of us that were killed? I don't know. These are questions for a philosopher. But that you have purposefully left your father?" He shook his head in disbelief, but his voice was not unkind. "Tell me, how long is it your plan to stay with me?"

I had never considered when I might leave, so sure was I of Chaim's need for my companionship. This is the hubris of the young, who cannot imagine that the old do not want to be with them. "Ten more days?" I asked him.

Ten days stretched into a month and then two. After we used what Chaim had stolen, there were still ten thousand francs left in my tobacco tin, which we spent on meals and bills for water and electricity and coal. I was glad that my money—my father's money—gave us a respite, that it "came in handy," as the Americans say. So while Roosevelt lay dying in Warm Springs and we learned of the liberation of the camp Buchenwald (named for Goethe's beech tree—Father, I thought of you), Chaim and I lived, if not in richness then in comfort.

Chapter Thirteen

I HAD ALWAYS PLANNED TO RETURN TO MY FATHER with my catalog of triumph and loss, but as the days extended and my catalog had only blank pages, it grew increasingly impossible for me to contact him. When I thought of him, I mourned. And then, as if Father had sent her to encourage me, I saw Madame Bernheim, immersed in *War and Peace*, across the Métro tracks at Sèvres-Babylone. So the other Jewish art dealers had begun their return to Paris. I set out to make my rounds of their homes, using my father's address book as a guide.

I began with Monsieur Léon Lethez, a collector of pre-Columbian art. However, when I knocked at his door, the woman who answered said her brother was in too poor health to see visitors. I replied that as I had trained as a doctor, I was understanding of those who were sick, and that I hoped he would allow me to call on him again in a few weeks when he was well. The sister eyed me strangely. I wrote down my address and went next to the home of Frits van Seyveld.

My resemblance to my father was useful to me under certain circumstances and a burden in others. In the pursuit of discovering the fate of my father's compatriots, our likeness was helpful in seeking information from those who had been made suspicious by the war. I was not surprised that many recognized me, for these were men whose business was recognizing a fake.

I rang the buzzer to the van Seyvelds' apartment on boulevard de Courcelles and waited. Before the war, this man had possessed the world's finest collection of Rembrandt drawings. Standing on the sidewalk for some time, I could not conjure his face, only that he wore a pince-nez. I was about to leave when the wind rattled the front door. It was unlocked. I leaned on the handle and entered the foyer, which opened onto a set of stairs, at the top of which was another door, this one covered with a lace curtain. I knocked and called out the Dutch dealer's name.

I heard voices behind the glass, the squeal of a lock, and before me stood two elderly people very small in size. A white-haired man in striped pajamas leaned against a cane. The woman beside him wore a black dress with a pearl necklace that draped nearly to her waist. She had on a hat and gloves, as if she had been preparing to leave the house.

"Monsieur van Seyveld?" I asked.

"Daniel!" He embraced me. Then he began to speak hurriedly in a language I did not understand. He grabbed my cheeks, looked at his wife plaintively, and barked a command at her.

She said, "My husband wants me to tell you how grateful he is for your visit. He has not seen anyone from the lost world since we returned to France. We were in Switzerland during the war and he suffered a terrible stroke. It's taken years to regain his ability to speak, but finally he can converse in Dutch, his mother tongue. He used to speak such beautiful French! I've discovered that he remembers the tunes to 'Frère Jacques' and 'Alouette' and 'Sur le Pont d'Avignon,' yet not the words! Are not our minds miraculous and terrible machines, Monsieur Berenzon?"

Frits van Seyveld clasped my hand and spoke again, his leaking gray eyes intent on mine. I understood that he was inviting me into his home, and so we began the long, slow promenade into their salon, which was a grand one, of the kind I had not seen since before the war. Brocaded curtains hung to the floorboards, and everything wooden was gilt. On the walls were prints of elephants and rajas and women playing stringed instruments.

I explained to Madame van Seyveld that I was in fact Daniel's son, and she conveyed this information to her husband, who nodded as if he understood, though in further untranslated exchanges I heard my father's name repeated.

The wife grew quiet, awaiting the explanation of my visit.

"I'm happy to see your home remained untouched," I said.

Madame looked down and twisted the emerald ring she wore over her gloves. Her skin hung loosely off her bones and her hair was nearly gone. Hence the hat, indoors. I imagined they had not responded sooner to my knocking because, unaccustomed to visitors, they had had to ready themselves.

"You see," she said, "the apartment is filled with furniture. Yet, aside from the stove and the bathtubs, none of it is ours. Neither the kitchen cabinets, nor the forks or the linens. Not the bedposts, not the prints of India, not even the doorknobs."

Her every belonging, Madame van Seyveld said, had been replaced by something that resembled its predecessor but was fundamentally different.

"The Germans emptied our home completely in 'forty-one. Then it was refurnished to house a Vichy official, who is now in prison. I can't recall his name." She asked Frits for it, but he turned up his palms and smiled, tapping his temple.

"I've gotten it into my head to find the lady of the house that was looted to stock ours with silver," she said. "If she is still alive, she must want it back." With a clink, she lifted a tarnished spoon from the table. "We had the same pattern, only the monogram is changed," she said. Without warning, her husband began to weep. The wife seemed not to notice as he wiped the tears with the sleeve of his pajamas.

I handed my handkerchief to Monsieur van Seyveld, who blew his nose.

Madame continued for what must have been forty minutes, explaining that she had tried to get the Bon Marché's wedding registries from the same decade in which she herself had been married to see if she could match the initials on the silver to a bride from the last century. The department store's records, however, were incomplete. At a certain point, Monsieur van Seyveld, still clutching my handkerchief, dropped off to sleep. His wife, though she appeared frail, continued. "We find the strangest things in the house—a child's penmanship book in one drawer, dentures in another, this hat I'm wearing, Frits's pajamas, bronzed baby shoes. No two things came from the same house. Rather, the Germans brought a desk from one place, an armoire from another, our bed from a third. I picture some central warehouse of furniture from all the Jews in Paris. I dream of it, in an airplane hangar, with towers of chairs, and tables stacked one atop another."

At length, I interrupted her. "What happened to your husband's collection of Dutch drawings?" I asked.

The old woman touched her husband on the wrist and pressed her lips to his cheek. I could picture them as young lovers: Frits, blond, speaking French with his rich Dutchman's vowels; she, skittish and stylish.

She recited my question in Dutch. He beamed at me, then spoke one sentence at a time, pausing for her to translate.

"Fortunately, the Rembrandt sketches are not big. We put one or two drawings in envelopes this size." She repeated his motions, as he held his hands out in a square. "We sent one hundred letters, registered mail, half to our address in Switzerland and the rest to our most trusted friends.

"Four did not arrive. We comforted ourselves: a few out of two hundred is not so bad to have lost. But then, when we came back here as you did, in the late summer, we found those four letters waiting in the postbox. They had been sent all over Switzerland, so it took them nearly twenty months to return home. On two, we had marked the wrong addresses. We learned from the stamps on the other two that a friend had died and we had not been notified."

"Where are the drawings now?" I asked, incredulous.

The wife straightened her hat and repeated the question to her husband.

He answered her and she translated. "We'll never tell."

. . .

I STRAINED AGAINST THE DOOR LEADING INTO CHAIM'S apartment building. At that hour, six o'clock, kitchen windows with grease-darkened panes had been thrown open across the courtyard, and from them fell the smells of onions and boiling cabbage. The branches of a summer magnolia tree draped over the cement wall, and the round loveliness of the blossoms seemed almost obscene. A baby wailed and a cat meowed plaintively, their cries intermingling until I could not tell one from the other.

A telephone rang—an uncommon sound in this neighborhood—as if to say, *Stop all this racket!* and everyone and everything hushed for a moment, straining to hear the news and how our neighbor would react to it, good or bad, miraculous or tragic. I listened, too, but heard only the wind sucking the curtains in and out of an open window above my head. They reminded me of lungs, inflating and deflating, and I remembered my horror when we operated on live dogs in medical school. We sawed through their sternums and opened the rib cages with the same gesture as one opens a window onto the street, which revealed the dog's lungs undulating beneath. I had given my poor subject too much chloroform, and it died mid-operation. I told Bertrand of the dissections. I hadn't expected to upset him so. For days he would not stop talking about it, lecturing me on the evils of modern science.

As if summoned, Chaim appeared in the window five floors above me. Chaim did not look out but seemed preoccupied with—it must have been—the contents of my valise, which was stored where he stood. His movements were furtive and quick. I entered the building and climbed the stairs. I could not be angry at Chaim for this—I had done my own curious (and ultimately heartbreaking) reconnoitering amid his family's belongings.

Before I reached the landing, Chaim had unhooked the latch and stood shaking in the doorway.

"You eat so much that soon we'll have nothing left. I can't keep a boy who gobbles up all my supplies." His anguished face reminded me of an El Greco. He seemed ready to howl.

"Please don't worry," I said.

"Then what will we eat?"

"I have ten thousand francs hidden away," I said.

"Let's see it," he snapped. I was lying.

The apartment was stifling. The night was cool, though not unusually so. However, Chaim was burning a broken chair in the fireplace. The blue paint peeled and cracked and glowed in the fire, and one leg stuck out at a strangely human angle. Everywhere I looked were Chaim's family's belongings—his wife's hat with dust on its brim, the box with his son's lock of hair on the mantelpiece, the shelf of children's books. Chaim put his arm on my own to steady himself as we walked to the valise, where I knew I had no money hidden. The fumes from the burning paint made me lightheaded. I felt Chaim's impatience shimmering behind me. I thought, He will know that all I have in here is the fake Manet *Ham*, a concert program of Mother performing Brahms's Concerto Number 2 in B-Flat Major in 1927, and the pink sweater with the pearlized buttons that belongs to Rose. I made a show of unzipping the case's inner lining, where the forgery sagged in its gaudy frame. I rummaged through a shelf in the pantry.

"I find your lying unsettling," Chaim said.

He sat at the table. We could hear the radio from the *chambre de bonne* above us, and the sound of emptying water rushing through a drainpipe.

"You should find your father," Chaim said.

"I know where to find him," I said, more harshly than I had intended.

"I'd like some tea," he said, his eyes darting around the still room. I wondered who and what he saw.

"I'll make tea," I said, jumping up. He waved me down.

"There isn't any," he said. "No tea, but I'll tell you a story." He gestured for me to sit beside him and patted my hand absentmindedly while he spoke.

"I remember visiting the family of a rich dentist when I was very young, in Wilno. They had a magical contraption in their house that kept the water boiling all through Shabbas, so we could drink tea at any time of day. I remember watching my mother envy it, and to see such envy in her eyes made me want to steal it or break it for her.

"I dreamed of that machine for years—until we left Poland, and I was already a grown man. But from the time I was five until, oh, twenty, that machine stayed with me, steaming away, and when my mind drifted or filled with envious thoughts, or when I felt wronged in some way that was small but bitter, there it was. I had loved my mother's samovar and tea set before we visited the dentist's family, but when we returned to our house when Shabbas was over, our samovar seemed common and tarnished to me, with dents in places I had never noticed before. It must have looked that way to my mother, too, because she put it away and stopped using it except when my father asked her to take it out.

"What is amazing, though, is that the dentist and his wife, who was also educated, a doctor—they were the richest Jews in town; they had a cook and two maids—still they only had an outhouse, just like my parents and I did. I remember the dentist's backyard, the kitchen gardens to one side, the chicken coop to the other, then the apple tree with the table beneath it, and at the edge of the property the whitewashed outhouse. Though they were assimilated Jews, my father's fondness for the dentist was greater than his disapproval. The visits, however, made my mother unhappy. She worked so hard. Father would tell her, *We're rich in all the things money can't buy*, and kiss her and bless her and then the children and the house. But my mother, may she rest in peace, was a more practical woman." Chaim clapped his hands against the tops of his knees, as if to say, *Enough of that.*

"The only goy I call my friend, Gilles Lalieu, is a tailor in the same neighborhood where I worked. His customers were mostly Christians and mine were mostly Jews, though there were some Christians who thought I was better than Gilles and some Jews who thought he was better than me. Yet"—Chaim paused—"I am truthfully the better tailor. When his billy-goat mother torments him, he drinks, and this makes his hands shake. And mine have never failed me. I am as deft as Houdini. I had not wanted to visit Gilles until I filled out. And now I say we should go. Come with me now, won't you? They, too, have the tea-making machine."

Chaim unchained the door, and I had to jockey on the stairwell to get in front of him. I preferred to walk ahead on the stairs in case he stumbled on the uneven steps. The heavy courtyard door swung shut behind us.

We descended rue de Sévigné to rue de Rivoli. The sun setting behind the gold-topped pillar at the Bastille filled me with a hope I had not felt in many months. A red convertible car honked its horn at two girls who carried a picnic basket between them. The men and women in the cafés were leaning over one another's tables and laughing, the women's elbows resting on the tables of men they did not know. A crowd had gathered before a hotel on the corner.

"What's going on?" Chaim asked the waiter at the busy café.

He wiped his hands on his apron and said, "Maurice Chevalier. He went into the apartment above the hotel two hours ago." A man in a tweed coat with a camera slung around his neck jostled the waiter. The waiter pushed the cameraman off the sidewalk, into the street. "Watch it," he said. "The café is still open here."

The reporter took a picture of the building, and at the pop of his flashbulb everyone rushed forward. The singer was nowhere to be seen. "Why's Chevalier in the Fourth?" I asked the blond woman standing next to me. She had a doll's face with a black veil drawn over her eyes.

"I don't know and I don't care," she declared. "Oh, it's been years since anyone has seen him!"

A teenage boy at my elbow said, "Chevalier's girl's a Jew—her parents live in this neighborhood." At that moment, the singing star appeared on the doorstep of the hotel wearing a white linen suit, with his famous boater cocked at its famous angle. The crowd cried out and pushed toward him.

"Tell us about Mistinguett," the newsman hollered. Chevalier took off his hat and looked into it. "To me, she is dead," he said.

"Tell us about Hollywood," a second newsman called, as he ran to join the crowd.

"I love it," he said in English, and gave a toothy smile.

"Mr. Chevalier, what about a song?" a woman called out.

"A song! A song!" The crowd began to chant.

"Sing 'Prosper'!"

" 'Ma Pomme'!"

"How about 'Dans la Vie faut pas s'en faire'?"

" 'Valentine'!" Chaim shouted, cupping his hands to his mouth.

"Chaim?" I said, amused.

He shrugged his shoulders. "What can I say? My wife used to love it."

"No, sing 'Ça sent si bon la France'," a voice shouted. The crowd quieted and the blonde to my right clucked. "What a faux pas." I recalled the song, written during the Occupation and popular with German troops and their sympathizers.

A young man in a narrow tie and a gray hat pushed his way to the front of the crowd. "Collaborator!" he shouted. "*Boche* lover!" A murmur rose up around me. The young man took a swing at Chevalier, who staggered back. The singer's hat was knocked from his head and onto rue de Sévigné. The wind lifted it and skipped it farther down the street. Two women gave chase, their high heels clattering.

The crowd parted. No one stopped the young man as he ran up rue de Rivoli, kicking his legs and pumping his arms, the tie dangling over his shoulder. The crowd fell silent and took a step back from Chevalier.

The waiter from the café handed a dishcloth through the crowd to the singer, who held it to his tanned cheek with one hand and smoothed his hair with the other. "Do you still want a song?" he asked.

"Yes!" everyone cried. Chaim and I looked at each other.

"Do you want to stay?" I whispered.

"Of course," he said. "It's Chevalier! It's not like we see him every day in shul."

"For the monsieur in the *impressive* black hat," Chevalier said. " 'Valentine.' " The crowd turned toward Chaim, who nodded to Chevalier above the stares.

Chevalier took the towel away from his cheek, and two splotches of blood stood out against the white cotton. "Well, I need a girl to sing to, don't I?" he asked and his eyes scanned the crowd, which had grown to fifty or so. Many customers at the café stood at their tables. A few remained seated and continued to talk in loud, deliberate voices.

"Mademoiselle—yes, you, *mignonne*, with the lovely black veil. Don't hide your smile. Come here and stand beside me," Chevalier said. He was pointing to the woman on my right, who did as he said. Chevalier held her hand in his as he sang. Chaim hummed along with the refrain, "*Elle avait des tout petits petons, Valentine, Valentine.*" The song rhymed the words "little breasts," "little chin," and "curly like a sheep."

Chevalier kissed the girl's hand and tipped an imaginary hat to Chaim. Chaim lifted the brim of his and then pulled on my sleeve. "Time to go," he said. We walked away as a few in the crowd shouted, "Encore!"

"He's not as good in person as he is on the records," Chaim said, and pulled at his beard. I wanted to know where Chaim had heard the records, because there was no gramophone on rue de Sévigné.

"He singled you out of the crowd."

Chaim shook his head. "He sang for the Germans during the war and went into hiding after, because he was afraid the Resistance might get ahold of him. So when the obvious Yid in the crowd asks for a song, he sings it to him."

We stopped in front of a bakery. Its blue awnings had been drawn earlier in the day to protect the precious handful of chocolates in the window from melting in the April sun.

"This is Gilles's house," Chaim said. A wind whipped down the street, sending dry leaves scattering along the pavement. Chaim and I shivered. "In the camps, I thought of Gilles only once, at the beginning, and I thought, How terrible I did not get to say good-bye to my friend. He was a good man. And here I am again." Chaim pressed the doorbell. As an afterthought, he added, "They're modest people. I don't think they would understand the lost paintings or be sympathetic to your cause. Perhaps it's best if you do not come."

Since I did not understand, I said, "Do what you wish. I'll wait on the street." The door buzzer droned and he entered the unlit hall.

It grew dark, and the lights in the rooms over rue de Rivoli sprang on with the randomness of a child hitting keys across a piano. I walked to the empty market stalls in the place Baudoyer and then back to the building that Chaim had entered. I reviewed what I knew of Chaim's history. In December of 1942, when he was called to the police station to renew his identity card, he was arrested immediately and taken ten kilometers outside of Paris to Drancy. This internment camp had been a public housing project for 700, later a police barracks, and a holding center for, at its peak, 7,000 Jews. When the Resistance killed Germans in Paris, tenfold were executed at Drancy. It was from Drancy that Chaim was shipped east to what he called the *lager*. I came to know it by the name Auschwitz. It was at Auschwitz that he learned of the German surrender at Stalingrad, thus locating his arrival there in February of 1943.

That same winter, I was in Le Puy, where the stark, bare tree branches were like Chinese calligraphy against the sky. After a storm, Monsieur Bickart enlisted me to shake the snow from their boughs so they would not be damaged by its weight. We all cursed the cold, except for Mother, who said it allowed her to hear more clearly. From the basement, she could differentiate the strike of a donkey's hooves on the cobblestone path from a horse's, as the donkey's rang more sweetly. A German truck skirted the village via the A-9 highway once a day, and Mother dutifully reported each evening whether it sounded laden with troops and weaponry or was fleet and quick, carrying only a single officer.

The winter Chaim was first interned, Mother embroidered handkerchiefs for us all and gave them out on Christmas morning, out of respect for our host. We drank a fierce hot cider, then Father and Mother played *belote* while Monsieur Bickart stirred the fire, lost in thought, with the flush of the fire and the cider in his cheeks. He said he preferred not to play, though I suspected that he did not want to introduce an element of competition into our cramped quarters, which was wise indeed. He had discerned something of my parents and their natures to which I had long been blind.

I heard the *rat-tat-tat* of shoes hurrying downstairs inside the building, and Chaim flung open the door. The meeting had lasted less than thirty minutes.

"Walk," he said, and we strode away, our shoulders hunched and coats drawn close to us.

"I should have known when he was surprised to see me that the visit would go badly," Chaim said after a while, his breath noisy.

"They're not sorry about the war," I said into the collar of my coat, which was moist and foul. Chaim nodded.

"Madame Lalieu was influenced by Pétain from the very beginning. Too bad I waited to see Gilles until I had fattened up." He filled his cheeks with air. "I didn't want to give them a fright."

We stopped at the corner of rue Pavée, near the synagogue. "I told them only the very surface of it, Max. The cold and the beatings." He looked up at the streetlamp and spoke to it, as its light poured over him. "Gilles said, 'It can't be as bad as you say, since you've come back to tell us.' "

I did not know how to respond. I raised my arms and dropped them. We stood in the halo of light made by the street lamp. Chaim's cigarette smoke clouded in front of our faces and dissolved. There was still the smell of wood fires. I recalled going riding with Bertrand and Fanny Reinach in the winter before the war started and the sight of the horses' breath in the cold air.

"In the *lager*, I worked in 'Canada.' In French, you would call it *Peru*, as in *all the gold of the Incas.* But we Poles say *Canada.* Canada was the collecting point. Diamonds sewn into the hems of clothing stripped from corpses." Chaim stopped speaking. Two men in identical hats and long coats, with pale faces and black beards and ringlets, passed in front of us. They lifted their heads at Chaim's last word, then turned away and hunched through the low synagogue door. "When the Soviets came, we had already stuffed seven thousand kilos of hair into paper sacks, which we labeled half a mark each. There were women's clothes, men's clothes, a mountain of prosthetic limbs. I stole precious stones, gold pieces, only things easily concealed, and traded them with the *Kapo.* We were searched very carefully, but I was never caught. And so I survived and did not starve."

He shifted the blue velvet pouch that held his phylacteries from under one arm to the other. "We've missed most of the service," Chaim said, tipping his head toward the temple door. "It's the final prayers. Kaddish. You'll come in with me, won't you?" For once, I agreed.

The temple was damp and quiet, as it had been when I first met Chaim. He handed me a shawl and skullcap, then offered me a prayer book from a jagged stack. "What good would it do?" I asked. I could not tell top from bottom of the dancing lettering.

"It gives you something to hold."

The men stood scattered among the remaining rows of empty pews. They faced the makeshift ark, their voices crying out at different intervals, as if the same desperate thought was passed along between them by an unpredictable electric current.

Chapter Fourteen

WHEN I WROTE NEXT TO MONSIEUR LETHEZ, I received a reply in a feminine hand that he was now well enough to see me. So it was that I climbed a battered staircase in the Ninth arrondissement to visit another man my father had inscribed in his book of addresses. Despair clung to this building and to the modest apartments. Lethez's sister greeted me again, wordlessly, with her finger pressed to her lips. Her movements were fluid and soundless, in the way that a nurse is always aware of the sleeping invalid nearby.

I followed her through a series of rooms without carpets or curtains, the walls of which were streaked with water stains but lined with vitrines of pre-Columbian art: flat golden heads and other works of metallurgy, three-dimensional figures in jade, humans with bird feet or fangs, jaguars, copulating men and women—dozens upon dozens, most no bigger than my thumb, marching in neat rows.

We passed the kitchen and the drone of the radio and the smell of vegetables boiling. The sister rapped on the door frame of the last room, and we entered it. Inside, a small man creaked back and forth in a rocking chair, his fingers worrying the white bandage on his head. He wore a crimson tie neatly knotted, which suggested the sister's hand in his careful attire. A youthful face ill-matched his widow's peak and, above it, the shock of white hair. He was pale and handsome and frail. He eyed his sister warily and did not look at me.

"This is Max Berenzon, Léon," she said. "You remember," and then closed the door behind her.

I looked back with alarm—why did she close the door? I did not want to be left alone with him. This thought struck me separately: I, who had nearly been a doctor, was still afraid of the sick. Staring at the door before I could catch myself doing so, I saw a pair of pajamas hanging on a hook. Their sight touched me distinctly, though I could not explain why.

I turned to Monsieur Lethez and saw him gazing at me, his hand still over the bandage, which was just larger than his palm. There was a plate of cookies on the table.

"Try these," Lethez said. "They are delicious."

They immediately crumbled all over my pants and the floor and stuck to my fingers. Lethez ate neatly.

"Wonderful," I agreed. He gestured for me to take another, which I dutifully ate. "I've made a mess," I said.

"Have one more," he said. I did not want it, but I ate anyway. My crunching and chewing seemed coarse in the quiet room. "Now, tell me, why you are here?"

My mind flipped through diagnoses—it looked as if a section of his skull had been removed—as I searched for the ailment and the operation.

I stammered and babbled, the man unnerved me so, thinking of one thing and saying another, and eventually formed the idea that I wanted to learn how he had survived the war and what had been the fate of his collection.

"What?" Monsieur Lethez asked, in a terrible and quiet voice. "I don't understand your question."

I tried it again. Lethez began to answer, but his voice dipped in and out of registers, his accent was very strong, the words slurred or trailed off altogether, and one idea caught the tail of another and dragged it down. I sensed that he had something important to tell me, and yet I could not understand him. All the while, the hand remained on the bandage and his forefinger stroked the cloth.

I tried to be simpler. "Were you in France during the war?"

His hand dropped to his knee. "In France the war was terrible," he said. His chest rose and sank. "In Lithuania, it was hell." Our eyes met for the first time, and I looked away. "But you haven't come here to ask me about that."

I could not form words to agree or disagree but sat mutely. Why must I upset this frail man with my idiotic questions? And what was it about ailments of the skull? Why could I not remember a single shard of information?

I named the lawyer who had given me Monsieur Lethez's name. I asked about the Bureau des Étrangers. "I served there until my medical problems became too numerous," he said, in his Lithuanian hush. "I thought we did a fine job. Now I hear many are unhappy with us." He raised his brows and made a very French noise of dismissal, "*Pf.*"

"Can you tell me about your art collection?" I asked. Again, whether it was my own agitated state or Monsieur Lethez's ailment, I could not grasp what he said. I fought the voice in my head, which was louder than Monsieur Lethez's soft one. Finally, I understood him to say, "If you had come here two months ago, I would have had so much more to tell you, but I had just had the first operation. Now it is all out of reach. Ask Anna these questions, she can tell you. Pernicious disease. Spiteful. Sometimes I am allowed to remember my life and the words I require to describe it, and other times not. To have survived Auschwitz and then to have this. What was it you wanted to ask me?"

"About your art," I said, to distract him from my nearness to weeping.

"It is all from South America," he said, "from the tribes of the Chavín and the Moche, on the north coast of Peru, intended to accompany their rulers from this life to the next. It was buried with them in their tombs."

FOR SEVERAL DAYS AFTER MY VISIT, I WAS UNABLE TO leave the house. Then, I dreamed that my father ordered me to go to the Nurse's Room on rue de La Boétie. I ran there at midnight and found a policeman standing at the gate with his hand on his holster.

There were wooden boards over the windows. "Move along," he said. "No loitering." The dog at his feet growled, or maybe he himself had growled and there was no dog. "Get going," the policeman said again. "Or are you drunk? I can arrest you for that, too."

I felt as if my father were beside me. I missed him in the marrow of my bones, and yet I swore I could not contact him until I had my own new exposition of old lost paintings to offer to him. And if I failed at this, then I was, at the same time, seeking out my father's compatriots in order to provide a blueprint on how to pursue one's shattered dreams. It was an urge both to numb myself and to awaken myself from a long and terrible nightmare.

I took to visiting the medical faculty's library at night, once it was no longer a polite hour to knock on the doors of elderly art dealers. The security guard at the library was the same as from before the war, and he waved me in without question. I researched ailments of the brain and skull, hoping to find some treatment or diagnosis that might help Monsieur Lethez. Then one day there was a new guard, so I could not go inside the library anymore.

Chapter Fifteen

ROSE HAD WRITTEN THAT SHE WOULD RETURN IN May, and when the month arrived I began to see her everywhere: in long-legged schoolgirls dressed in uniform, in a flash of pale face and dark hair streaming by on the back platform of a bus, behind the pages of a newspaper—VICTORY IN EUROPE, it shouted—held between slim gloved fingers. The Paris newspapers could not wait for the official announcement; we had begun to celebrate the night before. There were rockets over the Arc de Triomphe. And yet, I paid them little mind. I discerned after three nights beneath the windowsill of 13, rue de Sévigné, and one strange embrace with her concierge, that Rose's belongings had been moved—though not by Rose—from the Marais. If she worked at the Louvre, she did not access her offices from any of the usual aboveground entryways. I searched for subterranean portals; surely burrowed beneath the earth were tunnels that had once connected the Tuileries Palace to the museum. Once the unconditional surrender had been signed in Reims, once the British princesses had been allowed to wander through celebrating crowds at Trafalgar, I awaited Bertrand's return more keenly than ever.

At home, Chaim did his best to hide his impatience from me, but it was unmistakable. Three questions preoccupied him: when would he learn the news of his wife and son; when would I find a job instead of loafing about Paris; and when would I leave him in peace. We had not re-created the closeness I felt to him after his visit to the Lalieu house. It would be years before he would speak to me again about the war.

Thus, more to satisfy Chaim than myself, I found work filing immigration requests to Australia, a country that seemed about as imaginable to me as the moon. Shortly thereafter, I announced that I had taken an apartment in the Fifth, which was untrue. I told Chaim I would move in two weeks. Thus, I had two weeks to locate a flat and make my invention fact.

I understood that a career, or at least an office and a weekly salary, as well as a place for a young man to hang his hat, were important trappings of adulthood. Yet I did not understand that if the young man elects these trappings not because he wants them, but due to someone other than himself, they will tie him only loosely to the adult world.

And so I considered striking out on my own, always thinking of Rose. There she was, maddeningly shaped in a woolen bathing suit at the public swimming pool, swimming vigorous laps and knocking into the other swimmers because she had no goggles. Or glimpsed between the trees in the Luxembourg Gardens, in a beret with a basketful of artichokes on her arm and a little boy who held her free hand and waited patiently to ride a mangy pony.

Nonetheless, those days of looking for everything that was not there became more and more unreal. Then it was a sunless Sunday that belonged in February. I would find Rose, I decided, at Saint-Sulpice. Before the war, gloomy days sent her to that church and its frescoes. I rode the Métro from Saint-Paul, changed trains in the human jungle of Châtelet, and emerged two blocks from the church's plaza just as it began to rain.

I entered the sanctuary's damp hush. Saint-Sulpice was a good church for a Jew. The Delacroix was just inside, on the right, built into the first crook of it, with a mural on either wall of the nave and a small lectern in between, explaining the paintings and their significance as if one were in a museum. I told myself that if I stood in front of Delacroix's *Jacob Wrestling with the Angel* long enough, Rose would appear. I had learned the painting very well.

Perhaps due to my state of mind, upon my return to the Delacroix in May of 1945, I thought, This is a very erotic picture, and was confused by the androgyny of the angel, its purple flowing robes, and the pose of the figures that, at first glance, was as much about waltzing as wrestling. No lady angel, though, in the history of painting has such sinewy thighs or shoulders. I loved the white-blue flash of Jacob's garb and the effort and tenderness of his bowed head. He is muscle and strain, and his body gives the painting its movement, its crossed lines and limbs. The jab of his knee makes the angel's hem ripple like water. The angel's hands grip and grasp—the fateful touch on the thigh—but his celestial body shows no motion. The gray wings are uselessly leaden. The hind foot is raised but not flexed, the front foot is planted and the knee bent for forward motion, but Gabriel tips backward. He merely holds the struggling Jacob in place.

No, then I understood: this is the moment when the angel, still poised to wrestle, looks into the nothingness, accepts defeat, goes slack, and teeters under the weight of those ridiculous wings. Jacob still fights with all his might; he has not yet realized that he has pushed the angel away from, at least, the picture's center line. Or the son of Isaac cannot believe his victory. I marveled at the painting. Its time moves from left to right. How beautiful to capture the body so, in the flicker between movements. Jacob's form is Delacroix's technical miracle. The angel is the intellectual triumph, even if its execution is less compelling. Jacob is the one we want to watch.

My mother had read me this story once, decades before, in a book of biblical tales for children she had brought from Poland. She translated and summarized out loud, and I studied the lurid, lovely picture. I remembered the phrase, "The angel touched Jacob in the hollow of his thigh." It was very mysterious to me, but it was one of the few phrases that my mother translated identically each time.

Then I looked up to find Rose beside me.

"Rose." Drops of water stood out, silvery against her blue coat. The face so often imagined showed me its changes. I said, "You've grown younger." There was a shadow between her brows, a darkening under her eyes, yet she was more girlish than I had seen her look. Or, if she had aged, it had only made her more beautiful. It was all I could do not to clutch her to me. I had not, in the dim light, with my eyes playing tricks, realized how closely her hair was cropped.

"And you older."

"One hopes." I saw in Rose's hand that she had bought a box of candles from the church. I detected the honeysuckle scent that still made me dizzy. My hands trembled.

"You've seen the gallery," she said, and it was not a question. I nodded. "What of Bertrand?"

I shook my head, and she said nothing more as she followed me out.

IT HAD CEASED TO RAIN, THOUGH DAMPNESS WAS IN the air, and the plaza and its stones and statues were washed and darkened. The sound of the fountain was joyous. The piles of leaves blown against the trees glistened. The sky was cleared, as if a hand had brushed the clouds aside and left only stripes of pink against the blue.

Rose sat on one of the fountain's ledges, at the foot of an enormous stone bishop. The bishop's hands rested on his sturdy knees and he stared at the church before him, which I imagined bore his name. Rose tapped at the granite, saying, "Sit beside me."

She began to talk. Her thoughts darted like sparrows. I could not follow everything she said.

"I lived in your house for two weeks after you fled. Because Auguste and Lucie were kept on in the household, I was not afraid, and I did not know where else to go. Then one morning as we ate breakfast—and it was a morose affair without you—a man wearing a toupee appeared in the kitchen and announced that he was to take charge of the gallery. That the government had assigned him as its Aryan administrator. Naturally we all protested. Lucie went crazy. I conducted my research. Of course, it was convenient for Vichy to decree that Jews could no longer own businesses, because then we were less likely to note when the owners disappeared. Bureaucracy trundles on, unabated, through murder."

She touched her ear, that old self-conscious habit, checking that the earring was in place. I could not speak.

"Eventually, we got used to him, the Aryan administrator. The fellow was just a clerk and, in his person, mostly harmless. He checked the gallery's vaults at the Chase Bank and had just enough of a sense of duty and national Vichy pride not to pilfer from them shamelessly. Then he filed his useless reports riddled with spelling errors. Joslin, that was his name. He misspoke when he wanted to sound clever and did not really vex any of us much except Lucie. And after she threw another fit and then a table lamp, he kept his distance. I worried, really, only over the cruelty of the insecure man."

Rose shook her head. She did not object to my enfolding her small hand within my own, so I let her talk until she tired.

"Auguste always opened windows when Joslin entered a room to try to blow the toupee from his pointy head.

"This city became vile to me. Nazi flags draped down over rue de Rivoli, and everywhere you could hear the sound of jackboots. We bought candles at the churches because the electricity began to fail—and keeps failing." She picked up the box she had bought in the church and shook it.

"I was moved from the Louvre, which was by then completely emptied, to the Jeu de Paume." Rose named the king's tennis courts, now the museum of modern art, its collection made largely of gifts from Bertrand's uncle Isaac.

"The number of Germans working at the Jeu de Paume each day doubled. And how they complained of the Parisians' sourness, the shuttered city! Still, in every perfume shop, there was a Nazi officer, handing over a stack of money to buy toilet water for his mistress. The soldiers on the Métro platforms, waiting patiently, with their false passivity, letting the women enter before them." Rose shuddered. "Did you see children with rickets in the town where you were hidden? What was it called?"

"Le Puy," I said.

"Lentils and lace"—she smiled—"in the Massif Central."

"Yes." I wanted to lean in close, to press my face to her neck, to feel her hand on my cheek, to touch her chapped lips with my own.

"The children with rickets, here in Paris, bowlegged, with heads too big for those skinny hook-shaped limbs? I was grateful not to be a mother." I turned to look at her, but she kept staring in the direction of the bishop, at the church and its uneven spires, one square and plain, the other round and ornate.

"When did you leave our gallery?" I asked.

"November second, 1940. Late. When I returned home after work, Auguste stood outside, shivering. He had waited for hours to keep me from entering the house."

"He is a good man," I said.

Rose seemed not to hear me. This was the story she had waited so long to tell. Her speech was breathless. "Five moving trucks, he said."

"Who said?"

"Auguste. Pay attention! Five moving trucks had arrived at seven that morning and emptied the galleries of everything but the nails on the walls and the carpet in the main room."

The green carpet, like moss at night and grass during the day.

"They took the empty picture frames, the andirons from the fireplace, footstools, the Venetian mirror in the entryway—the Louis Quinze one with the acanthus leaf—everything. When the first five trucks pulled away, they returned for more. Auguste could still hear the engines turning onto Miromesnil when the next trucks arrived. The soldiers unloaded long tables and benches, from a library or school. The gallery was transformed into a soldiers' mess, with the apartments upstairs as a boon for a group of officers."

Rose paused, or perhaps she kept speaking. My mind returned to rue de La Boétie. I imagined an officer from this certain unit, thirty-two years in age, with a blond mustache and wiry, hairy legs. I pictured him taking my blue pajamas off the hook inside the closet door and hanging his uniform over the carved bedpost. (Surely no military man would drape his uniform so casually, but it hardly mattered.) Then with a sigh at the soft bedclothes, the heavy coverlet, and the good whisky downstairs, the officer pulled aside the white sheets and climbed into my bed. The bedsprings squeaked. He was a rigid man; he would be embarrassed if he was overheard, if he was not sure that all the other officers—in my father's room, my mother's dressing room, the guest bedroom, the Nurse's Room—were wishing that their wives could see their finery and be there to do this for them.

"When Father and I went there," I said, "it was so burned. We never saw what had happened upstairs, or if the upstairs even existed."

"It doesn't, any longer," Rose said.

It grew darker and colder. Lights appeared on the church's balcony and in the fountain behind us. They illuminated Saint-Sulpice's massive arched doorways and its Spanish-style veranda, on which two figures (a Madonna and bishop) were locked in an eternal pantomime. Saint-Sulpice would be a toy next to Chartres, to say nothing of Rome's landmarks. The temple my mother attended in Poland began two stories underground so it would not exceed any of the Christian homes in height.

"Look," Rose said, "an American." She gestured toward a woman in plaid.

"How do you know?" I asked.

"Such shiny hair."

Two priests in sweeping robes emerged from the church door. They walked diagonally across the square, in the direction of the Christian bookshop, nodding as they passed. The younger one turned to give Rose a second glance, which was not a kind look. Rose seemed not to notice. She withdrew her hand from mine, found a pack of Gauloises in the pocket of my coat, removed her right glove, and lit a cigarette.

"Lucie and Auguste and I returned to the house at dark, gathered our things, and fled. I did not ask after the paintings in the vault, because I did not know what information your father had entrusted to them."

"Everything, of course," I said.

"Then it is a pity I did not ask." She looked crestfallen. When she shivered, I put my coat around her shoulders. "No," she said, but left it on. "Let's walk. Then we won't be as cold."

I followed her. We paced around the perimeter of the square. It was strange to walk in her presence. The unreal version that lived in my mind had become more real than the one who strolled by my side, unaware that the too-long sleeves of my coat were brushing my leg, as if the trembling self who had been inside the jacket a moment before were coaxing the girl who now wore it to embrace me.

Rose pointed to a yellow wall across from the Christian bookshop, with bouquets at its foot. Two men from the Resistance were shot there, at a run, she said, as they tried to escape. All the neighbors could see and were afraid. We passed the Mairie and a circle of policemen in navy uniforms.

"They're like a fistful of pencils," I said.

"You see the funniest things," she said.

"And you say them."

She smiled at her feet. "I've missed you." My heart leaped. "Where did I leave off? At the Jeu de Paume, after I moved from your house."

"Yes?"

"Because I was French and young—"

"And beautiful," I added. I made her smile again.

"—the Germans no doubt had been told all these lies about French girls, which made my job at the museum far more difficult. Everyone had their eye on me." I examined Rose's cropped hair, which stuck out at odd angles. She must have cut it herself.

"It made me appreciate rue de La Boétie. I was so young when we first met. I didn't realize at the time how strange the arrangement could have been."

"But I saw Father knock at your door."

Rose straightened, frowned. "He never knocked."

I tried to take this in. He had entered directly?

"I don't know what he was doing that night. He didn't come in.

He was never at my door, as far as I know. That would have been very different, Max. I would have left the house in a moment, in my dressing gown, calling for the police and President Lebrun."

"Really?"

"What do you take me for?" She laid a warm hand on my arm, her second touch. "I cut my hair to become invisible," she said. "And it worked."

Somewhere within the Mairie, a siren started up. The circle of policemen scattered. One jumped on his motorcycle and, with a violent kick to the ratcheting levers, roared past. The church chimed again, seven o'clock.

"I'm invisible even now," she said. "Except to you, Max Berenzon."

I leaned down and kissed her. She tipped backward, repeating, "No, no, no."

"I don't understand," I gasped.

"I stand by what I said, that day, after we left Mother's hospital."

"When can I see you again?"

"Whenever you want." She removed my jacket. "Max, how have you managed without your coat? Paris is a Frigidaire!"

"Tomorrow."

"Tomorrow?"

"As early as possible. Before the sun rises."

"Old man." She laughed, imitating Bertrand, and we both grew serious again. Rose did not finish her sentence. I wanted to ask her about our paintings, but she was already pulling away from me.

"By the fountain, at five in the afternoon," she said, naming four days hence.

"Promise me you will be here."

She nodded solemnly. "Now turn," she ordered, and reached to put her hands on my shoulders, as one spins a blindfolded child on his birthday. "I don't want you to watch me walk home."

I walked toward the fountain. A flock of crows had landed on the head, shoulders, and knees of the great stone bishop. The birds shrieked. The statue seemed alive. I hardly knew what I had seen.

Chapter Sixteen

I WENT FROM THE CAISSE DES DÉPÔTS ET CONSIGNAtions, to the Office des Biens et Intérêts privés, to the Union Générale des Israélites de France on rue de Téhéran. At the last office, a young secretary whom I had met before said, "It's useless to try to find these paintings. At least, now it is."

I would ignore her. I left the building and gave the American soldier by its door a mock salute.

Then it was Wednesday and then Thursday, and Rose was beside me again, skin glowing and white and almost translucent at the temples, the crest of her skull visible through her cropped hair, her smile wide and her lips chapped. She wove her arm through mine.

"It's wonderful to see you again, to see you twice," she said. I smiled stupidly. "We are such old, good friends." She patted my cheek, waving at me the scent of her leather gloves and their mink oil. "Don't frown, Max. You are man and boy. One of your many charms. Tell me more about your parents. When do I get my audience?"

I said I did not want to talk about my father.

"How can we talk about your paintings if we do not talk about him?" she asked.

I told her my story, quickly, about Father giving up on the paintings and about the stolen hat, wallet, map, and address book.

Rose considered me in silence.

"I could use a drink," I said, with forced cheer. "One of Bertrand's haunts is nearby."

Georges was a bar below street level on rue des Canettes, where they served wine in jam jars and the walls were bare stone and medieval. A gypsy boy with wild licks of dark hair played flamenco guitar in the corner and howled and wailed, his voice breaking between the minor intervals.

"On Sunday you were going to tell me how to become invisible."

"I can still do that."

"Well, go ahead." I poured wine into our glass jars.

"In November of 1940, I worked all my hours at the Jeu de Paume. Researching Giotto, doing Jaujard's bidding—I hardly remember. We all moved like bees in the cold, sleepy, stumbling around, half dead. Then one morning we were shocked into motion by the sound of boots, marching in step, echoing through the museum. We congregated in the central hall, and there was Jaujard with a Nazi colonel he introduced as Baron von Behr. He had a wrinkled face with a sharp nose and wore a shining helmet and a long redingote with a wolf's-fur collar. The Germans announced they were to take over the Jeu de Paume and use it as a warehouse for *biens sans maîtres*, goods without owners. Vichy owned the belongings of all emigrants, von Behr said. The Reich deserved Jewish goods because of war costs, and by consolidating ownerless artwork in the Jeu de Paume they ensured state control over anarchy. My head spun with the details and the logic. This was a short-term solution for a problem easily remedied. They would handle all bookkeeping themselves—Vichy could sleep soundly—anyway, soon the 'collecting for safekeeping' would stop. Then von Behr explained that, since the Louvre's storerooms were all filled, the Jeu de Paume's new use was effective immediately."

"How is that possible?" I asked. The Louvre had hectares of underground rooms and corridors.

"Exactly," Rose said. "This was our first glimpse of the scale of their theft. The French curators were all dismissed, and we began to file out of the main hall. We had surrendered our museum in less than five minutes. Then, as if it had been planned, one of the electric bulbs high in the ceiling burst and scattered glass everywhere. 'There are maintenance issues to attend to!' Jaujard shouted, like a madman. 'The building will not care for itself!'

"The colonel pointed to me and said I could stay. Like that, I was assigned from one army to the other. To work for the *Germans* and maintain the Jeu de Paume's facilities. I remember shaking so violently that two colleagues held my arms. Jaujard said, 'Since Mademoiselle Clément will be here on behalf of the French museums, she will keep her own lists of artwork,' and von Behr conceded.

"Within an hour, a constant stream of men in the various uniforms of Parisian moving companies traveled back and forth in the building, wheeling in crates of artwork and carrying crates out as they were emptied. There was such a frenzy of hanging pictures! Half a dozen that I saw fell from walls and were kicked underfoot in the mêlée. A portrait by Santerre was stamped on and torn in two.

"I drifted from room to room, looking for my counterpart, the dutiful German doing his half of the double bookkeeping. Yet no one was writing. They were only hammering apart the boxes so that the air was filled with blows and the sound of splitting wood and the smell of pine. There was no bookkeeping. Von Behr, of course, had lied.

"I thought the walls could not support all the paintings they hung. Four hundred crates were carried in—and that was just the first day. Something rattled around inside me that had wanted to come undone for some time; maybe it had even been loose before the war. I can't explain it. I continued nonetheless to establish lists as complete and precise as possible. On the surface, this was to show the Germans that a Frenchwoman knew how to obey orders. Yet, without speaking to him, I knew Jaujard had named me for this task so that, when the day of our liberation came, we might begin to retrace the paths of the stolen paintings and return them to their rightful owners. At the time, we could not grasp that this would be difficult for the most horrific of reasons.

"I figured that it is twenty-eight centimeters from my elbow to my wrist and that the flat of my bent forefinger is four centimeters. This way I could measure the paintings inconspicuously. I worked quickly and was proud of my accurate records. I told myself I would be a model of French deference. If I demonstrated my obedience, I would become invisible in the epidemic of French submissiveness.

"Yet if I so much as pulled back my sleeve to try to measure a painting, one of Goering's men would appear, grinning, and ask me in horrid French was I too hot or did I need him to help me off with my coat. On the second day, I was warned to stop keeping lists and concern myself only with the building's maintenance, but I did not obey. I continued to draw up my lists in secret.

"The building's maintenance was a position of nominal importance. But I felt myself embody, for the Germans, their mania for discipline. It was more practical, and adhered to their sense of hierarchy, to address their collective complaints to me. I then reproached the personnel. Still, I used this to my advantage. If I were beloved by none, my work would be less suspect. And no one knew I spoke German.

"I had allies inside the museum, sent to me first by Jaujard and then through their own network, packing men who would visit my tiny office to say, 'Yesterday's shipments were all from the Rothschilds on avenue Marigny. Today they're from rue Saint-Honoré'—yet no ally could stay for long, because in the next moment he would be ribbed, within my earshot. 'Hah, sweet on Clément, are you?'

"The day I heard, 'Don't you know von Behr's reserved her for himself?' I panicked. I had let my hair grow out of superstition. I vowed not to cut it until your gallery was restored." Angrily, she rubbed her eyes with the back of her hand. "And then there was a sign in a wig shop that they would pay well for hair forty centimeters or longer. So I went to the woman and sold her my hair. She asked me if I cared how close she got to the skull, and I said, 'Cut it as short as you can.' If I was going to look as unwomanly as possible, I didn't want her to cut carefully. And I needed the money."

"Didn't my father provide for you?" I asked.

"I declined his offer, which frustrated him to no end. Remember, I expected your family to return any day. So the old wig weaver tied my pretty hair into three ponytails like I was a Chinaman, braided each one, and then lopped them off. She laughed a little when she saw me. When I looked into the mirror, I cried."

Rose paused and drained her wine. The glass was ringed with purple sediment. The gypsy boy sang and knocked his knuckles against the soundboard of his guitar. When he smiled at the crowd's applause, he could not hide his missing front teeth. He loosened a red scarf from his neck, used it to wipe his face, sang another ballad, and strummed its minor chords.

"And then at the Jeu de Paume, I heard one of the packers—there were hundreds of them, working shifts even when the rest of us were not allowed in the museum—say, 'Well, if the girl's cut her hair off, at least she still has her nice shape for us to look at,' and I thought, Oh, no, you don't, and found someone to give me a man's uniform. And when my transformation was a fait accompli, I felt a huge sense of relief, as if I were a thousand kilos lighter and heavier at the same time.

"I had erected a fence around myself," she continued, her voice as taut as a wire. "When, in my presence, the men began discussing the women whose bedrooms they could spy into, and their sweethearts and their whores, I could have skipped for joy. I see your face! I did this without any sadness, Max. When I understood what was most important to me—that I turn myself into a registry of lost art, a dictionary for when the missing returned—everything else fell away."

We were quiet for a while. The gypsy boy wailed in ecstasy. I pictured myself as a clock with its springs bursting out. Rose said, "Did I tell you how cold that winter was, in 1940? We crossed over the frozen Seine directly, rather than take the bridges."

I ran my fingers through her short hair. "And cold without your mane."

She tossed her head like a horse. "Terribly."

I reached over, draped a massive arm on either side of her slim shoulders, and lifted her onto my lap. "Sit here, I'll keep you warm."

"No, I shouldn't," she said, slurring a little.

"Everyone here is drunk," I said, which may have been true. "No one will notice."

I buried my face in her collar and closed my eyes and listened to her talk. She explained that for four months the Jeu de Paume processed only the collections of the Rothschilds. She saw *The Astronomer*, one of their Vermeers, but nothing from rue de La Boétie. The Nazi organization that ran the lootings, collecting, and dispersals east (via the Gare de l'Est or the airport at Le Bourget to the Reich's new and expanding frontiers) was called the ERR and was led by Alfred Rosenberg, who, Rose said, resembled a ferret.

The drunker Rose grew, the more sober I became. What she was telling me, I realized stupidly, the whole tapestry of it, was amazing and terrible. I lifted her off my lap and began taking notes on what she said on the newspaper that covered our table.

Rose continued, "Against the floorboards were generations of portraits. The family line laid out. Even portraits of pets. King Charles spaniels. A cockatoo! And then a Modigliani nude and a Chagall bride. Floating." Her hand drifted in the air as if she were hypnotized. "Only the Boucher was hung on the wall. See, the Boucher would be kept, and the modern works—mixed in with those of only personal value—they would go somewhere else. Every painting has a vanishing point, Max. In the Jeu de Paume, I was in the vanishing point of all of them." Her voice shook.

We were both silent. "And then the *chef emballeur* says to me, 'Reichsmarschall Goering will visit the Jeu de Paume tomorrow. With ten Germans here tomorrow for every one of us—and more! On the roof, in the gardens, on the balcony of the Crillon, in the Métro at Concorde—only those with an *Ausweis* signed by the Reichsmarschall can even come to work. So you may as well stay home.'

"But I had an *Ausweis*. So Jaujard was afoot in this decision. He wanted me to see what happened."

Rose took the pen out of my hand and tucked it behind her ear. Then she put her hand in my own.

"Sometimes I feel like you are my brother," she said.

I carefully folded my scrawled-upon newspapers rather than look at her as she said this.

"You've been heroic," I said. "They will give you the Legion of Honor. I heard you had been a traitor."

"And yet you still cared for me? That's bad morals, Berenzon."

"You are drunk," I said.

"And you are smart," she slurred. "And terribly handsome. It's a pity. And—write this down—I don't want the Legion of Honor. Not from any government that still has the Vichy stink on it."

"I'll walk you home," I said to Rose.

"Be a gentleman," she said. The barman winked at Rose as she left. "No winking," she called out to him. "The king has decreed it!" I was certain she was flirting. I did not realize that, in trying to hold back tears, she was exaggerating gaiety.

As we walked through the quiet square, we passed a father teaching his son to ride a bicycle along the empty streets. He ran beside the boy, flickering a flashlight across the dark cobblestones and holding the back of the bicycle seat.

Rose said, "For Goering's visit, there were yellow silk sofas and chrysanthemums everywhere, so that the museum smelled like the cemetery at Montparnasse. Ten times that year I smelled those flowers of evil, and ten times Goering came and stole. There were rooms of Gobelin tapestries and others of Flemish art. At the museum, the boys were disappointed when he came dressed in mufti. They wanted to count his ribbons. He was tremendously fat. I once had the eerie experience of seeing him decide whether or not to take a painting of Cronus eating his children."

Rose touched my elbow, and we turned down rue de Mézières. It was quiet and dark, though the moon lit a stream of light down the pavement as if the street were a river. Rose stopped before a white building, withdrew a jangling ring of keys, and pushed the door open. I hesitated.

"I want to show you something," she said. She called the rickety elevator while the concierge's dog barked and scratched at the door. The carpets in the building were all red and had once been rich but now were worn. We stepped into the tiny square of the lift and ascended, past the smells of onions and the sinister violins of a radio melodrama and the whistle of a teakettle. Rose tripped down the hallway ahead of me. "Wait till I show you, Max," she chanted.

She unlocked her apartment door and turned on the light in the cramped room. I took in the folded Murphy bed, the hot plate and dirty sink, the gold-leaf Giotto reproduction on the wall, the vase of tulips, the broken lampshade. Rose, in a room. But she had disappeared. "Where are you?" I called. The room smelled dusty and airless, like an attic.

"In the cloffice," she called from behind a green curtain. I pulled the drapery aside and found her in a closet, seated on a stool, grinning madly. On shelves that another tenant had built for shoes or sweaters were thousands of papers, some tied with twine, others sliding from their stacks into reams of unbound documents. The floor was a sea of blue wartime paper. Piles in the corner teetered higher than Rose's head. Drunk, she forced the joke. "Don't you see? It's a closet and an office!"

Whereas the mess in the Nurse's Room on rue de La Boétie had amused, even charmed me, this was something else. Rose, with her hair cropped like an invalid, looked unwell.

I remembered that Father had taught me a German word that meant *museum* and *mausoleum;* this was part of his explanation for preferring to own a gallery rather than a collection. He believed that collecting had a second motive that was an attempt to ward off death. *We must confront ourselves boldly and without delusion*, he said. So therefore the Camondos, in their attempt to re-create the ideal eighteenth-century mansion, had been blind in other ways. Rose, here, had constructed her own museum in her tiny apartment, of papers for paintings that belonged to Jews who, I presumed, were all dead, and Rose had entombed herself with them yet still would not love me, the living. Museum and mausoleum in one. "You don't take down the bed" was all I could muster.

She shook her head. "Not unless I am very tired." There was an armchair in the corner, with only a few stacks of paper on it. She must have been sleeping there. "And tonight I am very, very tired," she said. "I feel like an empty tin can. And rather sick." I picked her up under her arms and took her into the bathroom to splash some water on her face.

"Brilliant, Berenzon," she drawled.

The apartment had an unusually large separate bathroom, which ran the whole length of the single room. It had a bidet, a toilet, and a *baignoire sabot*—a short bathtub shaped like a Dutch shoe. "We could put papers on shelves in here," I said to Rose as she hung on to the rim of the sink.

She looked up at me, aghast. "Near the water? They would be ruined."

While Rose stayed in the bathroom, I stooped and lifted stacks of papers, trying to make room for the Murphy bed. In a moment, she hovered over me, wheedling. "Max, there is a special order. Everything had its place." I gently pushed her out of the way and pulled down the bed. Rose sat on it, reached for a pile, and then began handing me pieces of paper, letters—several in German—and photographs. I took them out of her hand and put them on the floor. My mind was blank. I lay down and she lay beside me. I touched her odd duckling hair, then her lips, her cheek, her ear and delicate earlobe and pearl earring. I kissed her closed eyelids. She let me unbutton the hundreds of buttons on her blouse.

"Max," she said, "I am a nun to all but my work." But she drew me to her.

My mouth found her neck. Rose's breath was fast. Uncertain about what was happening, I began to undress her, trying to be gentle, trying not to snag a zipper on skin or a button on her necklace. I did not want to hurry.

Then I realized she was hyperventilating.

"My God, Rose," I said.

"I would do this only to please you," she said.

I rolled away and sat up, without facing her.

"Do you want me to?" she asked, in a small voice.

I did not answer for a long time. "What a ridiculous question," I said first, bitterly. Then, "No, that would be terrible."

I handed her a dressing gown. Over my shoulder, she gave me my shirt. Without looking at her, I found my other things and put them on.

"Come here," she said, and pushed my head toward the pillow. "Now lie on your side." She stretched alongside me, her stomach to my back, put an arm around my waist, and I held her cold hand.

"Don't cry, Max," she said. I felt her shaking. "When everything has been disordered, then you try—" Her voice broke off.

We lay in the bed like that until, at some point after dawn, I fell asleep.

IN THE MORNING, WHEN AT LAST SHE AWOKE, HOURS after me, I asked her, "Please, Rose, tell me where my paintings are. You're the only one who knows."

She sat up, looking haggard and pale, and reached down to the pile of papers I had put on the floor a few hours earlier. She handed me a photograph.

"Goering," she said, "with a Corot. Look at them pouring champagne in the background."

"Next," she said. The newspaper pages were brittle, although they were not yet old. "This one is of Colonel Rosenberg—a German-Jewish name though he was anything but Jewish—surveying the storerooms at the Tolbiac sorting warehouse for domestic goods. They're Jewish prisoners, there, on the left, brought in from some camp outside the city."

I asked if the crates in the photographs were filled with art.

"No," Rose said. "Napkins, napkin rings, tablecloths, forks, spoons, silver baby spoons, pocketknives, combs, pens, writing tablets, hand mirrors. Children's rattles, toothbrushes, tooth powder, and eyeglasses. There was a whole room just for violins.

"German colonels made tours of the furniture storehouses and told their visiting wives or their local girls to choose new décor for their apartments. If any of the furniture was broken—well, no time to fix it. It was given away to a German of lower rank or, occasionally, a French employee. So," Rose explained, "every day there were a hundred minor accidents with the tables and chairs."

She handed me a report in German, marked, I gathered, SECRET. Rose read first to herself and then translated out loud in spurts. "It's from 1942, a report by M-Aktion. They dealt with furniture. By that date, 69,619 Jewish homes had been emptied. Of these, 38,000 were in Paris . . . *a matter of great personal pride and responsibility*—this is

Baron von Behr writing. . . . In the Jeu de Paume remain 2,703 paintings and 2,898 decorative objects."

She took the report back. "And this is why I brought you upstairs last night," she said, her voice catching. It was a work order for a moving company. Forty trucks were to be dispersed to the following addresses:

MM. Veil-Picard, 63, rue de Courcelles
David-Weill, château de Mareil-le-Guyon (S.-et-O.)
Alphonse Kann, 7, rue des Bûcherons, à Saint-Germain-en-Laye
Wildenstein, 57, rue de La Boétie
Berenzon, 21, rue de La Boétie

And there I stopped.

"Worst of all, after I saw this, I had to wait. Then there was your gallery, all at once: *Woman in White*. The Vuillard *Nude Hiding Her Face*. All those Sisley winter scenes. The Toulouse-Lautrec advertisements. Bonnard's *Breakfast*. When I saw *Almonds*, propped against the floorboards of the Salle des Martyrs, I knew that not only had the vault been discovered at twenty-one, rue de La Boétie, but that the coffers of the Chase Bank had been opened as well."

"And you could do nothing, when you saw them?"

"What, set them aside and take them home under my coat, one by one?" Rose said. "We were searched, very carefully, each night." She looked miserable.

I asked Rose if I could keep the paper and she said no. We sat side by side in bed. Rose continued, "The *chef emballeur*, Alexandre, collected the moving orders each afternoon so he could determine how many trucks to dispatch to the different arrondissements and how many men he needed on hand at the museum, how many paintings were being prepared to be shipped east and therefore brought to the station, and so on. Each night Alexandre gave his papers to me, and I took them to a man with an illegal darkroom in his basement who photographed them. This way we preserved what documentation we could. We also carried on the pretenses of an affair to avoid suspicion. I had my own lists—of what paintings I knew were going where, of where I believed they had come from when no information was available. I went home each night with my mind bursting with all I had to remember."

She handed me a photograph of a room filled with paintings.

"This is the Salle des Martyrs," she said. "So many modern paintings passed through this room. Because of my training with your father, I could guess which collection a painting came from, even if I had never before seen that painting itself. Your father turned me into an encyclopedia." She gestured at the stacks of papers. In one, I could just make out the word *Rembrandt*. "And now I have had all my pages torn out.

"I took note of each painting's departure, hoping to coordinate it with what I knew of its arrival. Then I gave copies of Alexandre's orders to the rail workers in the Resistance. Thus they knew which boxcars contained paintings, and I knew which paintings were on board the train. The Resistance, in turn, told General de Gaulle in London which trains should not be bombed and even which parts of a train should be spared. We were piecing together clues for the day when the Germans were defeated and the reassembling could begin. In the morning, I returned the packers' and the drivers' orders to Alexandre's office, carefully filed. Toward the end of the war, the photographer was killed and so my work was greatly slowed and many documents were lost. I copied everything I could by hand."

"You must help me to find our paintings now," I said. Rose looked pained. "Isn't this the easiest thing I've asked of you?"

She shook her head, unfolded herself from the sheets, and stood by the window smoking, tapping the ash into the courtyard below. An hour passed like this and the sky grew light. We heard the clink and whir of the flower market stalls unfurling their awnings.

She finished another cigarette and said at last, "My life is a life of negativity. I see my future in negatives, a future of what I did not do, what I did not find, what I could not explain, what I could not answer. I was predestined for this."

"I want to find my father's paintings."

"You can't."

"Then some."

"No."

"Then just *Almonds.*" I was not even certain why I said it.

"Why that one?" Rose asked.

"Because it was the only one my father wouldn't sell."

Rose finally left the window and pressed her cheek to mine. The thought that she had been deciding whether or not to leap from the window coalesced and evaporated. "We're corresponding shapes."

"I couldn't understand you less," I said.

"Don't try."

"All I do is try."

"That is why we're halves."

"We lasted the war."

"It's true." Rose took my hand.

"Your apartment is terrible," I said. "Let's go out and I'll buy you some flowers."

"Flowers make everything look better," Rose said. "The table, the walls, the furniture, you, me."

"Me, not you," I said.

"Especially me. They make up for what I lack."

"What do you lack?" I asked.

"We don't have time to discuss it," she replied. We left the apartment and descended in the elevator.

We bought daffodils, because they were the brightest and the least expensive. Rose looked as if she were carrying a lit torch wrapped in paper. We returned to her building and I made a motion to follow her in the door again. She shook her head, but touched my face and said, "The owner of the Galerie Zola was never known for his morals. Not before the war, and certainly not now." How strange it was to name the gallery after Zola—Zola, who had defended Dreyfus; Zola, preoccupied with the heredity of violence. Rose put her hands on my shoulders again and said, "Go there."

As I walked back through the flower market, I compared my father to the workers around me, jovial, uncomplicated men who worked with their hands. Further along—around rue de La Boétie and the surrounding neighborhoods where once I had sat in the empty chair next to my father (tilted backward, neck and cheeks white with foam) or watched him in a mirror as a man with pins in his mouth hemmed Father's pants—I felt as if I could conjure his outline from those that had once cared for him, these men who had cut his hair and shaved his chin and shod his feet and clothed his back. Yet none among them were there. I understood then another horrible calculation in the formula of the war. One class that had always served another served it one last time by being killed first. I remember my father marveling, with his appraiser's eye, at the beautiful artistry of our false papers. Chaim had shown me his, and they were imperfect work indeed.

Chapter Seventeen

THAT SPRING, THE FIRST AFTER THE WAR, WAS A cruel trick. Even in May, grayness flooded the city from sky to street, from the pigeons roosting forlornly on lampposts to the granite plaque on rue Bonaparte where, as it read, Manet had been born in 1832, when the street was called rue des Petits Augustins.

I walked along the damp cobblestones onto rue des Beaux-Arts, past Manet's birthplace, stopping at the granite facade of the Galerie Zola, where Rose had sent me. Inside, I saw a woman dressed in a man's black suit, with hair the shade of a sunset in a Technicolor movie.

I tried the gallery's door, but it was locked. The woman in the suit reached under her desk, the door buzzed, and I pushed it open. A man beside her stared at me from behind a pair of bottle-rimmed lenses.

"Better him than Léon Blum," he said, turning back to the orange-haired woman.

They both laughed and then stopped abruptly. The man said something in a hushed voice and the owner said, "*Tsk, tsk.*"

While they spoke, I stood by the door and examined the gallery. The walls were covered in a brown fabric that gave the air a muddy quality. Picasso prints, all signed in 1944, filled the front room.

"Is this open?" I asked, stepping into the unlit side gallery.

"Yes, yes," the orange-haired woman said, in a voice indistinguishable from a man's, and turned on the dim lights.

Even before my eyes could adjust, I saw the Morisot emerge from the gloom. My father's *Woman in White.* At last.

I took it off the wall. My hands shook. Behind me, I heard the gallery owner hurrying her customer out the door. I strode over to her.

She gave me a quick, alarmed look and said, cowering, "Please, be reasonable."

"This belongs to my father," I said.

"Fine," she said, backing away toward her desk. The light reflected off her witchy shoes.

"You even kept the frame," I marveled.

"You can have it," she said. "I bought it for a song. I always thought I would have to give it back, and here you are. But now you must never come back here, and you must not tell anyone how you acquired this painting. I don't want to ever see you again. Don't even tell me your name." The fright was gone from her voice; this was a speech she had planned to give. She walked to the front door and held it open, waiting for me.

It can't be this easy, I thought. "How did you get this?" I asked.

"Do you want the painting? Because if you want the painting, then you shouldn't ask any questions. Let's keep this simple."

I paused. I thought of Bertrand then, who wouldn't have listened.

"Leave," she said, and this time I obeyed. I ran toward the Seine, clutching the painting under my gray coat. My feet felt like lead. I could not move them quickly enough.

THE SENSATION THAT THERE WAS A REAL WOMAN IN the room with me, and that she was lovely but remote, was nearly painful. I leaned the Morisot on the glass table next to my valise, wedging its corner into a jagged crack that streaked across the tabletop like a bolt of lightning.

It was Friday evening and Chaim had already set out for the synagogue, so I could study the Morisot alone: the half smile, the averted eyes, and the hatch of paint blurring the middle of her lips. In her dressing room there were a mirror, a washbasin, some jars suggesting powders and paints. A few shelves with perfume bottles, linens. I cupped my hands on either side of my eyes, as if peering in a store window at midday, and looked at the Morisot again.

The gesture, familiar all of a sudden, conjured an afternoon with my father in May of 1940, before the city fell. The days were lengthening and the gray sidewalk in front of the gallery was scattered with geranium petals from the flower boxes on the building's upper floors. The weather was so glorious, it nearly promised victory. However, at home, in addition to news of the bank panic and fear of the German invasion, my mother had been unable to find a reliable piano tuner. Father and I were in the gallery, trying not to listen to her argue with the day's third browbeaten tuner in the parlor above. The gallery darkened and then lightened as if cued by the intervals upstairs. Father shielded his eyes to look at the Morisot on the wall before us.

"I find it helpful to study Morisot like this. You do it, too," he instructed me, and then I saw what he saw. There was a claustrophobia to Morisot, or the sense of standing too close to someone else. I always wanted the painter to paint from one step farther away, as in Morisot's portrait of her unlovely sister Edma, mountainous in a black frock atop a floral settee.

Now with my hands around my eyes, I looked at Morisot's *Woman in White*, and the model's averted gaze suggested she knew I was there and looking. The circular mirror in the painting reflected nothing back, and the mottled impasto on the model's chest was a lighter shade than on the figure's face. Her left hand was engaged in pulling off the right sleeve. Soon, one hoped, the whole nightdress would follow.

"When Manet died in 1883, five of his portraits of Morisot were part of the estate," my father had said. "Manet kept the pictures he had painted of his sister-in-law for all those years, out of a sense of love or propriety, that no one else should possess such an intimate sight. What makes one man keep a painting when he could have a thousand others? It pleases me to think we've reunited Morisot and Manet here, even for a few days. They can whisper to each other in the gallery after dark."

Father leaned closer to the painting. "The Impressionists respect me," he said. "I like the unfinished quality of their work. It may be what I like best. And Morisot leaves her paintings unfinished as well as any of them. She says to you, 'Let your eye finish the picture. Let it notice what isn't here and add it in, let it resolve the features on this woman, see what I saw in this moment, what stood out to me, what remained and what did not.' There's a modesty to that vision that I admire. One that respects what the viewer will see.

"I'm not a modest man," my father said.

We heard Mother pound an angry arpeggio and scold the piano tuner.

"Your mother isn't modest either," he said. "But Max." He said my name almost plaintively. "Somehow, you are a modest fellow. It is a great virtue, and I admire it in you." I flushed and tried to look into my father's face, but his eyes were still fixed on the painting. A flock of swallows glided past the skylight in formation, and their shadows flew across the illuminated patch of green carpet. The sounds of the piano tuner were comical and sporadic.

I ticked the time off on my fingers: by that evening in Chaim's apartment, it had been five years since I had last seen the Morisot. The church bells outside tolled eight-thirty. Somehow I had missed the intervening hour and a half, lost in my thoughts and the study of the painting. Chaim had left me two unripe apples, the day's newspaper folded in two, half of a baguette, and a hard triangle of cheese. I was touched by his silent generosity even while he worried about how much money we had left and the dwindling number of cans in the cupboard.

I polished off the apples, followed by the bread and cheese, hid the Morisot in the valise, tucked the newspaper under my arm, and went in search of something else to eat. I crossed over rue de Rivoli and out of the Jewish quarter. I found a grocer selling sardines for a good price near where rue de Rivoli becomes rue Saint-Antoine, bought a tin and a stale roll, walked to the church of Saint-Paul, and sat down on its steps. I unfolded the newspaper and read an account of the American battle for the Chinen Peninsula. Okinawa was nearly theirs. In Paris, the wife of Robert Wagner, former district leader of Baden, committed suicide upon her arrest. The newspapers were always especially curious when women were involved.

I ate my sardines on the roll, soaking the stale bread in the oil at the bottom of the tin. The oil dripped and spattered onto the newspaper, and two pigeons with iridescent heads and lidless beady eyes waddled over to inspect.

On Friday nights, before the war, Bertrand and I might have tried to sneak into a movie or have loitered in the place de la Sorbonne to see if any girls wanted to talk to us. Tonight, I licked the sardine tin clean and walked back to Chaim's apartment and to my painting, which I propped next to my bed. Before succumbing to sleep, I considered that my father would be proud of this recovery. It was nearly enough to take me back to him.

THE NEXT MORNING, A SATURDAY, I AWOKE TO THE sight of the Morisot.

I rolled over in bed and turned away from the window, the light streaming in from the open shades. I watched the dust motes and fell into a languid half sleep.

In a dream, Rose appeared at the foot of my mattress, carrying a child in her arms. The bundle cried out twice, sounding much like Chaim's neighbor's cat, and then vanished. Rose was the girl as I remembered her before the war, in the same gauzy *déshabillé* as the Morisot woman. I could smell her laundered nightdress and her damp skin and its talcum powder and perfume. The collar of the *déshabillé* brushed against me. But this fantasy was broken by a second one. In the painting was a mirror. I dreamed then of a second mirror, covered with a black sheet. Where was *this* memory from? When the Count de Camondo died when I was thirteen? Yes, and another house as well, with lotus flower wallpaper. But I could remember nothing more.

I woke with a cry and leaped from bed. It was essential to hide the painting, which I did, behind the giant armoire in Chaim's hallway. Then I set out in the direction of the rue des Beaux-Arts.

I ARRIVED ONCE AGAIN AT GALERIE ZOLA AND PEERED in its window. The owner's elbow was propped against the desk and she was engrossed in an auction catalog. A long ash dangled off her cigarette and piled on the page opened before her. I rang the buzzer and she started, then walked to the door but did not open it. She touched the glass, leaving the cloudy imprint of five fingers. Judging by how she had sent me away, I was prepared for a fight. But to my surprise, she pressed an unseen button and let me in.

The gallery was stuffy after the brisk air outside, and I could smell the wilted flowers rotting in the wastebasket. I noticed an ashtray that bore the name of a Swiss hotel.

"Please sit down," she offered. I sat.

"So you're Daniel Berenzon's son." She could not hide that she was impressed. So my father's reputation had meant more than my own efforts.

She eyed me down the length of her Camel. I looked at her hands. They were ringless, with nails bitten to the quick.

"Don't bother asking how I know that. I had heard a whisper that you were back in town. And you look just like him. I realized it last night, after you left. Before the war, I attended the openings at your house. Beautiful gallery. Paris is just *un petit village*." She laughed.

I took a calling card from its tray on her desk. *Claudine de La Porte des Vaux*, it read, and gave her address and telephone exchange.

"I apologize about the difficulty yesterday," Madame de La Porte des Vaux said, as if she meant it. "I'd heard that the Jews coming back to France are all practically deranged. So listen: The cheese man sold his cheese during the war. The baker sold bread. I kept the gallery open and sold the paintings that fell into my hands. And I was better than most, Monsieur Berenzon."

"Better than most Frenchmen?" I asked.

"True, though my point is finer than that: better than most of your father's and my colleagues. You want to know how I got the painting? The Germans asked me a question, I gave them an answer, and one day a man—in civilian clothes, mind you—knocks at my door and gives me the Morisot. He says, 'Thank you for providing Herr Rosenberg with the necessary information,' and disappears. I didn't even know who he was talking about. I didn't want to get mixed up with the Germans at all. But if you find out who Herr Rosenberg was, and you probably will, you could let me know."

"What did you tell them?" I asked.

She sighed. "You think I was a collaborator, but I was not. The month was January, in 1942, and I was alone in the gallery as I always am. Two German soldiers came to the door. They were very polite and apologetic that their French was limited. I, however, know a little German, so we were able to converse. I was courteous—I value my life, after all—but not friendly in the least.

"The soldiers showed me a piece of paper with the name *Rose Clément* on it. In their uncouth way, they were asking me what I knew about her and whether or not she was a respectable young woman. I praised her honestly: her intelligence, beauty, the enormous responsibilities that your father entrusted to her, and so on. I hope you will not mind my saying this, but I heard that she had rejected your suit. So I told the Germans this, too—that she had refused a Jewish man.

"The soldiers nodded to each other and one wrote down little phrases in a notebook. We stood talking by the gallery door the entire time. No Nazi ever set foot in this establishment.

"Then three months later, a bald man appeared. He wore lovely shoes, I remember, and handed the Morisot to me. At the time, I had no idea why—I thought he wanted me to sell it for him, which surprised me because he was so evidently well-off in those lean times. But then he made it clear that it was a gift for my cooperation. What cooperation? I thought. After he left, I remembered telling those two polite young men about Mademoiselle Clément, and I figured the events must have been connected. I was so relieved the soldiers didn't deliver the painting to me. Then the neighbors would really have been suspicious! So you see, I wasn't a collaborator at all. And I may have saved your friend's life." She looked out the gallery's window in a dreamy way, as if she were sitting for her portrait. "Now I have helped the house of Berenzon twice," she said, and patted my hand. I withdrew it. "Just remember. In this business we say, any bad arrangement is preferable to a good lawsuit."

"Did you know the painting had belonged to my father?" I asked.

"Certainly not. I gave not a thought to its origins. I hung it in my own home for several years and forgot all about it—something new eventually becomes so familiar it grows invisible. However, my financial situation has been more difficult of late, so Lola, my daughter, reminded me of this small Morisot and suggested we sell it.

"Mr. Berenzon, I pity your plight, I really do. I can't imagine how I would behave if I were as distinguished and established as your father in this field, and if all my life's treasures went *poof*!" She made the shape of an explosion with her hands. "Where *is* the elder Mr. Berenzon? Why doesn't he make these inquiries?"

What could I say? That I had seen my father unhinged? "I don't know," I said.

"Oh, you're just a dear young boy." Madame de La Porte des Vaux wrapped her bony fingers around my wrist. "You have suffered. I know how you must have suffered." She tightened her grasp. "I want to help you, Monsieur Berenzon. But I've done my part in the war effort, no? I see that you're a fine young man, if lost in the world. I know you will be tempted to come see me again, but resist this urge. The urges we feel most strongly in life are the ones most essential to resist. If you do not make me regret my kindness, I shan't mention to the other dealers that you're on the hunt. If I do, your search will run as dry as the desert." She buzzed the exit to the gallery and, wordlessly, I left.

WHEN I ARRIVED ON ROSE'S DOORSTEP AND TOLD HER I had found the Morisot, it made her call out as if in ecstasy.

"With one name from you, I found this," I said. Rose nodded. "Did you know it was there?" Rose said she did not, and for the first time I doubted her honesty. She refused to look at me yet invited me in. I joined her in the wire elevator, not with the sense of elation that a young man should feel in a small space with a girl but with the dull desperation of an action he feels powerless to defy. We did not speak. She opened her door with a key on a ribbon, took my coat from me, and hung it in the closet-office, out of sight.

"Give me another name, like Madame de La Porte des Vaux," I asked.

"You're a pawn," Rose replied. "She's suspect, so you've just allowed her to privately dispense with some of her looted goods. She's a shrewd businesswoman. She will be pleased to have you frightening other dealers to sell quickly or, better yet, to give you their paintings outright. A Morisot is not nearly as precious as a Manet. What she has parted with is not priceless—which is in comparison to the high personal value that she correctly imagines you place on it. She has made the better deal, still."

"Of course," I said loudly. I had not thought about the value at all, only the sensation that this was the first of many doors unlocking, at the end of which stood my father.

"Hush," Rose said. "The neighbors will think—"

"Your neighbors are all indecent," I said. "Unless you tell me they've been in the woods with the partisans." I gripped her arm.

"Max, I'm sick," she said. "That hurts, let go."

I put my hand on her forehead. It was clammy. "Have you seen the doctor?"

"Look, I'm going gray," she said, and parted her hair for me to see. It was streaked with white. "Max, I want you to have ordinary happiness."

"What?"

"May I have a cigarette?" Rose asked. "I think that you are looking for extraordinary happiness, with me, with these lost paintings, and it is not here. Not in this lifetime. Only aspire, Max, to ordinary happiness. It makes me feel hopelessly sad to see you, when you are so alive and gay, and it's wasted on me. Go back to medical school. Stop looking.

"I know you're asking me for another name. But don't you understand that if you appear at the door of every suspect art dealer, and they draw the line connecting you and me, they'll know I know about their trades and I'll be unable to carry on my work?"

"We're running out of time."

"Some will sell, but some will not. I'm only one woman. No one understands what has happened like I do."

"Let me help you."

"Don't be ridiculous. You're made entirely in your father's image. You don't know what you're stumbling into. I told you—let me carry on with my work."

Rose stood and filled the teakettle. After four silent minutes, it whistled hysterically.

I sat in Rose's chair and listened to her story, which was not told in a single breath but, rather, with several pauses, over the greater part of the night. At times she narrated it to me; at times, when I neared sheer exhaustion, it seemed as if I told the story to myself. Rose was lucid and detached as she spoke, and for the first time I wondered if she had completely survived the war. She performed a strange, hypnotic dance around the piles of papers in the main room and in the closet-office, lifting the tilting stacks midway, as a magician takes any card from a deck but knows its number and suit, and then she would read out loud the list of figures or addresses or paintings' names. I realized that these tens of thousands of documents were, in fact, all ordered according to the system she had arranged in her miraculous mind. The only other person who could also do this would have been my father.

"It was with your collection that I understood how Goering had organized a new economy. It benefited Hitler first, Goering shortly thereafter, and next the French art dealers. For example, in your case, Goering's insatiable lust found a French art dealer's *Portrait of a Bearded Man*—Italian school, sixteenth century—and a scene of the hunt supposedly by Jan Weenix. Dark masterworks of debatable authenticity. The market was flooded with forgeries precisely because the Germans wanted this so-called Aryan art, from centuries past, with no 'degeneracy' or modernity to it. Thus, at the Jeu de Paume, the *chef emballeur* was told to gather *Nature morte aux fruits* by Braque, Cézanne's *La Douleur*, Degas's *Madame Camus au piano*, three paintings from the Kann collection, one of your Sisley winter scenes, *Maternité* by Corot, three Matisses, and Picasso's *Mère et l'Enfant* for shipment. All together, twelve of the best-known paintings in modern art, exchanged for those two morose Old Masters. No money changed hands. The Jews' art replaced the need for currency. Goering kept his two paintings, and the French dealer obtained twelve masterpieces that he would quickly sell and set adrift on the active art market. Hitler's acquisitions are much easier for me to trace, since he insisted on 'paying' for his. He had a middle-class attitude toward finances. Goering, the rich man, took what he wanted. Abetz, too. They say he reconstructed your father's entire office as his own, on avenue Marigny. It's all dismantled now, of course.

"In July of 1941, a light on the roof of the museum was left on. In a hateful coincidence, the Reichsmarschall had visited that very day, and we were to entertain an audience of Feldpolizei the next. The word *sabotage* was quick on everyone's lips. As a French citizen, I was naturally suspect for attempting, during the blackouts, to send a signal to the Allies. What luck that my first interrogation was for a crime I had not committed. Later, I could assume the same righteous manner when I was, under the circumstances, guilty. I adopted a German attitude during questioning; I reaffirmed my position over and over, without embellishment and without heat. I had only detachment, and my curmudgeonly reputation, and my ugly hair and clothes.

"On another occasion, a German soldier spied me copying the descriptions of paintings. He confiscated my notebook and delivered it to his superior, who tore it to bits. That was my second interrogation—which followed much as the first: the German's rapid-fire questions and my stubborn, repetitive answers—and this satisfied the soldier. I went home that night in a fever to re-create the notebook from memory, which I did.

"In May of 1943, a large shipment left the Jeu de Paume for Germany. Many of the staff went on holiday, as we were told there would be no work to do at the museum. Still, in the Salle des Martyrs—the so-called degenerate art repository—and in the storage rooms of the basement, there were more than five thousand paintings left behind. Their abandonment was a matter of concern. I complained to the soldiers who remained in the museum of the faulty wiring in the Salle des Martyrs and the basement and, after I undertook a quick tour of these rooms' lamps and sockets, though I nearly electrocuted myself in the process, I had a dozen easy reasons to stay behind.

"I walked among the paintings that had not been shipped—Masson, Miró, Picabia, Valadon, Max Ernst, Léger, Picasso, Kisling, La Fresnaye, and Klee. On May 26, they disappeared. On May 27, I arrived at work almost at dawn, and already a column of smoke greeted me above the terrace of the Tuileries. By sunset, the fire still burned, fueled, I assumed, by the five or ten thousand paintings that our occupiers considered so dangerous. After that, the museum was quiet, as if in hibernation, for almost a year.

"On Bastille Day of 1944, Alfred Rosenberg's organization, the ERR, issued an internal report of European confiscations. Its author was modest, admitting that the numbers did not include the seizures of the East and regretting that ten thousand objects had not been cataloged at the time of the report's completion. Still, this balance was its own account of the German victory. The 22,004 works of art were categorized as:

10,890 paintings, watercolors, and drawings
684 miniatures, paintings on glass and enamel, books, and manuscripts
2,477 furniture pieces of acknowledged historical value
583 textiles: tapestries, rugs, and brocades
5,825 objets d'art: porcelains, bronzes, jewels
1,286 archaeological pieces from the Far East
259 objects from antiquity, including sculptures, vases, and jewels

"There was enough furniture to fill 29,436 railway wagons. As the summer progressed, and the rate of convoys leaving for Germany reached breakneck speed, I had a sense of the German army gathering its loot and preparing to evacuate it by rail, as that trip was much faster than the one by road. The ERR did not wait until the last minute to pack its bags. After the landings at D-Day, the Resistance grew bolder and their acts of sabotage increased. That was after the SS massacre at Oradour.

"Another grand shipment was arranged, with an air of finality about it. A museum's worth of Cézanne, Gauguin, Modigliani, and Renoir paintings were brought to the train station. There were twenty-four works by Dufy, twenty-eight by Braque, twenty-five by Fujita, four by Degas, three Toulouse-Lautrecs, eleven Vlamincks, ten Utrillos, sixty-four Picassos, ten Segonzacs, more than fifty by Marie Laurencin, and eight by Bonnard. At the Gare de l'Est, forty-seven railcars awaited the shipments from M-Aktion, the agency that collected quotidian goods and fine furnishings. M-Aktion moved slowly, and I had time to notify the Second Armored Division of the presence of this train. The convoy's destination, we believed, was the château of the Prince of Dietrichsten, in Nikolsburg, about eighty kilometers from the Austrian capital.

"The men in the railroads orchestrated their resistance. It went like this: When Colonel von Behr gave his orders for the train to depart, the tracks were in use! There was no one person who could be blamed for the masses of locomotives waiting to load, unload, refuel, cross, enter, and depart. Still, there was such traffic in Paris as had not been seen in years. The Germans were angered but hardly surprised. They looked for any excuse to point out our national disorderly malaise. Several more days passed, and finally the long train full of paintings made its way out of the capital, only to break down at Bourget. The mechanics explained it was too laden for the tired engine. In Aulnay, a pause was necessary to replace the locomotive. Engineers swore up and down that it would be ready to depart by six o'clock on July 27.

"And this was the opportune hour, the time that the men of the railroad had arranged with the Second Armored Division. The approaching armies of Leclerc arrived in Aulnay, seized the town, and stopped the train. The important story, that of the artwork, ends there, when the art was returned to French hands.

"On August 19, as de Gaulle's forces approached Paris, I returned to the Jeu de Paume to keep track of any remaining stores when the Germans retreated. I recognized the uniformed men on the museum's roof. They waved to me, and I waved back. There was fighting during the day and at night. I dozed at the desk in my office, wakened at three a.m. by gunfire in the distance and again at five by gunfire overhead. At dawn, I counted nine bodies in brown sprawled dead around the museum. From the shapes they made in the dust, I gathered that they had fallen from the rooftop. Another gun battle lasted two more hours, and then the three hundred soldiers that held the Tuileries surrendered.

"I watched as our countrymen rejoiced. But I could not leave my post to celebrate with them: as soon as the Americans captured the German gunners in the Grand Palais, the Jeu de Paume was surrounded by razor wire and turned into a prisoner camp. I thought, This is what they mean by a war museum.

"Soon the Jeu de Paume was breached, filled again with the sounds of marching men, most of whom would have never set foot in a museum before. Three maintenance men and I, trembling all, were hidden at the back of the building. I went out to greet the conquerors first, hoping that the presence of a woman would calm them and that the lives of the maintenance workers would be spared. With a submachine gun trained on my back, I led the Allied soldiers through the museum as they kicked empty crates and flung open closet doors and dynamited the locks on the vaults, looking for the Nazis. I was lucky that no German soldiers were found. When I returned the following day, no trace of the *Boches* remained—not a single helmet, gun, leaf of stationery, flag, or plate bearing the insignia of the Reich. Somehow my papers, though they had been rifled through, remained an intact collection. In this, again, I saw the hand of Jaujard.

"In November, after the liberation, we formed the Commission de Récupération artistique, the CRA, of which I am the secretary, naturally, as I am its sole woman." For a moment, the old humor crept into her voice.

Rose explained that her work depleted her entirely, and that she often dreamed that she was buried in sand. As she choked, she envisioned her lungs glittering with the pigments of paintings, gold leaf, and lazulite from Badakhshan. To the Rothschilds had been returned their Vermeers. Yet what of the rest? They had been hidden in salt mines, in caves, in châteaux, in underground bunkers, in banks. The

Americans' art recuperation corps—dubbed the Monuments Men—predicted that, in coming decades, much would be found in America, home to the new millionaires. "At night," Rose said, "when I am unable to sleep, I repeat to myself, *Mon action après l'ERR n'avait pas été inutile.* My actions were not useless.

"You should end this rift with your parents, Max," she said. "Go to Le Puy. You never know when they will die."

She touched her ear and its pearl jewel, opened her door, called the elevator, and waited with her back to me. We parted, she turned. I watched her face rise above me as the elevator descended. I stood outside for a while on the stoop. I felt indistinct, distant from the street, the parked cars, the dead bird by the gutter, and the flapping blue awnings. Had she said I was not myself without my father?

I could no longer remember if I had asked Rose for one more name, for the name that would lead me, at least, at last, to *Almonds.* But I knew she would have refused. As I left her room, I had let my gaze drop—it did so unconsciously and of its own volition—to the sheaf on the nearest stack of documents. The word CAILLEUX leaped out. I knew it but could not recall its origins.

I opened Father's address book and found Cailleux on rue Washington, the same gallery that had sold the Matisse forgeries in March 1939, before the war. If at the time I felt a pang of guilt over betraying Rose, I quelled it with my conviction that a discovery was close at hand.

I had been standing on the street for an indeterminate amount of time. I watched the red flickering light of the radio transmitter atop the Eiffel Tower as it spread news, predicted the weather, damned the politicians, and warned airplanes of a metal spire in the clouds. I thought of Bertrand. I had grown accustomed to missing him.

Chapter Eighteen

THE CLOUDS THAT MAY NIGHT LOOKED LIKE dendrites—a word and image that floated to the surface of my mind from the glossy page of a long-neglected textbook. As I neared the Parc de Monceau, scraps of a dream I had had early that morning returned to me: I was running through the park with another child, hiding in the shiny leaves of the rhododendrons, hand attached to sticky hand. The dream memory of running quickened my pace until, with a leap, I had to step back up on the curb to avoid a car. *Il a brûlé un stop.*

I tried not to think of Rose, or of the peevish exchange with Chaim when I returned home. We were seated at the table, drinking the end of our twice-used coffee grounds. "Today is our last day's worth of food, Max," Chaim said. He had threatened this before and it had not been so; I suppose I was dismissive of him.

I shook my head to clear it. A veteran from the Guerre de Quatorze roasting fragrant chestnuts shared the street corner with me. The smell, and the sound of the heavy nuts falling into a customer's brown paper bag, was pleasant, and my spirits lifted. Above us, a soprano practiced an aria, and the veteran stopped scraping at his tin tray to listen. She sang Puccini, "*Chi il bel sogno di Doretta,*" from *La rondine.* Her voice soared upward between two impossibly high notes and seemed to join the sudden wind that swirled, swooped down the street, and snatched a newspaper from a man's hands. The traffic light changed and the cars rushed forward with their loud *shush*ing sound. Mother said Mussolini ruined Puccini for her by giving the oration at the composer's funeral, and my father said he didn't care.

I turned onto rue Washington, where two women hastened in opposite directions from the doors of the Cailleux Gallery. The sun had dropped from sight, but its low rays made the steep mansard rooftops glint like the rubbed tip of a pencil. The gallery's sleepy yellow glow, too, suggested that some evening festivities were dwindling.

I pushed open the door to find a teetering, red-faced man gripping a bottle of champagne. "We don't have any glasses left, so you'll have to drink out of this!" he shouted, and tried to embrace me, though I ducked out of his grasp. This was Mr. Cailleux, the gallery's owner.

"Don't expect to buy anything because it's all been sold, sold, sold!"

I edged past his enormous girth, out of the entryway and into the room. I had not been to a gallery opening in five years, but the smells were the same: toxic fresh paint, sweat in wool suits, acrid cigarettes, wine, and Roquefort cheese. I scanned the twenty or so canvases before me and saw a red dot—sold—beneath each painting. One wall was Cocteau: thin, whimsical drawings and portraits by the opium addict. Ten Gustave Cariot studies of Notre-Dame borrowed Monet's trick of painting cathedrals at different times of day. Cariot's Notre-Dame was wan and sandy at 9:30 a.m. By four in the evening, the church was as pink as your tongue with a sky as green as grass. Two couples lingered by a table filled with empty wine bottles.

Underneath *Notre-Dame, Vue du Port aux Vins, 1 heure de l'après-midi* were a pair of round sofas, red like the divans in my father's lost gallery. On one, beneath a cloud of cigarette smoke, lounged two women, each with her legs crossed toward the other, their limbs nearly intertwined. The darker of the two was shoeless, and a girl with her same complexion scuffed the floor between the sofas, shuffling in her mother's too-large high heels.

"*Tesoro*," said the barefoot woman, her eyes thickly lined in kohl, laughing as I started. "And who are you, with your pretty face and big eyes? Are you wanting to buy Bernard's paintings, too?"

"No—yes. But I was told they are all sold. My aunt had wanted to come herself, but she is suffering from bunions so she sent me instead."

"And who is your aunt?" The woman flexed her stockinged foot and smiled at me.

"Claudine de La Porte des Vaux."

"Then come over here," shouted Cailleux. "You can settle a bet for us. It's two against two, and you'll be our deciding vote."

"But he doesn't know anything." The speaker had a nasal voice and a beard pointed like a spruce tree. He made a tent out of his fingers and flexed them back and forth.

"No, no, his aunt is Claudine de La Porte des Vaux, a marvelous art dealer," Cailleux told the bearded one. *And very rich*, he mouthed. The two remaining couples kissed the women good-bye. "*Buona notte*, *congratulazioni*, *arrivederci*," they called from the hallway.

Mr. Cailleux had rolls of fat on his forehead where another man might have had wrinkles. He wore a gold ring on his first finger, which he kept jabbing into the bearded man's chest. He wheezed while he spoke.

"We're talking about the bad old days," said an American in golfer's clothes. "Back when Cailleux was thin and hungry!" He gestured at our host with his glass. Its ice cubes clinked merrily.

"Listen to Mike," the barefoot woman cried, pronouncing the golfer's name *meek*. "Now you are too fat even to go sailing!"

"*Haw-haw!*" Mike laughed like a donkey. "Too fat to go sailing!"

A fourth man did not speak but stared at me from behind black-rimmed glasses. I tried not to look at him. Had we known each other? He rubbed his bald head over and over, thinking, I worried, of the same thing.

Cailleux turned to me. "Listen carefully. I say there were four great art dealers before the war: Berenzon, Paul Rosenberg, Wildenstein, and one other. I was one of the petit greats, yes, but not of the same grand tradition. Not yet!" He puffed at his Gauloise quickly, as if to indicate his excitement. "No one can remember the name of the fourth. Mike will pay whoever can come up with it. Or maybe Oskar will." Mike looked over at the bald man, who was busy cleaning his glasses. The bald man returned the glasses to his face and squinted at me.

"David-Weill?" the bearded man offered.

"No, he was a collector, old boy. Try again."

"We have ten thousand francs resting on this," Mike the golfer told me, grabbing my elbow. "You've got to remember the name of the fourth. You've just got to."

I didn't understand their bet, nor did I really want to help these men. But the question was too easy. I couldn't resist showing off. I imagined the Bernheims' salon: two purple and crimson tapestries running the length of the walls; the black marble fireplace with its veins of mica; the Lipschitz andirons in the shape of coiled snakes; the display case in the corner, lightly covered in dust; the too-soft leather couches; the hordes of children in varying states of undress. "Could it have been Bernheim-Jeune?" I furrowed my brow.

"Jesus Christ, ten thousand francs!" Mike shouted in English. "Oskar, pour this young man a whisky." Bald Oskar lumbered to the bar. Mike thumped me on the back.

There were more paintings in the gallery's hallway and antechamber. I wanted to stand and examine them, to look for the clue Rose had recorded. I made as if to leave, but Cailleux grabbed me by the wrist. He didn't seem to have noticed that he'd just lost a bet. An idiotic grin stretched across his drunken features.

"Did you know the Bernheim-Jeunes?" I surprised myself by asking.

"Sure," said Cailleux. "Here, hold this." He handed me his cigarette while he reached in his lapel pocket for some pills.

"What about Wildenstein?"

"Good riddance," he said, with the pills on his tongue. He took a slug of whisky.

"And Berenzon?"

"Daniel Berenzon," he said with relish. "Did I know him!"

"Who didn't," sneered the bearded man.

"Did you like him?" I asked, still holding the cigarette.

"Who could like him?" said the bearded man.

"But who couldn't? *Un momento*, who gave you that?" Cailleux asked, and I handed the Gauloise back. He gestured for the little girl to come to him, and she shuffled over in her mother's shoes. He lifted her onto his lap, and she reached into his lapel pocket and took out a lighter.

"At first Berenzon was so cocksure, a bastard," the bald man said, glancing at me.

"Slipped Matisse away from Bernheim," Mike added.

"Like a bride from her garters—"

"It wasn't nice," Cailleux sang. The daughter began to flick the lighter on and off.

"Oh, no, it wasn't nice."

"But it was brilliant."

"His timing was impeccable."

"Like a Swiss watch."

Cailleux leaned back and snatched the lighter out of his daughter's hand and smoked another Gauloise. He stared at the end of the cigarette. "Matisse was tired of the Bernheim brothers. He had begun a new phase, in the Oriental mood, and they weren't selling, until Berenzon put one up in his window and it was a smashing success."

They fell quiet.

"Remember that wife of Berenzon's?" The golfer asked. He reached over my legs for the bottle of Glenfiddich and made a low moaning noise. My eye started to twitch, and I raised my fingers to its lid to stop the spasms. A repugnant two-second image played in my mind in which I saw the golfer, in his white varsity sweater with the green V collar, atop my struggling mother.

"Oh, you have no idea, young man," Cailleux said to me. "What a face. A thousand ships. Troy could have happened all over again."

"And not just a face." The bald man wiggled his hips. When I met his eyes, he snarled.

"That Berenzon wooed her—"

"Like every other man in Paris rich enough—"

"Even Cailleux asked Eva out for dinner." The golfer laughed. "And I was already married!"

At this, the tanned woman glared from the other sofa. She unclipped her earrings with two noisy clicks and spoke in rapid Italian to her friend. My mind raced to find an excuse to look at the paintings or to join the two women.

"Berenzon wasn't afraid to take on a Jew—"

"Berenzon was a Jew, too!"

"Who wasn't a Jew then, in this business? They were everywhere."

"A Jew, though not a cheap one."

"But crafty."

Cailleux dropped a hand, heavy as a paw, on my knee. "Berenzon visited this very gallery once, long ago—1938, maybe. Right before I had a show of Utrillos. Strolled in behind some workmen even though there were curtains up in the windows. He sauntered over to my desk, picked up the price list, and read right through it. I was so angry! I almost taught him a lesson right there. But listen to this: Berenzon said I was underselling the Utrillos. If I didn't make them more expensive, no one would want them and I wouldn't make any money or pay off my gambling debts." He sucked at his teeth. "I don't know how he knew about those debts."

"I didn't know you had them," said the golfer.

"Not anymore. That show got me, as you say"—Cailleux turned to him and switched to English—"out of the red."

"Berenzon's wife was barred from the casinos," the golfer replied.

"She had a gambling problem?" Cailleux asked. "Cheated at poker? Counted cards?"

"I know the story," I said. I told them about the thirty-seven slots on the roulette wheel that my mother could envision as keys on the piano. I described her mountain of casino chips, the cheering crowd, and the unhappy portly owner. My mother had recommended he install fans to distort the wheel's perfect pitch. We were given his white car and its chauffeur for the day. Did it really happen? It seemed as far away as the memory of a childhood dream.

"That's ridiculous," sneered the bearded man.

"Well, it's true," I replied.

"How do you know?" the bald man asked.

"I heard it from my aunt."

Cailleux sat forward on the sofa, drawing his breath in starts, eager to tell the end of *his* story. "I sold every last damn painting in the show. Even the paintings Gabriella said were ugly." He looked down at his daughter, sleeping in his lap, one shoe fallen to the floor. He kissed the part in her hair. "It was nearly a miracle. Utrillo was so happy, he embraced his boy in front of me when he learned we'd sold everything. Sold everything, just like tonight!" Cailleux and the bald man clinked their glasses. The bearded man had his eyes closed. His slack jaw revealed a mouthful of weasel teeth.

"Utrillo, one of those?" Mike asked, in a skimming voice, light and dangerous.

"How could you not know this?"

Cailleux called over to the women's group, "Sometimes the women don't mind, eh?"

"We need sensitivity." The dark woman's French sounded like Italian.

"*Haw-haw!*" Mike laughed again and stood up, stretching. "Listen to La Macaroni!" He mimed a golf swing.

The Italian raised her voice, tossing her words over the backs of the sofas. "Mr. Berenzon knew how to talk to women."

Her companion spoke for the first time. "He listened carefully, not interrupting, not giving advice."

"*Bof*, it's not even all that," said the Italian wife, gesturing with her hands as if she were opening a book. "He'd experienced sadness."

"What sadness?" Cailleux asked.

My skin pricked.

"I heard his kid joined the Free French. Then, when the son was approaching Paris, they stopped a Nazi train bound for Germany, and on board were all of Berenzon's paintings." I swelled at this heroism, misattributed though it was.

"No, that was Paul Rosenberg's son," Cailleux's Italian wife said. "I read a piece in *Libération*."

"I can make some coffee," her friend said. "Who wants a coffee?"

Everyone nodded, and the two women disappeared through a Roman arch at the back of the gallery. The room was still, except for Cailleux's wheezing.

"Let's turn off the lights in here and just sit with candles," Mike said.

"You have the strangest ideas."

"It will be beautiful," Mike insisted. He lit the candles and turned off the lights. The faces floated around me, glowing and rosy.

"So what happened to Berenzon?" Cailleux asked, yawning.

"His kid ran away," I offered.

"His boy ran away?"

"I didn't hear that," the bald man said.

"No," said the Italian wife, returning with the tray of coffee. The other woman stood behind Mike and put her hands on his shoulders. "I mean the daughter."

I could barely make out their words over my own thoughts. This is it. This is what I have known all along. It has finally come. I watched us from the ceiling.

"Oh, that's true, that was decades ago, right—I'm tired. I should get going, boys—born with a problem in her skull. It couldn't grow—my cousin's wife had that, too, the baby seems fine at first, but then it doesn't develop like it's supposed to. The soft part is fused . . . or she had a horrible fever. That's what happened to his baby girl." The women clucked their tongues. "Poor thing. At least they had another. And then there's that Picasso picture of her with her rabbit." It flashed before my eyes, as if lit by a bulb, its blues and grays.

Micheline.

"That's when he gave up collecting, had that huge sale. Did you purchase anything? I didn't go the first day. They say it was empty. It felt like tomb looting. He even sold the portrait of the daughter. Then Stefania made me go. I bought a gorgeous Renoir. It was still expensive—he wasn't giving away the stuff for free—*Au contraire*. I sold the Renoir last year for ten times the profit." Cailleux wheezed, and I heard a little whistle while he spoke. "Drouot's was amazed I had a Manet still life in my collection, asked how I possibly could have acquired it. They know I'm not the biggest cat in the chicken coop. I sold it privately, of course—why hang it in the entryway, then? To boast! When I sold the Renoir, the buyer was worried that all the papers were in order."

Coffee cups clinked and the candlelight reflected one hundred times in the gallery's windows and off the bald man's glasses and my head spun, dizzy with the flickering light.

I remembered the baby we examined on the last day of the anatomy semester, under its awful square of rubberized cloth: its too-small skull. *Failure to thrive*, the doctor said. *Note the link between microcephaly, craniosynostosis, and what we call* kleeblattschädel, *the beaten copper pattern on the inside of the child's skull.*

You would make a wonderful pediatrician, my father said, after that day's lesson. *Yes*, my mother agreed, *there are never enough good ones*.

Cailleux's cigarette crackled and hissed as it lit. I was sitting so close to him, he could have been my father smoking in the dark in the gallery on rue de La Boétie. He, who never told me. I wiped my cuff against my eyes. I needed to leave. Her name was Micheline. I knew it then but I had also always known it.

Cailleux asked, "Who got us started talking on this? You did, Mike." "Not me, he did." They were talking to me, at last. "Why do you want to know? Don't I recognize you from somewhere?"

I wanted to flee, but if I ran would they suspect me? I stood up, and my hands scrambled around on the dark sofa for my overcoat.

"You say Claudine is your aunt?" one of the men asked me.

In the entryway, I swayed a moment as I leaned into the door, and the gust of wind blew the candles to and fro. I steadied myself against the door frame and the jerking candlelight illuminated what Cailleux's hulking frame had blocked as I entered: There was Manet's *Almonds*, with a little red dot on the wall beneath it.

Chapter Nineteen

I STUMBLED BACK IN THE DIRECTION OF RUE DE Sévigné. I lost my key somehow and banged on the peeling door of Chaim's apartment with a closed fist. Chaim answered, already chattering.

"I just can't see the worth of keeping this when I could starve and you could starve or you could not care. It's not even a picture of someone in your family." Chaim's words ran over each other, and I could neither understand what he said nor to what he referred. "After I did it, I knew I did something terrible to you, Max. I thought, I don't know Max very well, but I know I have done something that will make him spin away from me like a top." He made a frenzied gesture with his finger. "But you did not seem to understand how close we were to starving, and this morning at the aid society, once the grenade came through the window, and the explosion, I thought the smoke was gas and—"

I held him by the shoulders. "Be calm, please." The war wrecked his mind, I thought. He's deranged, just like Madame de La Porte des Vaux said.

Chaim pushed my hands off. "There was a grenade at the aid society today! Someone threw it in the window after I had waited in line all morning, just when I got inside. They say it was some anti-Communist, but I didn't realize it was a Communist aid society for political prisoners. I thought they would still help me, but when the grenade went off we all pushed out of the building and I fell and they stepped on my hands until I grabbed on to the legs going by so someone would help me up."

"And then what happened?" I asked.

He looked down. "I sold your painting."

"What? Where? To whom?" I sputtered.

"I don't know. In the Eighth. Or the Sixteenth." There were dozens, if not scores, of galleries in those two neighborhoods.

"We'll retrace your steps," I said.

Chaim said, "I have to sit down. You, too."

We sat speechless next to each other at the kitchen table. "I know it was a very valuable painting," Chaim said. "I did not realize what a treasure it was until I sold it. But once I gave it to the art dealer, I could not stop myself. I thought only of how we would buy ourselves food and that I needed to go to a doctor."

He held up his left hand. It was purple, and the first three fingers were swollen and askew at the knuckles.

Chaim was calmer now. "The dealer called all his associates over when I took out the painting, then had his wife come downstairs from their home on the floor above. 'Where did you get this?' he asked, then said, 'No, no, don't tell me, I don't want to know.' He took a special picture of it and had his assistant rush it to the Curie laboratory. With this I can go to the doctor. What do I know with money anymore? I have not had money for years. I think we could buy an automobile. We could buy two. I don't know how much it is worth. He said a huge sum. Max, if you had explained to me it was a once-in-a-lifetime chance, your prized possession—well, I suppose you tried to tell me you had hidden savings but you sounded like a liar to me. If only I had believed you! But would you have sold it if we were starving? We were starving and you didn't sell it. You kept it from me."

"Do you have the money with you?" I asked, suddenly calm.

Chaim stood and began pulling ten-thousand-franc notes from his pockets. "The man tried to give me a bank check but I said I wasn't going to trust the banks, so his assistant opened a vault behind a bookcase. At first I thought there were bricks in the vault, and then I realized they were blocks of money." Chaim pulled money from one pocket and then the other.

The bills began to blow around the room and underneath the table. He dropped to the sofa, sitting on four hundred thousand francs or so. I gathered up the notes and tucked four and then a fifth into the velvet bag where Chaim kept his prayer shawl and phylacteries.

Then I wrapped a blanket around Chaim's shoulders, led him to his room, and filled the kettle. I had a sister named Micheline, I told myself while I waited for the water to boil. *Almonds* is in the Cailleux Gallery. The teakettle whistled. What a lot of money the Morisot fetched. My father would be proud.

From the *chambre de bonne* upstairs, someone who did not know how to play violin was playing slow open-string double stops on an untuned instrument, arcing the bow over the strings in ascending and descending pitch. I kissed Chaim's forehead. He slapped my cheek and then gave me the hot tea bag, which burned my palm. I opened the cabinets. They were not bare. I bought a bottle of whisky from our neighbor, whom we all pretended was an honest-dealing man, and watched Chaim while he drank some down. I took him to the hospital, and though I dreaded it was a mistake, it seemed criminal to do otherwise.

We returned by evening. I left the apartment again immediately and hitchhiked a ride with a young doctor who was driving in the right direction. He wore a khaki-brimmed hat and a coat of the same color, like a man on safari.

I held his black bag on my lap. "Now all the babies are being born," he said. "New armies of French sons, every day. We'll be ready to fight Germany again in twenty years." To what hospital did they take my sister? Where did she die? Where was she buried? I pictured a small headstone, chiseled with my last name, rose-colored stone turned gray by city soot and creeping graveyard moss and mold.

"You all right?" the doctor asked me.

"Yes," I said. We were idling at a red light, and he turned to look at me. The car's engine thrummed in my bones.

"I'm done for the evening. I can let you off at your destination," he offered. I said I would be much obliged and asked him to take me to rue Washington.

The doctor nodded. "I know it well. A week ago, a Sicilian lady called me. She had been married two weeks and her husband became possessed with the idea that she was unfaithful, so he slashed her face, in the old tradition of scarifying one's lover to make her unattractive to other men."

"Barbarism," I said.

"Everywhere," he replied, and we did not speak again until he deposited me on the street corner and his car sped off into the distance, driving, as all Parisians did, with only the low parking beams, a lingering habit from the days of the blackouts. There were many traffic accidents.

When I turned to the Cailleux Gallery, I was surprised to find its owner standing in the doorway. His eyes were beady and wine-brightened and his mouth purplish and slack. He opened the door. I glanced over his shoulder: *Almonds* no longer hung on the wall.

"Monsieur Berenzon, at last," Cailleux said.

"I want *Almonds* back," I said. I did not tell him that I had 400,000 francs in my pockets.

"You're making an offer?"

"There's no offer. This is theft." Yet in fact, I *was* prepared to make an offer, should we come to that. I was less interested in justice than in the painting itself. I had long given up on justice.

"I can ask *Almonds*' owner to name his price, but I warn you it will be very high. Eight hundred thousand. Maybe a million. My client has had his eye on that Manet for decades. Your father did you no favors today, Berenzon, by making it so dear. It's a prize now"—he put his hands around my neck—"like a stag's head." I pushed Cailleux away. "May twenty-fourth," he said, naming two days hence. "I want this for you, Berenzon, I do."

"Meet at this same time," I said.

Cailleux nodded, scratched a match, and unsteadily lit his cigarette. I could tell that he was nervous and this pleased me, though it should not have.

I turned toward home. The streetlamps, the closed shutters, the line that separated the sidewalk from the street, the grate over the gutter—everything seemed too sharply outlined. I had a sister and her name was Micheline and she would have died when I was too young to remember and young enough to be lied to. I ground my teeth. A vagabond half lay across the sidewalk, as if he were a legless doll propped into a sitting position. Eyes shut, he thrust a tin cup toward me. Had he seen Bertrand? I asked him. He said he had. They were sailors together at Gallipoli. I gave him some coins and wandered away.

Bertrand was missing in the vast sea of humanity. I yearned to numb my mind. I tried to reel in the long loose trail of my memory. There was a photograph on my mother's dresser that she said was me, but it did not resemble my other baby pictures. A lock of hair. It is too late now, Max, I thought; too much time has passed. You have memorized too many other things. I cursed my father for filling my brain with paintings. Had he hoped that all those names and pictures would crowd out the sunken tragedy? I gripped my head and wished I could pull from my coiled brain the Cézanne, pull from it the Bonnard, the Morisot, and, last, the Manet. Give me my sister.

Here I stopped, as if fixed to the flagstones. The church bells began their banging and echoing. My hands were clenched. My palms were sticky with sweat. A girl with sticky hands had danced with me before *Almonds*, singing a nonsense song—or the garbled speech of an imprisoned brain. She had not been a dream at all.

I returned to Chaim's apartment and, as I unlocked the courtyard gate, saw the concierge's liver-spotted hand draw back her curtain. I walked up the five flights, resting at the fourth, and wondered how Chaim had found my Morisot's hiding place. I had shoved the monstrous armoire in his hallway with all my might in order to squeeze the picture behind it, and then forced it back into place with my shoulder.

When I entered Chaim's hallway, there were his wife's lavender gloves waiting on the table, next to a note in Chaim's left-handed scrawl that said he had found a man to drive him to Pithiviers, near Orléans, where he hoped to find word of his wife and son. I felt like weeping but told myself it was only the fatigue.

Pithiviers, Pithiviers, Pithiviers, I chanted as I studied the armoire to see how far Chaim had moved it in order to extract the Morisot. It was nearly flush against the wall and there were no scrapes on the floor. How hard I had to push to move the armoire! I thought. I heaved against it again, for good measure, and heard a crash. When I withdrew the broken object, I held the Morisot that Chaim had sold, the *Woman in White*, ever averting her eyes, receding further into her quiet mysteries.

He had sold something else, then. But what? I looked out the window, into the courtyard, and saw a man in a felt hat checking the sky for rain. Standing where he stood, I had seen Chaim's face in this window days before. I had returned home from my second visit to Madame de La Porte des Vaux. That day we had burned one of the chairs from the kitchen table because we had not had sufficient fuel, and we argued and I threw a teacup against a wall and it did not break. I recalled thinking that Chaim was rummaging through my luggage but had not concerned myself with it further, because the valise had nothing of more than sentimental value inside. I threw open the case. There were the playbills of my mother's performances, a comic book of Rose's, her first letter to me, and my father's scarf with the moth hole at its hem. And then I understood: Chaim had sold the *Ham.* The fake Manet. The talisman of my hubris and failure. Someone had bought it for a handsome sum because he believed it was real.

Chapter Twenty

MY NEXT VISIT TO MADAME DE LA PORTE DES Vaux was brief. I found her sitting at her tall desk with a liquor bottle beside her. I knocked at the window, she reached out of sight to press the buzzer, and the door clicked open.

"Have a drink with me," she said. "Courtesy of the Russians. They admired my suit. They're my dead husband's suits. Not a bad one in the lot." She fingered a lapel. "Didn't you behave poorly at the Cailleux Gallery opening! I had to hear all about it from his wife. Why are *you* here again?"

"He has *Almonds.*"

"Oh?"

"But it's already been sold."

"So you buy it back. No one wants a row, that I can assure you. It will be easy. That Mademoiselle Clément, she is causing messy scenes."

"I haven't spoken with her since before the war."

"She's crazed—a vigilante. Accuses everyone: Christians, Jews, art dealers, buyers, the prime minister. Now, share some of this with me." She slid the vodka bottle toward me. I touched the violent Cyrillic on its label.

"I haven't the money to buy *Almonds.*"

"*Bah.*" She rolled her eyes and poured more vodka into her glass.

The Russians' drinking glasses were pushed to the far edge of the high table. She swept them over its rim and they shattered in the dustbin below. "Look what you've made me do," she said.

I ignored her.

I figured whoever had bought the *Ham* from Chaim might have bought another Manet—*Almonds*, for symmetry's sake. But there was an additional symmetry for me. The *Ham* could lead me to *Almonds*. I could circumvent Cailleux.

"Have you heard of another Manet for sale?" I asked.

She twirled a silver pen between her fingers. "I don't know anything about what you are asking, but here's an intuition. An American opened a new gallery on the Right Bank. Only Americans have money these days. Goodman, Gutman, Gutfreund—you figure it out." Her voice seemed to pick up. She was pleased, I suspected, to have me off haunting another dealer. "Yes my boy, try him. . . ."

I stood and hurried to the door. "Thank you, Madame," I said, from a safe distance. "You are always so kind to me." She poured more vodka from the garish bottle and lifted the glass to me.

"*Santé*," I said.

"*Dosvedanya*," she replied. "That means *You have a pretty face* in Russian."

As Madame de La Porte des Vaux had predicted, my path was easy, or nearly so. That same afternoon I found the new American dealer, Hans Gutman, who was not American at all but Swiss. He was plump with gray hair drawn across his scalp and bifocals perched low on his nose. I explained who I was. He seemed happy to see me. Yes, he had bought the *Ham*. No, he didn't know anything about *Almond*'s buyer.

"Cailleux sold it, right? I assume you asked him. And I assume he didn't tell you. This is happening everywhere." I was silent. He told me that he had always admired my father's taste in the avant-garde.

"The man who brought me the painting, he is who exactly?" Gutman asked.

"My uncle," I said. "Of a sort."

"Your uncle," he repeated. "How is his health?"

I told him it was much improved, and he said he was glad. We stood in the gallery's main room, each waiting for the other to speak. At last, he motioned me into his office, where a Rembrandt portrait of a young woman in a fur collar was propped against an easel. The desk itself filled much of the room. It was as long as an operating table and twice as wide. Four odd lamps stood at each of its corners: a Deco gooseneck, one with a fringed shade, a kerosene Rayo lamp, and a plain metal light such as one might see on the bench of a chemist in his laboratory.

Gutman stood by the door with his hand on a switch. "Let me begin by demonstrating my latest technological curiosity." He turned off the lights and passed behind me in the darkness. "I thought this would be of particular interest to you, because, if the rumors accurately retell the Manet's history, when you bought it at Drouot's everyone thought you were a fool. They judged it a fake, and with good reason. The poor painting has more varnish on it than the string section of an orchestra. Nor is its perspective altogether convincing."

The room went dark except for the glowing purple bulb of the chemist's lamp. "I have here a black light," he said. I looked up at Gutman, who gave me a violet and toothy smile.

"Remarkable, isn't it?" I agreed. Next, he lifted the Rembrandt portrait from the easel and held it flat beneath the light.

The signature, *Rembrandt*, with its wide swooping *R*, seemed to float above the surface of the painting and shone with the same purple light as Gutman's teeth. "We say it *fluoresces*," Gutman said. "Anything illuminated indicates new paint." The fur collar, too, shone. Dimly visible beneath it was painted a plain white strip of fabric. Ghostly lines shimmered around the woman's mouth and eyes. "Someone has tried to give this woman more of the famous Rembrandt sensibility and to dress her up as a noblewoman rather than a housemaid. Hence the fur collar, lightly painted on in later years. To the naked eye, it maintains the same *craquelure* as the older parts of the painting and hence seems all of a piece."

"A forgery," I said.

"Yes, which I can say with certainty because of this miraculous light. My economist friends tell me fakery is a market response to a demand."

"Why do you keep it?" I asked.

"I can't destroy it, and to sell it would be irresponsible. It makes an excellent teaching tool," he said. "This forgery has been in my possession since before the war. The director of a museum in Berne was so dismayed to discover it was a fake that he gave it to me practically for free. I've performed all other sorts of experiments on it. Linseed oil, for example, dissolves the newest paint pigments—it's a mystery why. I haven't a degree in chemistry, but it works."

I asked to see a *Ham* under the light. Gutman's breath was audible. "That was sold the same day your friend brought it to me." He turned on the lamp with the fringed shade.

It seemed obscene to me, like the short dresses of the women at Le Chat Noir on the evening of my birthday and my rift with Bertrand. The wrinkled man continued. "Surely your father had the same arrangements with his collectors as I do—that I will buy any Boucher or Fragonard or, as in this most recent transaction, Manet, that appears on the market. My client accepts it sight unseen."

"Everyone at the auction told me it was a fake," I said. I remembered the crooked white number 6 over the auction hall door at Drouot's, and Rose's shame on her pale cheeks. I touched my own cheeks, and they were fiery.

Gutman nodded in a pleasant, comfortable way, unaware of my growing agitation. "Your picture had new canvas stretchers and that horrid varnishing. But the black light showed me that nothing new had been painted onto it. "

"Perhaps you'd prefer not to know," I said. "A lawyer visited the forger in prison, who confirmed it was his work."

"And why would a forger ever tell the truth? He was in prison, no? What did he have to lose by telling you the Manet was his own? His reputation as a copyist could only be improved when others learned he fooled the house of Berenzon. Satisfy yourself with having recognized a master when others could not."

"It was Baron von Horty," I said. "He's infamous."

Gutman smiled. "That daft fellow's a hero now. During the war, a woman who worked in the Louvre—or was it the Jeu de Paume?—sprang him from prison to paint fake Vermeers, van Eycks—anything Dutch. Goering and Hitler bought them up, every last one."
Rose? I was seeing her hand everywhere.

"I'd like to offer you another rare piece from my collection," I said hastily. Gutman sat back in his chair. "A Morisot. It's only fitting to buy a Manet with a Morisot, is it not?"

He sniffed and nodded at my satchel. I withdrew the painting. He offered me a good price. I asked for thirty thousand francs more. He nodded silently. "It does make a man look twice to see a painting in which one woman has drawn another undressing."

"I've never seen a Morisot nude," I said. Gutman's voice lowered. He was as excited as I by the *Woman in White*.

"Cézanne could barely paint them either," he said. "You'll do well to take eighty thousand,"—which was twice his original offer. We stood and shook hands. His fingers were damp and fleshy.

"You're a fine young man. I'm pleased to do business with you," he said. "I shall certainly tell your father as much when we see each other next at the association meeting."

"Association meeting?" I asked.

"Of Art Dealers, at Drouot's, on June thirteenth."

"I had forgotten," I said. A lie. I had heard of no meeting, of course.

Unbidden a well-dressed young man appeared and wrote out a draft for the Morisot. I did not know if I had enough money for the price Cailleux would name, but I hoped that I was close. Gutman and I bid each other good-bye.

I had sold my first painting, I was ready to purchase my second, and yet I felt desolate. I went to the bank to exchange Gutman's check for currency, and then to the Louvre to find Rose. She was not there, so I returned to Chaim's and washed my shirt, shaved, nicked my upper lip, brushed my teeth, ironed the shirt, and dressed in it again, though the collar was still wet, bought a bottle of cologne and some flowers, and appeared again on the stoop of Rose's apartment on rue de Mézières. It was May 24 and eight o'clock at night. I would meet Cailleux at eleven.

After several minutes, Rose came to the foyer to greet me. As unwell as I had felt, she looked worse. There were dark circles under her eyes and her clothes looked like they were hung on a metal fame.

"Have you been eating enough?" I asked.

"Doubtful," she said.

"My God," I said. "Please, let's eat dinner."

"Is it dinnertime?" She looked up at the pale solstice sky. There was a restaurant still open along the Luxembourg Gardens, and I practically carried Rose there. When she first looked at the menu, her eyes welled up. "Only the crème brûlée sounds good," she whimpered.

"You're absolutely right," I said, and we ordered two of those, and wine, then omelets. Rose devoured hers, then much of mine. I drank my glass of cloudy water. Color crept back into Rose's cheeks. Her eyes shone at me. If she were not half-mad over the food, I would have mistaken the light for passion.

"We're in a medieval calendar," Rose said, and her laugh too was a sound from another time. Bright clementines dotted the trees around us, and the sky unfurled like a blue fan.

The air smelled like rain while the park's keepers watered the garden's dusty paths. I hummed the Satie *Gymnopédie* that my mother had taught me to play as a child. Rose peeled apart the bread in the basket and gave me the crusts while she ate the soft parts.

Rose tipped back in her chair. "This is pretty, old man," she said, using Bertrand's nickname for me, as if she could replace him. My friend, I wondered, where are you? I imagined my father, sitting on the lowest rung of the ladder that led to Monsieur Bickart's root cellar. Where was he now, in Le Puy? In the South? Would he forgive me when I returned?

"In a month I will have to go away again. Back to Germany."

"Stay here," I said. "I found *Almonds.* I am going to buy it back tonight. It belonged to a little sister—or an older sister, really—who died before I was four. She was kept a secret from me. Her name was

Micheline and the painting belonged to her. At Cailleux's, they talked about my father starting the gallery after she died."

"Cailleux?" Rose asked. "How did you know to go directly to Cailleux? You found his name in my room, didn't you? You spy!" She was white-faced again. "Cailleux didn't know I suspected him, so he kept operating in Paris and selling to Parisians. Now he knows. Don't you understand, Max? Cailleux will be gone by now. You've frightened him away. Why didn't you consult me first? You've ruined it all."

Chapter Twenty-one

WHAT HAPPENED AFTER CAILLEUX'S DISAPPEARance is difficult to recall. I moved from Chaim's flat and left him a rambling letter, for when he returned from Pithiviers, and a small fortune tucked under the chocolate bar he kept in his bedside table. I rented a student's room in the Latin Quarter, as it was close to Rose and to the medical faculty. No one knew I was there.

Whereas I had attended medical school in a desultory fashion before the war, I now visited its facilities religiously. As I had been expelled under the *Statut des juifs*, now I was readmitted without question. My anatomy course began again as if I had lifted the needle from a record in the spring of 1939 and laid it down in the same groove in June of 1945. The semester had stretched into summer because of the interruption of the war. I found some solace in memorizing the bones of the body, in my classmates' singular obsession and competition, and in the ornate writing of my textbooks. I walked along the quays, singing to myself, "The ethmoid bone is a light cancellous bone consisting of a horizontal or cribriform plate, a perpendicular plate, and two lateral masses or labyrinths." Labyrinth indeed!

The lectures continued with their comforting air of déjà vu until the professor announced that the next week our lessons would take the form of case studies on the classification of synarthroses, amphiarthroses, and diathroses—joints of the immovable, slightly movable, and freely moving variety. I had missed these lectures years before. Yet I recalled Rose asking me if I wanted Ivan Benezet's notes on the subject.

I arrived late on the third day of case studies. "In healthy children at birth," the professor intoned, "the bone consists of two pieces, which later become united along the middle line by a suture which runs from the vertex of the bone to the root of the nose. This suture usually becomes obliterated within a few years after birth. This was not the case, however, for today's study, a child of Polish decent, whose death certificate was issued in 1923 at age four."

I tore myself from the lecture hall and was soon outside in the summer air. This was the illness that Cailleux's wife had spoken of. So my sister's case made it into my textbooks as well. A coincidence, perhaps, but not such a great one when I considered how many we studied. Was it possible, then, that Micheline was also in Ivan Benezet's lecture notebook, dated March of 1939, right before the fall of Madrid and the suicide of Professor Negrín?

I understood then that Rose had known, for as long as she had known me, of Micheline. When I had named a sister, my sister, buried from word and memory, Rose was not surprised. She could have first learned through artistic circles, or perhaps my parents had told her. She slept in the Nurse's Room, after all. If Rose had once kept Micheline from me, now she wanted me to find her, if only because the tragedy would stop me from interfering with her work. Rose had, after all, encouraged me to return to medical school. Whereas Father had not wanted me to look for his paintings because any search would lead me to Micheline, whom he and Mother had so carefully buried. I understood it all only as betrayal. I did not take into consideration my parents or Rose's separate grief, only my own.

My steps brought me to the Marché aux Puces, as they might bring one man to his church and another to his whorehouse. A flea market would be the lowest circle of Purgatory for a painting, here amid carpets and paste jewelry, sandals from Calcutta, enameled pots, Czech beads and Scottish tartans, Moroccan leather, maps cut from old books, birdcages, patched tires, and engine parts for cars no longer produced on Europe's great assembly lines because their cities of origin were now piles of rubble.

A voice like a barking dog interrupted my reverie.

"On the subject of outlandish! Here is the son of my nemesis, hat in hand."

The speaker was blowsy, bald, and much too tall for a Frenchman. If there was any man in Paris whose career had been the twin to my father's, it was this Jew from Mannheim, Daniel-Henry Kahnweiler.

"You mustn't tell anyone you saw me here, aux Puces," he said.

"You're rather recognizable. But you have my word if you want it." I wondered, Had Kahnweiler known of Micheline, too?

Kahnweiler rummaged through a shelf filled with paintings and made the frames clack one against another.

He held up a cheap Abstract imitation. "For this dross, this whole nonsensical *movement*, I blame Rousseau with his student paint kit and taxidermified animals. And also that pedophile in Tahiti. In the Cubist's work, the viewer is coauthor. What he sees of the painting is reconstituted in his mind; the pieces reassemble. This Abstract school"—he made a spitting sound—"there is no point of entry on the canvas. It is only calligraphy, only brushstrokes." Oblivious to the effect his German accent had on those around him, he studied another painting in a battered frame. "I still have an eye out for my paintings taken in the fiasco of 1914," he said.

This was the root of his enmity with my father: Kahnweiler had been Picasso's dealer until the outbreak of the Great War. Yet because he had never bothered to obtain French citizenship, with the archduke's assassination he was classified as an enemy and forced to surrender all his belongings to the French state, which auctioned off his trove of Cubist masterpieces at fire-sale prices to his competitors. Meanwhile, Picasso had been awaiting a payment from Kahnweiler and was enraged when the suddenly penniless man could not produce it. And so my father extended his hand to Picasso and the painter took it.

"And from this war?" I asked Kahnweiler. "Have you seen any of your paintings here?"

Unable to resist a smile, he said, "I've no need to look. They're in my gallery, just as I left them. A miracle, you think? No, of course not. When my brother in Munich told me about the mobilizations, I transferred the title of my gallery to my Catholic daughter-in-law, and my wife and I passed the war in the Norman countryside. We read Trollope and Dickens. Pity you didn't think to marry that gap-toothed girl working for your father. You might have had the same arrangement, too."

Kahnweiler thrust his face closer. He smelled of camphor ointment.

"I told myself that if I lived to be seventy years old, your father would have passed the gallery down to you and I would get back in the old gladiator ring, where my intelligence would win over your youth. By all accounts you were a terribly bright child. How this gave me unhappiness! Then it occurred to me, as I watched my own son falter in his adolescence: wait until the Berenzon boy turns sixteen, that fateful age when his father's own dearest papa was killed. And falter you did, no?

"I remember the day of the accident well because it was on the same day as the Salon des Indépendants, which your father and grandfather were on their way to visit. Paul Rosenberg had witnessed the crash, so within the hour the whole salon knew that Abraham Berenzon had died. Of course, at the time I had no premonition of the importance your family would hold for me, or that my suffering would mean your father's good fortune and now, conversely, that his is mine."

Across the lane, a canteen in a rickety shack opened. A woman slopped a bucket of water over the tables outside.

"Does your father ever mention me?" Kahnweiler asked.

"Never," I said.

I roamed through stall upon stall of paintings. The market would close soon. Here was a stall, run by a child. I moved from crate to crate and made my way through her wares.

And, for the second time, fate flung me a painting. It was a study in oil of a fat, muscular, white Percheron horse, the punctilious work of Rosa Bonheur, who had perfected her painted animals by dissecting real ones and visiting the slaughterhouses in which they were killed.

The study was small, no bigger than the cover of a novel. I lifted it from the crate and looked over my shoulder. It was not Kahnweiler staring at me but another man in the lane. On second thought, he appeared not to see me at all, but to look right through me. I saw his yellow shoes first. I said to the child, "Let me show my friend this painting. I'm not stealing it, you have my word," and ran into the street after the man, who wore the same shoes as the *absents* at the Hôtel Lutetia.

"Do you have any money?" I asked him.

"No, thank you," he said, stepping away.

"I'm an art dealer's son," I said. "Let me show you something: it's a Rosa Bonheur. You haven't heard of her, but she's Géricault in a dress. Not as good, but she has the same movement and theater and horseflesh. This horse is being put through his paces. This outline in the left corner is the hat of a prospective buyer. Can you see it? How much money do you have?"

I spoke too fast, as if the tightly coiled spring inside me was about to be released.

"Whatever it is," I said before he could answer, "we can get it for less. A tenth, a twentieth of her price. Then take it to Madame de La Porte des Vaux at Galerie Zola. Z-O-L-A."

"Like the writer," the *absent* said.

"She's on rue des Beaux-Arts, right near the café La Palette. Don't sell it for a centime less than—" and I named an enormous sum.

"Why are you here," he asked, "*in the foul rag and bone shop of the heart?*" His Viennese accent was as delicate as marzipan.

My glance flickered across his shoes. "I haven't the money," I said, "and it is not the painting I am looking for."

The man approached the girl, and I joined the crowds exiting the market.

THAT SUMMER I WALKED BY THE WINDOWS OF MADAME de la Porte des Vaux's gallery nightly, studying the pictures in the light from the streetlamp. Though the display changed regularly, *The Horse Fair* study never appeared. Perhaps the man with the yellow shoes did not purchase the Bonheur after all. Perhaps Madame de La Porte des Vaux was unwilling to buy it. Or perhaps he had kept it.

Chapter Twenty-two

I ANTICIPATED THE FIRST POSTWAR REUNION OF THE Association of Art Dealers with a tingling sensation—excitement, surely. I could not admit that I hoped for my father to attend.

I arrived at Drouot's at eight in the evening. Save for the queue of idling cars, it could have been a scene from the last century: the men wore round eyeglasses, pocket watches, and sideburns in the old style.

We walked up the sloping entrance of the building, then followed signs to the second floor and Room Six, where men sat in white chairs and inspected each other. My father was not there. Neither were Madame de La Porte des Vaux nor Cailleux. I had prayed that the latter would be—I had brought the nearly half a million francs with me, buttoned into every pocket and folded into a pouch that dangled, beneath my shirt, against my chest, in preparation either to buy *Almonds* outright or to bribe Cailleux. A few men met my eyes and raised a hand in my direction. Though their faces were all unfamiliar, I greeted them, too.

I began a mental tally, looking for Paul Rosenberg, or Wildenstein, or David-Weill, or a Bernheim, but they were nowhere to be found. Not even Kahnweiler was there, since his Catholic daughter-in-law now owned the gallery. Those who had ruled the art market before the war, those who had championed the lovely, deluded, polyglottal art that marked the first half of this century, were gone. Was I the only one left? But I had never been among the greats.

At ten past eight o'clock, when the room was full and growing warm, the association's president and his board appeared on the auctioneer's platform. After a few pleasantries, through which the audience continued to talk, the president called the meeting to order with his gavel and announced that the association's most pressing concern was the issuing of a report to the Direction Générale des Études et Recherches about the association's members' commercial activity under the Nazi fist. I was shocked to see what was happening. Could the organization be so open about its collaboration?

A young man rose from his seat on the platform to speak. "Lefranc and Fabiani, members of this same union, have done a grave disservice to our profession. I too read *Le Monde*'s story of their arrest and the suicide of their commander in Paris, Colonel Kurt von Behr, with great interest. However, I have little more information about their fate, other than that they are held in Prison S—— in the town of Le B——." Immediately, I understood the scheme: Lefranc and Fabiani, then, would be blamed, and no one else.

At this moment, as the men failed to stifle their sighs of relief, a broad-shouldered man appeared next to me and asked for my membership papers. I opened my wallet (in fact, my father's wallet) and, from behind a half-stamped card to the swimming pool on rue de La Boétie, which my father had last visited on May 2, 1940, I withdrew, to my surprise, my father's membership in the Association of Art Dealers. This was delivered up to the platform and handed to the president. He whispered to my inquisitor, who returned to my side. I could feel the heads turn toward me.

"We must ask you to leave, sir," my inquisitor said. "This card has expired and you are not Mr. Daniel Berenzon."

"I'm his son," I protested loudly, as the men eagerly (now given an excuse) swiveled to stare. "He sent me in his place."

The inquisitor jerked me out of my seat by the elbow.

"Please," he said. As I was hustled to the door, I saw Hans Gutman.

Help, I mouthed to him. He grimaced and raised his hands, as if to say, What can I do?

A FEW MOMENTS LATER, I FOUND MYSELF ON THE street. My knee was scraped where my trousers had torn. I sat on the curb and considered ways to reenter the building. With the eyes of a stranger, I studied my reflection in the darkened glass of the auction house. The war's rations had exaggerated my thinness, so that I seemed taller than ever, with wide shoulders but not enough flesh below them. My curls were in need of a shearing, like a caveman in a diorama I had seen once, long ago, in London, with my mother. Why had we taken that trip? I wondered. A doctor. *Micheline.*

Minutes later, the door to Drouot's slammed again and another man was shoved out onto the sidewalk, this one with a childish face and a balding pate. He too had torn the knees of his pants.

He squinted in the darkness in my direction. "Come out, don't lurk," he said. "I know who you are."

He took a step toward me, examining my face with a frown.

"You're a friend of Bertrand's!" he exclaimed, after a pause. "That's it. After they threw you out, there was a fair amount of clucking from the hens in the audience, and the rooster had to quiet them down, saying you weren't who the card said you were and it had expired five years ago. Well, anyway, as soon as they got rid of you, I figured I'd be next. I'm Artur Stein." He thrust his hand toward me. "Picture me with a full head of hair. Then you'll remember."

I tried to, and conjured up a night of Bertrand, Artur, and me on bicycles, following a taxicab with Fanny Reinach and her companion, en route to the Odéon movie theater.

Artur smiled. "Now you recognize me?"

I said I did. "Have you—" I began.

"Heard from Bertrand?" He shook his head. "Nothing. These days no news is the worst kind of news." He lit a cigarette. "They were going to leave Paris at the same time we did, but some distant relative named Le Tarnec had connections to the police and promised to keep the Germans off their backs. A protector. You know how connected those Reinachs were. And Léon, too, Fanny's husband, with his father running the Villa Kerylos in the South and practically every Manet, Renoir, you-name-it painting in the Jeu de Paume donated by their uncle.

"At first, Bertrand argued in favor of leaving," Stein said. "He was always pessimistic. Said they would be punished for indecision. That it wouldn't be so bad to leave the city, since they could always come back. But Léon and Fanny were worried about the Camondo museum.

"Just a month before all this, Bertrand had written a play. He called it *The Collector.* He mailed the script to some types he knew in the theater but hadn't heard any news. It sent him into one of those terrible depressions. It made him want to flee this cursed city even more. But then a theater troupe wanted to stage it. They idolized him, said he was the next Molière, and if you're a fellow who's been searching and searching and found nothing you like except hashish and Antonin Artaud and then—*whoosh!*—these twenty unwashed bohemians think you're better than Ibsen, and some of them want to sleep with you, too? So Bertrand convinced Léon to stay. That's all I know."

We sat in silence on the curb, and the sewers murmured beneath us. In the sky, the stars were bright, sharpened by a dark city in which most people still used their blackout shades at night.

"And Fanny?" I asked. He shook his head.

"There's some central office where you can see if someone was arrested or not," Artur said. "There's a red book where all this is printed. I've known about it for months," he said miserably, "and I haven't gone."

"I've known, too," I admitted. And yet Chaim went twice a week.

"Where did you hide?" Artur asked.

I told him about Le Puy, Monsieur Bickart, and the root cellar. As I spoke, I pictured my mother's hands playing piano concertos on the bottom rung of the ladder that connected the kitchen to the cellar. She said the ladder had three octaves. Her right foot pumped an invisible pedal.

It was later than I thought. Artur would catch the last train to Vincennes. We walked south along rue Drouot, past the yellow post office and its raised portcullis, toward the Métro. Artur said his family had also hidden in the Massif Central, with a widow who ran a grocery. His grandmother had been rounded up from a hotel in Nice. The family believed she died on the journey to Poland. (I pictured a woman in a white fur coat.) Artur had one brother, younger by ten years.

We descended into the station and waited. Our train arrived, and we changed it for another at Strasbourg-Saint-Denis, then made our way toward the Gare d'Austerlitz.

We approached a flock of pigeons crowded on the pavement beneath the sign posting tracks and times. When we drew too close, the birds took flight and, as if on cue, each slot on the Departures board became a whirl of flying letters and numbers as its information changed. Artur's train did not leave for another thirty minutes. We sat in awkward silence.

"Our business has always been furniture," Artur began. "That's how we got to know the Camondos. My father sold the kind of furniture Bertrand's grandfather collected. *Tout est Louis.* Very traditional, Louis Seize, gilt. Can you imagine trying to tuck a chandelier or a harpsichord out of the way? Of course not. When we came back, everything was gone. Mother bought some mattresses for us and we moved back into the house. My parents have started to buy a few pieces, mainly chairs. Father always said that to build a collection one had to start with chairs, since they make the measure of a craftsman's art."

Artur rubbed his hands against his scraped knees.

"Father can buy furniture again because other pieces have reappeared at our gallery. We'll look out the window during breakfast to discover six fauteuils on the curbstone, as if someone would sit on three-hundred-year-old armchairs on the street. Or a truck will rattle our saucers, and the next thing we know a Chinese chest is on our stoop. Or someone will ring the bell late at night, and when we go to the door there's no one there, but instead of some swaddled orphan child there's a set of console tables.

"My parents say, 'Isn't this nice, a neighbor must have known what happened and they're trying to help.' But you and I know it's more sinister. These mysterious donors can either burn their loot, or keep it until they die. But then, when the children sell papa's desk, they'll find out that their sweet dead papa was not such a good man after all. We have arrived at the end of the great shuffle."

"Or the beginning."

"Six weeks ago, my younger brother and I were at an auction preview. I lost sight of him for a moment. Then I heard him shout, 'Artur, this is ours!' so loudly that everyone in the room looked up. The dealer turned seven shades of purple and ran over. There was my brother, on his haunches, staring at the shelves inside a mother-of-pearl-inlaid armoire. My brother recognized the armoire when he bent down to look at it—because that was the height he had been when we went into hiding.

"The dealer rushed us into another room and offered to sell our own armoire back to us. He gave me a fair price, probably what he had paid for it—that is, if *he* paid for it. He said to me, 'A bad agreement is better than a good lawsuit,' and Father bought it that day."

The same well-turned phrase had made its way around Paris. Was this how the dealers comforted each other when, on a rare occasion, they were forced to correct their collections?

Artur's train appeared at the far end of the station, its front window a glowing band in the gloom.

"Come to the deportees' office with me, tomorrow?" I asked.

"Where?" he asked. "When?"

I told him the address: the Service Central des Déportés Israélites, 23, boulevard Haussmann, Ninth arrondissement, where I had left Chaim before.

The train stopped with a screech and a pneumatic sigh. "Till daylight, old man." Artur hung from the train's open door. "At nine, a few short hours from now."

I walked across the pont d'Austerlitz, planning to visit Chaim. Yet as I approached his apartment, I feared I might frighten my friend if I were to wake him, and so I changed my course.

Streetwalkers loitered on both sides of the boulevard. They had dead-looking hair like the wigs in the wig shops that flanked the arcades. Three pimps lurked nearby. One in a leather coat talked with the women, while two others leaned in the shadows, sleeping.

The women called out to me.

"You're beautiful," I said. "But you would tire me out. Plus, I'm as poor as the pavement."

An ancient whore, her hair pinned by a sequined bow, trotted alongside me. "Sweetheart," she said. "A special rate for you." She eyed the pimps.

"Not tonight, young lady," I said.

"They think you look like a rich man pretending to be poor," she whispered, her painted cheek against mine. "So run."

I ran. For what felt like an eternity but could not have been more than three or four minutes, I thought I could outrun the two men who had pretended to doze against the wall. But they were faster than I anticipated. Their breathing sounded like dogs'—easy, animal, enjoying the hunt. In a moment, they were upon me. One wrenched off my overcoat and tore the money pouch from around my neck, and the other knocked me to the ground. The taller of the two loomed over me, raining blows on my cheeks and jaws and kicking my stomach. I heard my keys chime against the metal sewer grate before they landed with a splash. Then the men were still. The taller one sniffed the air. "Enough," he said, and ran off. The other followed until they were running with their legs in unison.

I lay over the sewer grate until I was certain they were gone. The street was silent again. I dragged myself to the curb, felt my face and stomach, and ran my tongue across my teeth. I thought of all that missing money. Two paintings' worth, lost, found, and lost again. I vomited in the sewer. Blood slicked my nostrils.

I struggled to my feet and began to walk. My father had been right—the paintings were not to be found—and had turned back as soon as he sensed this, which was almost instantly. I had gone on, blindly. I was a work on paper: weightless, sketchy, all impulse.

I heard no bells that morning as I continued on to the Service Central des Déportés Israélites. I leaned against the door of 23, boulevard Haussmann until a figure appeared, pawing the ground with two crutches, then swinging her body between them. She wore a kerchief over her dark hair.

"Excuse me," she said. "The office will open in exactly fifteen minutes. You will have to wait outside. I'm sorry. It's the rules." She peered at my face. "Do you need a doctor?"

I shook my head.

When her back was turned to me, I studied her legs. At first, I thought they looked like the limbs of a starved person. On closer inspection, I realized her calf muscles had been entirely cut away. Only the femur and ulna were wrapped in skin.

The girl on crutches returned to the door. By the puckering and jumping of her mouth, I understood she was asking a question. She stood back, and I gathered I was permitted to enter the building. She pointed to a toilet and held out a towel to me. "I haven't any bandages," she said.

When I emerged, I told her Bertrand's name, as well his sister's, mother's, and father's. She wrote them down in neat script on a pink slip of paper. Behind her were rows and stacks of books, which resembled photograph albums. She asked me a few questions: Were there alternate spellings to the Reinach name, and did I know the year in which they were deported? No and no, I answered.

"We don't have a precise system yet," she said. "The Red Book is a list of all the people we know who are alive. The convoys, with the names alphabetized, are on the shelves in order of deportation date. I'll ask you to keep the volumes in order. They're quite heavy. If you put Convoy Forty in the place of Twenty, it's no chore for you to move them, but it's hard for me." She looked at me fiercely.

I waited another half hour before beginning my work, hoping Artur Stein would still appear. At a quarter to ten I gave up and entered the reading room, which had empty bookshelves but twelve long tables. I began to read through the Red Book.

I did not find Bertrand's name under R-REINACH. Next, I scoured the book looking for anyone named BERTRAND or CAMONDO, his mother's maiden name. I closed my eyes. I could hear the thump and swing of the girl moving about the office and the unintelligible rise and fall of voices on the street. Sometimes the building shook with what surely must have been the Métro running beneath. A shade was raised too quickly, and it wound around its roller with a snap. The telephone rang and rang. Single men came and went from the room; there were very few women. When a couple did enter, they were father and son.

I moved to the black books, which were heavier for me than the girl had predicted. The sun traveled across the floor as I lifted book after book and skimmed through the names.

By the twentieth book, my eyes were exhausted from reading. I heard the girl on crutches speak in Yiddish to an old man in the hallway. Eventually, he shuffled into the room and began to work on the black books, too. He was unkempt, with crumbs in his beard. I felt badly that he had no wife to care for him. He grunted with each book he lifted down, and flicked through the pages quickly, licking his finger from time to time. I heard a strangled cry come from the old man.

I found Bertrand in Book 35, Convoy 62, which departed Paris on November 11, 1943. My friend was the 887th person listed on the convoy, with his sister as 888th and father 889th. As if Bertrand had stepped forward first, and announced his profession: carpenter. *Schreiner.* I continued to read.

Seven volumes later, I found his mother, in a convoy of 1,501 persons, deported on March 7, 1944. How had Madame Reinach née Camondo been separated from them? I could not fathom anything. I thought of what Chaim had said about Drancy and how children there wandered, forcibly separated from their parents, too young to know their own names. If an older child knew a younger one, he wrote the infant's name on a piece of wood and tied it with twine to the baby's neck.

OUTSIDE THE BUILDING, I LAY ON A BENCH AND FELL asleep. Eventually, I heard the crutches of the injured girl. Night fell quickly, and a policeman appeared who knocked at my legs with his baton. "Move along now," he said, tapping in time to the syllables.

I had the idea that I would like to sleep in the Bois de Boulogne. It took me most of a day to walk there, and as I walked I thought about Rose. The one time I thought I had made her weep with pleasure. The pearls pinned to her ears that she always worried she would lose. I spoke out loud to her as I walked, asking her why she would not love me, telling her that I had not heard all there was to hear about her bravery in the museum. I pictured the fire she had seen burning in the courtyard of the Jeu de Paume. Five thousand or ten thousand pictures, she had said. A fire that burned all day.

I left the Seine, crossing the offices belonging to La Radiodiffusion Française. I could hear its transmissions crackling, and the sound of my mother's piano returned to me. I recalled the strange feeling of sitting at my mother's feet as a child, arranging my toy train set—laying out tracks, placing the stationmaster beside them, putting down a barricade striped like a piece of candy, building a bridge with a miniature pine tree and gaslight beside it—and hearing my mother play on the radio. I had the uneasy feeling that Mother was not really there or wholly near me. That some part of her had been stolen someplace else. I might touch her bare feet just to make sure that she was with me while I tinkered with my train set.

I found a wide bench in the Bois de Boulogne and fell asleep in the sun. I blessed the springtime. I did not know the month or the day.

OVER THE COURSE OF MY WEEKS IN THE BOIS, I SAW many figures from my past—most often my father, and then Bertrand, Fanny, Mother, the Hungarian trumpeter who had lived across the courtyard on rue de La Boétie, and my grandfather who died on avenue de Breteuil and gave Father his limp.

With my eyes closed, with the sun beating down on my face and the rain misting it, I tried to remember my sister. In the sea of my memory, a few details rose to the surface, memories without any mooring that I began to affix to Micheline. A little girl with garbled speech. A face so close to mine I could not see it, buttoning my coat with the utmost seriousness. Me, waiting patiently through the ritual, knowing its importance, growing stuffy indoors wearing my winter layers. A sticky hand holding mine. Sharing a bag of sweet nuts. Her arms around my head, she kissed my face and nearly strangled me. I put my hands in the corners of her elbows and struggled from her arms. We jumped up and down in a field of mossy green.

I opened my eyes. The Bois was the greenest stretch of Paris. I looked out at its fields. The grass was not the color of the moss in my memory, as green as seaweed waving on the bottom of the ocean floor. I saw myself from behind, a little boy in short pants and a sailor suit, standing next to my sister, Micheline. I could not see her face. Turn around, I begged the two figures. My sister and I don't hear me, though. We stand on the mossy green rug of the gallery, sharing a sweet bag of almonds, underneath my sister's painting with the same name.

A face stared into mine as my mind was breaking. Bertrand held a bottle to my lips. "*Les mariages du Bois de Boulogne ne se font pas devant Monsieur le Curé*," he told me. The night fell. The trees bloomed and their blossoms blew against my chapped skin. At night, I shouted, "Turn around, show yourself to me!" How had I been her brother but forgotten her face? Micheline. I had always known it.

It grew warm. Someone stole my blanket. Micheline still did not turn around. Eventually, my mind grew tired of pleading. I thought about *Almonds*, and how the unshelled nuts clustered together like rats. I wanted to see my father, but first I needed a bath.

I slipped into the apartment building on rue de Mézières behind an old man fumbling with his keys. Then I knocked on Rose's door. When she answered, the sight of her with short hair and crescents of darkness beneath her eyes distressed me anew.

Finally, I asked, "What day is it?"

"Tuesday," she said. I saw the chain was still on the door.

"No, I mean date, month." My voice creaked. I apologized. "I've barely spoken in weeks."

Rose said, "July 7, 1945," and, "I can see." She paused. I had been in the Bois nearly three weeks. Rose asked if I needed a doctor, or dinner, or a bath. I said the last.

I stood between the bed and a bookcase with documents on one shelf and tin cans and torn paper ready for the toilet on another. Rose rummaged in the bathroom. I heard the sound of running water and soon the steam from the tub began to cloud the windows.

"Go in there," Rose ordered. "I'd give your clothes to the Red Cross, but they probably should be burned."

"I've nothing else to wear," I said, amazed at the practicality of her speech. It followed the pattern A, B, C, while my senses were darting around the room like gnats. I tasted honeysuckle in the air. Something was clotting at the back of my throat. My eyes smarted. My friend Bertrand had a woolly head like a lamb. The snot had coagulated in my nose. I couldn't hear. I couldn't think. The humming feeling in my blood meant worry—Rose looked ill. The throbbing between my ears made it hard to follow the logical conversation.

Rose stood back and I entered the bathroom, shut the door, shed my clothing, and stepped into the shoe-shaped tub with a splash. The water was fragrant and its surface iridescent. Rose had added some salts or oils to it. I shouted my thanks.

"You're welcome. Have you drawn the curtain?" she asked. I gave it a rattle on its rings.

In she came. Rose said, "I have had my heart stomped upon. With a boot."

I felt a sharp pain in my chest. I slipped beneath the oil swirls on the surface of the tub and came up only when I needed to breathe. I moved aside the curtain to study her face. Rose now wore a silk dressing gown over her mannish clothing. I reached to touch it and left a damp stain on the silken sleeve. "Is it from an American?" She nodded, sobbed, and turned away.

"What is his name?" I asked.

"I don't want to say it."

"He's a damned fool," I said, careless and callous, like the boy she had known before the war. "I thought you were a nun to all but your work."

She shook her head no.

"You'll arrive here," I said, pointing to myself, "to anger. Now you're only hurt, split in two. Eventually, you'll be mad." It was a direct translation: my experience into hers. Thanks to you, I charted this terrain first, I thought.

Her shoulders heaved. It was terrible to see her mourn, so much so it almost knocked my own grief from its pedestal.

"We could still marry."

She looked at me as if I were crazy. I stood up in the bath (Rose gasped), wet and unpeeled, and walked into the main room. I dressed myself and stood in the doorway, my untoweled hair soaking the collar of my stinking shirt.

"You knew about my sister," I said to Rose, who wiped her tears with a napkin.

She nodded and I stepped out into the dark hallway. A wind, somewhere in the city, sucked the door shut with a slam.

Chapter Twenty-three

I RETURNED TO RUE DE LA BOÉTIE. SINCE I NO longer had the key to the front gate, I grabbed hold of it, expecting to shake it violently. I would enter at any cost.

A voice from inside, rough and suspicious, called out, "Who's there?" It was my father. Chains rattled and stiff bolts unclenched their bite.

"Come in, come in quickly," he said, and opened the door. We studied each other in the half light. He had grown a beard and his clothes were little better than mine. Father cupped my face in his hand. "You've broken your nose," he said, and suddenly, convulsively turned from me with his hand over his eyes.

He led me through the gallery, through the ruined rooms, over the uneven wooden floorboards. I closed my eyes, which was nearly unnecessary in the darkened gallery, and heard my father moving about: clanging a pot, turning a creaky spigot, the lonely piddle of water in the teakettle. I wondered if I had not, in fact, come home at all but was instead a ghost, brought back to witness my father's comfortless state. In my mind's eye, I saw a figure ascend the stairs to the emptied rooms, pluck a withered leaf from the floor, tuck it into his lapel, and float through the roof, into the night sky. How had I forgotten that a son must care for his father, too?

Father returned to his office, and we sat on the mattress pushed into the far corner of the walls, where his filing cabinet had once stood. He explained that in fact he had not left Paris at all but had stayed in a hotel in the Eighteenth, hoping to find me. He had searched the hospitals, the DP services, the garden chairs of the Luxembourg, the benches of the Bois, the fleabag hotels near the train stations, and the alleys of Belleville and Pigalle, to no avail.

On the day he had given up and conceded to return to my mother in Le Puy, he received a telegram from Rose. I had been sighted in the Bois, she informed him. Still, even then, I had not been found. On the way back from the park, my father decided to visit 21, rue de La Boétie, one last time, and found it open and empty. The Communists were at a rally. He entered, barred the doors, discovered the telephone in operation, and called first a locksmith and then a lawyer. He had remained barricaded inside for the last three weeks, with the lawyer—a young man my own age, I realized, to my chagrin—providing Father with his necessities. Father explained some contested French law, about apartments left vacant without their owners reverting to the possession of the State or their occupiers after a certain passage of time.

I, in turn, told him about the Morisot, Madame de La Porte des Vaux, *Almonds*, and Cailleux. I could not bear to say Bertrand's name.

Father replied, "I knew when I said we would return to Le Puy that you would keep looking. The bank account was reopened the day I told you I could no longer tolerate staying in Paris. Did you notice that day how I paid for everything in large bills? Didn't you think I carried an awful lot of money with me? I was fairly certain you would take it to buy back the Cézanne and the Sisley that the Americans had stolen."

So my father had foreseen the single independent decision of my adulthood. I hardly knew what to say. "I did not anticipate that you would abandon me," he continued. "That came as a blow."

I asked after my mother. He said, "If you're here, she will forgive me for being away a while longer." He smiled wistfully. "If you can believe it, the war was nearly good for your old father and mother. I don't know who relented first. Yet somehow during our time in that cellar, we forgave each other certain things."

"Like my sister," I said.

Father grabbed my hand and held it. Rather, he clenched my four fingers as if they were bundled stalks. I did not know the last time I had held my father's hand. In front of *Almonds*, my sister had gripped my right hand and someone clasped my left, and I understood then that it had been Father. We were the family trio.

"Your mother never wanted me to tell—or, rather, to remind you," he said. "I thought this choice was a mistake. It prevented me from speaking frankly to you. After a few years we stopped commemorating the night she died. And when we gave that up, many traditions fell away."

Eventually, my father stood and let go of my hand. I sat on the mattress on the floor, listening to the wind in the ruined chimney and the rustle of papers waiting to be burned in the fireplace. I heard Father talking to himself in the other room. It occurred to me that the child believes his parents' behavior has everything to do with him, always, and that this will then be the source of a life's worth of misunderstandings.

Before dawn the next morning, we were awakened by a knock at the front entrance. It was the young lawyer. Through the crack in the door, he handed my father a brown sack of food, a bottle of milk, several cans, and an envelope wrapped with twine. Introductions and handshakes, too, through the narrow wedge. The lawyer asked my father to give him more ration tickets. Father reached into his pocket and withdrew the strips of coupons, geometric patterned things, printed in carnival colors. The young lawyer looked nervous outside in the dark, checking over his shoulder. He promised to return later in the day with more supplies and to "pick up those papers." I was glad that he was on the outside and my father and I were inside, and that Father had not returned to Le Puy, leaving me here in his place.

Father read out loud from the papers. "Jews who have suffered a loss of property fill out this form . . . estimate value . . . will be treated with all due haste, return by the deadline—that's three days from now—be assured of most distinguished sentiments, et cetera, et cetera." He threw down the papers on the bed. "What an extraordinary waste of time. But our legal counsel will be cross if we don't do as he says."

So again we walked around the gallery's main room in circles, stopping at intervals to name the Vlaminck, Dufy, Braque, Picasso, Morisot, or Matisse that had once hung there. This time, for reparations. Father and I had not rehearsed the paintings, as we had done for so many years of my childhood and adolescence, while in hiding. At first my mind creaked in protest, and the paintings' details ran together. It brought to mind the sensation of trying to recite verbs for Latin class after the summer holidays. *Amitto, -mittere, -misi, -missum.* To send away, to let go, to let slip. Hence, in general, to lose.

We spent an entire day on the task. Three times I named paintings that had been sold before the war, and each time father scolded me. The nib of his pen scratched through the paper. When we had finished, Father said, "Let us never speak of this again." He placed one hand on my head, as if in blessing. He raised the other to touch the wall, as if it could yield to him what it had seen.

Epilogue

FOR THE FIRST EIGHTEEN MONTHS OF MY LIFE AS an American, I worked for the German government—or, more specifically, for a Pole, a psychiatrist named Emanuel Senek, who was paid by the German government to interview survivor émigrés in the Great Lakes region for matters of reparations and pensions. Senek, a survivor himself, worked in Polish. I conducted interviews in French, though few of those whom I spoke to and whose interviews I later transcribed were actually French. They were the orphaned children of Jews from the Pale who had fled to France but were unable, as we all now knew, to save themselves. At first, I found solace and meaning in this work.

When later in Ann Arbor, despite myself, I asked a man who had been deported on Convoy 62 in November of 1943 if he knew Bertrand Reinach, this was correctly deemed unprofessional and may have precipitated the illness for which I was hospitalized on the day prior to the election that won President Truman his second term in office.

When the crisis abated three months later, I was advised not to return to my interview work with Senek. Before my release from the hospital, I spoke often with one of my doctors about my own haphazard medical training in France. As unorthodox as it strikes me now, he suggested I sit for some exams in Anatomy and Physiology at the University of Michigan Medical School as part of my cure. I passed these, then several more, then began attending lectures regularly. Seamlessly, or so it appeared, I made the transition from patient to student to doctor.

For some time, I possessed an aversion to the idea of visiting New York City and a fear that I would encounter someone from the old world there. Most of the art dealers who had left Paris had taken refuge in Manhattan; a few were in London, a few in Los Angeles. At the height of the McCarthy era, Father reported that two or three had returned to France. This aversion remained until one day, a glimpse at a Sotheby's catalog revealed one of my father's Toulouse-Lautrecs—*La Goulue with Her Partner*, the dwarf painter's muse with the man who was called the Boneless One for his flexibility. I rushed to New York to claim it. Yet the seller disappeared and the auction house remained mute and uncooperative. Rather than return home, as I had no real belongings or friends in Michigan—and my kindly landlady agreed to ship to me what few things remained—I saved the money of the return ticket and stayed on in Manhattan.

I first caught sight of my future wife during the month of October, in my first year as a resident at New York Hospital. The young Ellie Berger remembered all the patients' names but forgot the doctors' (including mine). She was unshaken when the survivors of a school bus accident were brought to our emergency ward. I overheard her tell another nurse that her fiancé had died over the Pacific. When I introduced myself a second time and asked where she had been raised, she said, recognizing my accent, "Nouvelle Rochelle," waited for me to smile, and then explained the joke. Through the glass of the nurses' station, I watched her complete crossword puzzles with terrifying speed. We were married in four months' time.

Now I understand that more complex forces drew us together. Ellie's own father (a Berliner by birth) hanged himself following the crash of the American markets on Black Tuesday of 1929. Her mother took in boarders and put her daughter to work. My family's life must have seemed a miracle of ease to her.

Our older daughter Sophie is to be married to a lawyer of Irish extraction in the winter. I cut the engagement announcement from *The New York Times* and sent it to my parents, who have it framed in their kitchen in Le Puy. The younger, Michelle, I am told is almost identical to me as a child. She is long and loose-limbed, with unruly brown hair and a dreamy look and disposition; perhaps it is true. I am a fortunate father, for they are doting daughters. During their childhood, I took them often to the Museum of Natural History and the New York Public Library, but never the Metropolitan or the new Modern art building on Fifty-third Street. I supposed they were both ignorant of art, though at Sophie's graduation from Barnard she received a prize for an essay on Ruskin. We may have something to discuss in our later years, after all.

Chaim remained in France two years after I did, still searching for word of his wife and son. When at last he learned of their murders, he followed me here. He seemed to bury his grief in his work, opening a store that sold winter coats to the women of Milwaukee. Chaim chose Wisconsin, which he refers to as *Veesconseen*, because he was told that its climate would remind him of Poland. He remarried, to another survivor, though they have no children. He spoils mine instead, and Michelle is his favorite.

In January of 1965 he went back to Auschwitz for the twentieth anniversary of its liberation. "I was freezing the entire trip, Max," Chaim wrote, in a handwriting I now know only we Europeans use. "I thought only, 'I could not survive this now. Surely I would have died.' I could not believe I survived it then."

Chaim, perhaps unexpectedly, took up fishing, and I followed suit. We visit him and his wife each summer. I did not tell Chaim of my stay in the sanatorium in Michigan; hence, he thinks I am a man apt to disappear for long stretches of time, as I did when we lived together on rue de Sévigné.

ON THE OCCASION OF MY TWENTY-FIFTH WEDDING anniversary, I arranged for three weeks' leave from the hospital and had the travel agency on our street corner book passage for two to Paris. Neither of our children would come. Sophie was at a piano workshop in Aspen and Michelle was meditating at Esalen. Ellie and I reserved rooms at the Hôtel Rousselet in the Seventh. My parents had a neighbor care for their dogs and took the train from Le Puy. My mother's seventy-fifth birthday was a few weeks hence. It was to be a celebratory visit.

Despite myself, I thought of Rose. I could find her in a crowd of a thousand, by the Greek vases with their scenes of love in the longest gallery in the Louvre. I had thoughts like this many times. And though their frequency did not lessen with the years, their yearning quality did.

During our second night in Paris, from the depths of a deep sleep, I heard my mother shouting my name. I rushed into my parents' room. With deliberate, untrembling hands, I administered chest compressions and breathed my breath into my father. This prolonged his life by several days. The chest compressions, as sometimes happens in older men of a delicate constitution, shattered his eardrum. He was half deaf for the final days of his life. We all had to shout our love at him, which, it occurred to me, I had been trying to do my whole life.

On the morning he would die, Ellie said, "Max, you're always on the other end of the camera. Take a picture with your parents." Her motive seemed so transparent, as if to ask, how much time do you three have together? I protested, but my father beckoned me. He pulled me to him and kissed my forehead, holding his lips there during the long time that Ellie fumbled with the F-stop and the focus and the flashbulb. The click came too soon. My father had never embraced me for so long.

When I learned that my father had died in the night, I ran to a camera shop, as if the photographer's strong-smelling solvents might bring him back to life. I ran past the post office on rue de Sèvres and wove madly through a bakery line. I crossed the avenue while the traffic was still moving and heard it screech in my wake.

The camera shop owner must have recognized my distressed state. Although he still wore his street coat, he complied with my request to develop the roll of film with my father's last photograph. I lifted the heavy camera from my neck—I had not trusted my shaking hands not to expose the film or drop it in a gutter. He took the

Nikon into his darkroom and returned a moment later. "I'm terribly sorry," he said, his mustache working up and down above his lips. "There is no film in this camera. Perhaps you took it out already?" And so my father's picture joined the other images in the lost museum in my mind.

WE BURIED FATHER IN OUR FAMILY'S PLOT IN MONTparnasse, beside my sister. Micheline's grave was gray, and time had darkened the letters of her name. She lay next to Abraham Berenzon, whose tombstone looked as if it had been burned. A tower of five or six stones rested atop each, laid by an unknown hand. While the rabbi conducted the service, a jet plane flew overhead and drowned out the sound of his singing. The jet's trail evaporated in the sky, though we could hear its roar after it had disappeared above the clouds.

"Please join me in Kaddish," the rabbi said. In a voice husky with tears, my mother chanted with him, loudly, as if hoping Father would hear her from the beyond. As a child, when I first heard these words, I thought they were Polish.

Our feet sank into the cemetery's damp grass. The ground trembled when a train passed deep beneath us, steaming out from the massive station. The graveyard's whitewashed walls, with their scatterings of red moss, could not block the sight of the sleek office tower that had been erected in 1972. I thought it a black shard of glass piercing the earth.

ELLIE DIRECTED THE SHIVA RITES, COVERING UP THE mirrors in our hotel suites and somehow procuring black ribbons with a single tear, which we affixed to our clothes, a symbol as if we had rent them in mourning. On the seventh day, Mother said, "Now he's gotten out of going to the memorial service."

"Who?" I asked. "What memorial service?"

"Your father. The anniversary of the roundups. Because of the

Camondos." She still referred to Bertrand's family by his mother's maiden name. "Every year, a battle with your father. He never liked to go. I've never missed one."

She wiped her beautiful, fluttering hands on her apron, cupped my cheek with her damp palm, and said she was going to lie down.

"Please, Mother, don't smoke in bed," I asked. She had singed a hole in the hotel blanket the night before, and I had woken to the smell of burning wool.

She shushed me. "It is one of life's great pleasures."

Ellie went out and returned with one of my mother's early recordings, and the concierge brought up a gramophone. We listened to Brahms all afternoon. My wife and I bid each other a happy anniversary at midnight.

BECAUSE THE SEVENTH DAY OF SHIVA HAD PASSED, I proposed to Ellie that we attend an auction. It was time to get out of the hotel. I kissed her and thought how we were both growing old. I would turn fifty-five the next month, as would she.

Father was on my mind in the taxicab, as we crossed the Seine. I told Ellie how men at Drouot's elbowed one another when he appeared at the back of the auction hall, framed by the double doors, the pomade in his hair shiny, everyone and everything seeming instantly to dull by comparison. The taxi passed through the courtyard of the Louvre and its long queue of tourists with visor hats and sensible shoes. I thought of Rose then, for the second or hundredth time that day: in her red coat with her cheeks flushed in the cold at 5 a.m., Bertrand beside me, his cap at an angle as we watched *Winged Victory* roll from her pedestal in a wooden crate. The phalanx of white trucks, the exhaust from their running engines brown in the wintry air.

That morning, at the reading of my father's will, Rose was bestowed a not insignificant sum, as a "pension for a former employee." I felt my mother's eyes on me but did not meet them. There was no need to upset Ellie. The will told me that Rose was most likely in Paris, and I felt a vague unpleasant anger toward the dead. How often had my father been in contact with her during my decades of faithful silence? With what knowledge had he died?

We sped under an archway and swerved to miss a dog. The Comédie Française passed in a blur of columns. I had proposed the auction visit on a whim or, rather, out of an old familiar feeling that I desired to shake off and that I could not resist. It was 2 p.m., and that seemed a reasonable time for an auction. I paid the taxi driver and, forgetting that I was in France, gave him a tip. I grabbed Ellie's hand and pulled her out of the cab. "Come on, old girl," I said. "*Vite, vite.*"

"*Vite, vite,* yourself, old man," she said, as we hurried across the marble entryway. I sensed that the few people milling about were listening to our English. "There's no rush. You haven't been here for thirty years. And you can't buy anything anyway. You have two daughters to marry off."

THE ROUNDED WINDOWS OF THE CASHIER'S BOX caught my eye. CAISSE, the tarnished brass letters read. Inside, hunched over the cash register, raising with each keystroke a torrent of ringing mechanical bells, was the gnome from my youth, from the day I purchased Manet's *Ham.* He raised his head and I looked quickly away.

"All the big auctions happen upstairs," I said, tugging Ellie by the strap of her handbag.

"No bidding," she said, and slapped my hand.

"*Ça va,*" I said.

Room Six was choked full of bodies in suits. Even in the hallway, we could feel the heat from inside.

"Good God," Ellie said. "We can't go in there."

"Come on," I said. "It's always like this." She made a face and disappeared between the broad shoulders of two men. Her hand reappeared and grabbed my sleeve.

"*Mon mari,*" she said, in her broad American accent, and smiled at the unhappy men, who parted to let me through. Ellie looked around the room, searching for a seat. "Everyone has a catalog," she said. "Why didn't you get one?"

"If I'm not allowed to buy, what's the use?" I whispered.

"I wish I had a catalog. Or at least a seat." She smiled, announced, "*Je vais défaillir,*" and accepted a young man's chair, surrendered with a sigh. Now nearly everyone seated was female. We were separated by sex, as if Drouot's were an old-world synagogue.

The men stood pressed against each other, arms bent close and awkward, pale auction paddles flattened to their lapels. The heat settled around me like a bath. A Vlaminck sketch sold for 100,000 francs. Then an ugly Picasso vase went for half a million.

To the gentleman on my right, I said, "*Très bon marché*"—the prices were startlingly reasonable, even cheap. He smiled and touched his brow.

"So you have not been in Paris for many years?" he asked. "You are forgetting de Gaulle's currency adjustment. Everything, divided by ten!" We laughed. It was a delight to be there. A moment later he said, "Make way for the woman in the chair." Somehow, this made me shiver.

I turned to look and gazed quickly into the face of the plump blonde who pushed the wheelchair. She gripped the auction catalog before her.

"The next lot is from the collection of Madame de Chambrun," the auctioneer announced, loosening the knot of his tie. There were whispers in the audience. The gentleman beside me hissed and pushed his way out of the room. I eased into the space he left behind.

A portrait, attributed to the Cranach workshop, sparked heated bidding. Next in the lot was a series of Paul Klee sketches from the 1930s. Unusual, I thought, that Madame Le Chambrun, whoever she was, should collect paintings both from the German Renaissance and the prewar period. I shrugged my shoulders. Both artists were German. Stranger things have happened.

"Lot Fifty-one: Matisse's *Intérieur vert et bleu,*" the auctioneer announced, smiling at the commotion this incited in the crowd. I felt it too. A row of assistants were poised with telephones at their ears.

"Bidding will begin at forty thousand francs," he announced. "Do I hear forty thousand five?" And on we flew. The lemons seemed to float on the surface of the canvas. It was one of Matisse's color experiments, where a table and a wall and a chair were all the same block of green.

I felt my heart race and my leg quiver. It was a beautiful Matisse indeed, with rich colors that vibrated against each other.

"Fifty-five thousand," I called out. Ellie turned around, eyes wide with warning.

I ignored her and entered the fray again at seventy thousand. Ellie rose from her seat and made her way through the crowd. "Why are you doing this?" she said. "Please don't do it just because I asked you not to. This has all been very difficult, darling, I know. Remember—your father loved art, but he loved your mother more. Now let's just enjoy the auction." She hung on my arm, so I would not raise it.

One by one, the auctioneer's assistants hung up their telephones until there was only a single telephone bidder, a Dutchman, I gathered from the assistant's responses, and the invisible woman in the wheelchair. At the last moment, an ill-shaven fellow in a motorcycle jacket began shouting out bids before the auctioneer could ask for them and had to be reprimanded. Then the last telephone bidder hung up the line. The motorcyclist, growing red in the face, kept gesturing *Up, up* with his paddle. The plump blonde looked ready to faint, as if she were holding on to the handles of the wheelchair for dear life. Several moments later, her companion won the Matisse and a smattering of applause broke out in the room. I joined the clapping. The blonde reached down and touched the invalid's shoulder. Then she wheeled the chair toward the door.

"Wasn't that exciting?" I asked Ellie. She said it was. There was a Cézanne next.

"The more expensive the painting, the hotter the room gets," Ellie said. "God forbid we see a Monet." I looked at my wristwatch—we had been at Drouot's for less than an hour.

I tried to hide my disappointment. It was our last full day in France. I had hoped, against hope, that *Almonds* might be for sale, or even the *Woman in White.*

We pushed our way through the wall of people into the muggy air of the hallway and stood on the moving staircase, letting it lower us into the vestibule. The desire to turn back gripped me; it made my head spin, past the image of the great Ferris wheel that was erected at the foot of the Tuileries Gardens each summer of my childhood, past the memory of Bertrand clicking a bullet into the chamber of a gun, saying, "We won't play Russian roulette, but imagine if we did, and I go first," and shooting the gun into the woods and startling our horses, spinning until I could hear my mother humming *Orphée et Eurydice*, when Orpheus calls out to the Eurydice he has lost forever.

At that moment, a young Drouot's employee blocked our path. He held a painting crate in his hands.

"Mr. Berenzon," he said, "you can't leave without your painting."

"You didn't—" Ellie protested.

I looked up, into the quiet cashier's booth. The gnome was inside, twirling a pen in his ear. "Max Berenzon," he said to me, though I hardly knew my own name, "we've been waiting. For all these years."

"I did not buy a painting," I said.

"I know," the young man said, wiping his brow. "A woman pointed you out and told me to give it to you," he said. "The one in the wheelchair, with the Legion of Honor pin. I almost thought you had left. That would have been a disaster."

IN THE TAXICAB, ELLIE AND I PRIED OPEN THE CRATE'S latches. Inside was the Matisse *Intérieur vert et bleu.*

"Monsieur," I asked the taxi driver, "who is Madame de Chambrun?"

"Has she died?" he asked. I looked at his fat fingers on the steering wheel and the jumping dials on the dashboard.

"I don't know," I replied. The Matisse had come from her collection.

"Everyone knows," he said, "but no one will admit it."

"Who is she?" I asked again.

"What are you saying?" Ellie begged for a translation.

"She's the daughter of Laval," he said, and spit out the window.

"Who's Laval?" Ellie asked, now following the exchange.

"The prime minister of France under Vichy," I said, and turned over the painting. It was stamped:

Daniel Berenzon
21, rue de La Boétie
Paris 8ème

Did this mean that a son's love and grief for his father triumphed over all? Or that, in a moment of reckoning, I had seen and remembered nothing? I understood then that Rose had begun to bid only once I had stopped. She had been sent to Drouot's, or went of her own accord, in case I had forgotten what I would see there.

"Let's go back to the hotel," Ellie said, her hair whipping in the open window. "Your mother will need us now."

"Yes," I said. "I need her more than ever." Ellie put her hand to my forehead. I took it and kissed the knuckle of the finger that bore the ring my mother had brought with her from Poland in 1917.

We passed a protest and a blockade of policemen in riot suits, as black-shelled as beetles. I examined the painting as the taxi raced through the hot street's mirage. There were fumes in the air, of asphalt and gasoline. The shimmering of the city was also a part of the canvas: Matisse's lemons seemed to float above the table and the white plate on which they might have rested, if they had been given rest. It was a still life that had not been granted stillness. I thought of the dimensions of the painting, of its flat and hovering planes, and that somewhere, in between the two, lingered those whom I had lost.

AUTHOR'S NOTE

The tragedy of France's looted artwork is but a shadow of its Jews, who numbered three hundred thousand at the outbreak of World War II. Seventy-six thousand were deported. Eight thousand of those deported were children under the age of thirteen. Three percent of all of those "sent East" returned.

While Max Berenzon is entirely imaginary, many other historical figures appear in this work of fiction. To the best of my ability, all the references to the wartime activities of Reichsmarschall Hermann Goering, Colonel von Behr, and Ambassador Otto Abetz are true. Daniel-Henry Kahnweiler, the Bernheim-Jeune brothers, and Paul and Léonce Rosenberg were all art dealers in Paris before the war, as were the Wildensteins, Cailleux, Lefranc and Fabiani. The latter quartet remains under suspicion to this day for collaboration or shady dealings (Maria Dietrich, Hitler's art broker, was one of Cailleux's clients); the former left their brilliant, indelible print on the course of Modern art by fostering the twentieth century's most visionary painters. Drouot is still one of Paris's busiest auction houses, and the Lutetia one of its most glamorous hotels, with little trace other than a plaque on boulevard Raspail of the painful scenes that took place there in the spring of 1945.

Rose Clément takes her name and story from Rose Valland (1898–1980), the former curator of the Jeu de Paume. The Nazis mistook Rose Valland's unassuming manner for timidity and allowed her to stay on in the Modern art museum as a supervisor to its maintenance men. Their mistake is history's triumph, as her meticulous documentation of looters, the looted, and the destination of the spoils saved thousands of paintings for their eventual repatriation. Valland's communication with the Free French and Allied forces guaranteed that the thousands of railcars of looted artwork were neither bombed (at the outset of the war) nor allowed out of France (in the war's final hours).

I have relied heavily on Rose Valland's 1961 autobiography, *Le front de l'art: défense des collections françaises 1939–1945*, for her account of her work at the Louvre and the Jeu de Paume, and have incorporated some of her descriptions of the looted artworks' arrival, sorting, selection, and dispersal into my text. All of the lists that my Rose shows Max in this novel are actual ones that the real Rose surreptitiously obtained during the war. Rose Valland received the Legion of Honor and the Presidential Medal of Freedom, and yet, *Le front de l'art* has gone out of print. Her country, it seemed, was eager to brush her aside. Lynn Nicholas, in the definitive *Rape of Europa*, describes Rose's increasing isolation:

> After a time [Rose Valland's] persistence and her knowledge of collaboration and shady deals began to make her unpopular among those not wishing to be reminded of the events of the war. She was particularly reluctant to set a final date for claims on the unidentified and not very high-grade leftovers which remained after the better objects had been distributed among the museums. These had become an administrative headache for everyone, and many felt they should be sold. By 1965 Mlle Valland's stubbornness had driven the director of the Musées de France to suggest to her that it might be time to look forward to peace and fraternity, forget the past, and leave the disposition of the works to the living, which "would take nothing away from the respect for the dead." But Resistance heroine Valland never would compromise, and in her last years retreated entirely into her world of secret documents, which at her death

were relegated, unsorted and chaotic, to a Musées storeroom in Malmaison.

Bertrand Reinach, too, once lived in Paris, though I have been able to find almost nothing about his person and character. There is a photograph, a picture of an impish boy with big ears, wearing his school uniform, slouched in a giant armchair. There is an almost identical photo of his older sister, Fanny, in which she wears the same uniform and sits in the same chair. His deportation file tells us that he indicated his profession as *Schreiner*, or carpenter.

The Musée Nissim de Camondo, Bertrand's grandfather's private residence and collection, remains to this day one of the most beautiful and haunting museums in Paris. Located alongside the parc de Monceau, it is the ornate collection of the Count Moïses de Camondo, a Turkish Jew who loved French culture so wholly that he modeled his home on the Petit Trianon in Versailles. Camondo collected Catherine II's silver service and Marie Antoinette's tiny inlaid reading tables and vases of gold and petrified wood, amassing the country's finest collection of late-eighteenth-century furniture, silver, and china. When the count's son, an airman in World War I, was killed in action over the Atlantic, the count bequeathed his collection to the French state in Nissim's name. One can imagine, then, how this family, with a war hero and a national French museum—in the same union of museums as the Louvre—thought that they were safe.

The scenes of the Louvre's evacuation are also drawn from firsthand accounts. Jacques Jaujard, director of the national museums, and René Huyghe, the Louvre's curator of painting, oversaw that astounding maneuver. The *Mona Lisa*, for example, alongside many of the Louvre's other treasures, went first to the château in Chambord. After the invasion of France, she was brought by ambulance stretcher to the Abbey of Loc-Dieu in the Midi. *The Rape of Europa* retells the painting's odyssey:

> The museum people, like everyone else, listened late into the night to the BBC, whose programs were laced with cryptic messages to underground activists all over Europe. Thus they knew

that information on the relocation of the collections to Loc-Dieu and later to other refuges had been received in London when the message "La Joconde *a le sourire* [The *Mona Lisa* is smiling]" came crackling through the night.

A meeting of the Association of Art Dealers did take place after the war. There, these dealers, who had profited from the looting, agreed not to report to the French government or the Direction Générale des Etudes et Recherches on their members' wartime activities because, in fact, so many would have been implicated.

All of the paintings reproduced here, and many of those mentioned, with few exceptions (the *Ham*, for example, which hangs safely in Glasgow), are still missing. *Almonds*, *Woman in White*, and others all appear courtesy of the Bernheim-Jeune Gallery's heirs. Unlike the photographic plates belonging to many other Jewish art dealers, the Bernheims' plates endure because a blackmailer swindled the family into keeping his collaboration a secret in exchange for the photographs, which documented the family's stunning, lost collection.

Pillage accompanies most wars. Yet the systematic looting of art would not have occurred were it not for the voracious appetites and bureaucratic meticulousness of the Reich's two most powerful men: Adolf Hitler and Hermann Goering, commander in chief of the Luftwaffe and Hitler's second in command.

Hitler, who as a youth had been rejected from the Academy of Fine Arts in Vienna, planned to build a museum in his hometown of Linz, Austria, dreaming it would become the world's greatest. By 1941, there were 497 paintings in the collection of the future Führermuseum. In 1945, its stores numbered 8,000—four times more artwork than was displayed in the Louvre, according to Jonathan Petropoulos in *Art as Politics in the Third Reich*. (By comparison, the National Gallery in Washington, which was dedicated in the same year, possessed a collection of 3,000 artworks only by 1991.) Later, this collection was stored in the salt mines at Alt

Aussee, a labyrinthine tunnel no more than six feet high, cut more than a mile deep into the mountainside. Many of the iconic photographs of the American Monuments Men, General Patton, and General Eisenhower posing with looted artwork were taken there.

Goering, a World War I hero, bon vivant, morphine addict, and art connoisseur, used the looting to enrich both his person (he was said to keep emeralds in his pockets for fondling) and his home, Carinhall, which was named for his deceased wife, Carin. The Einsatzstab Reichsleiter Rosenberg (ERR), led by propagandist and racial ideologue Reich Minister Alfred Rosenberg, was charged with confiscations first of fine art and, later, through M-Aktion, of furniture and household goods. Colonel Kurt von Behr was its chief in France.

Yet Hitler and the ERR did not want *all* art. Hitler had a taste for Germanic and Old Master paintings (though not religious ones) and an obsession with scenes depicting Leda and the swan (for which a market immediately sprung up). In 1937, the Nazis held the infamous Entartete Kunst (Degenerate Art) exhibit, which was but a preview to the purging of sixteen thousand contemporary paintings from German museums in 1938 and their subsequent sale in Lucerne in 1939, when Picasso's *Absinthe Drinker*, van Gogh's *Self-Portrait*, Gauguin's *Tahiti*, Matisse's *Bathers with a Turtle*, and Chagall's *Maison bleue* were among the canvases auctioned off.

As soon as Paris fell in June of 1940, the ERR began its French operations. In October, the first four hundred cases of looted artwork arrived at the Jeu de Paume museum, and from November third through fifth, Goering visited and made his first selection: twenty-seven of the finest paintings in the world, including Rembrandt's *Boy with a Red Beret* and Van Dyck's *Portrait of a Lady*. He knew better than to touch the Rothschilds' Vermeers; those were for the Führer. Due to the conditions of the armistice, the French museums were, much to Hitler's chagrin, off-limits—unlike the national collections, for example, of Poland, which was officially defeated and therefore plundered completely.

Still, France was the most looted country in Europe, with over one-third of all privately held artwork falling into Nazi hands: in all, over 100,000 works of art and several million books. According to the Mattéoli Commission report issued by the French government in 2000, 61,233 artworks were recovered after the war, of which 45,441 were returned to their owners. Two thousand works whose owners could not be identified were placed in national French museums, which inventoried them in "recovery collections," under the code of MNR (Musées Nationaux Récupérations). In 1954, 13,500 objects of lesser artistic value were sold, and for nearly forty years no further research was carried out to determine the legitimate owners of the plundered art. The locations of some 40,000 art objects remain unknown. They are in public and private collections and, many believe, in the former Soviet Union, plundered a second time by Stalin's Trophy Brigades.

Midway through *Pictures at an Exhibition*, Daniel Berenzon tells his son that the paintings will reappear, not in his lifetime, but in Max's. The more times an artwork changes hands, the more likely it is to be distanced from the person who knows why it should be hidden. In recent years, the rate of high-profile repatriations has increased.

Two thousand paintings in France remain unclaimed. For decades, until the publication of Nicholas's *The Rape of Europa* (1994) and Hector Feliciano's *The Lost Museum* (1995), the ownerless MNR paintings languished in French museums, detectable as war loot to only a few. Today, no major museum is untouched by the burden of proving the wartime provenance of its holdings. As of July 2008, the Metropolitan Museum of Art in New York lists 535 paintings (out of the 2,700 in its European collection) with "elusive gaps" in their Nazi-era provenances: neither the paintings' ownership nor their sale can be accounted for during the war years. These include Monet's *Camille Monet on a Garden Bench*, Caravaggio's *The Denial of Saint Peter*, five Cézannes, two Chagalls, five Degas, two Delacroix, works by both Brueghel the Elder and the Younger, Fra Bartolommeo, Picasso, van Gogh. . . . Think of a painter, and he is most likely on the list. Laudably, over the past decade, private and national museums have grown more transparent about this question of provenance and wartime history.

If you are ever in France, and from a distance you see a painting that looks roughly handled for a masterpiece—in the Musée d'Orsay, Pompidou, or any of the other hundreds of museums—look closely at the placard beside it, and you will likely see the letters *MNR*. I can still recall the first time I saw them, next to a Sisley with a torn corner.

ACKNOWLEDGMENTS

I am deeply indebted to the scholarship of Lynn Nicholas, Hector Feliciano, and Annette Wieviorka, and to the autobiography of Rose Valland, *Le front de l'art*, parts of which appear throughout this book. To interpret the works of Manet and Morisot, I have relied particularly on T. J. Clark's *The Painting of Modern Life* and Anne Higonnet's *Berthe Morisot.*

I wish to thank the following individuals and organizations for their support of this novel's research and completion: Nathaniel Rich at the Hald Hovedgård colony; Martha Heasley Cox and Paul Douglass of the John Steinbeck Fellowship at San Jose State University; the French Fulbright Commission; the Ludwig Vogelstein Foundation; the Avery Hopwood Awards at the University of Michigan; and the staff at the *Centre de documentation juive contemporaine* and the *Bibliothèque nationale de France.*

My professors and classmates at the University of Michigan's MFA program read multiple versions of early drafts of the novel, with insight and patience: Charles Baxter, Peter Ho Davies, Nicholas Delbanco, Reginald McKnight, Eileen Pollack, and Nancy Reisman; Laura Jean Baker, John Bishop, Andrew Cohen, Melodie Edwards, Laura Krughoff, Rattawut Lapcharoensap, John Lee, Patti Lu, David Morse, Michelle Mounts, and Catherine Zeidler.

My gratitude as well goes to: Tara Abrahams, Kate Aherns, Andrea Beauchamp, Rachid Bendacha, Orion Berg, Danielle Berger, Alice and Arthur Berney, Lexy Bloom, Jean Manuel Bourgeois, Micaela Blay-Thorup, Mary Burchenal, Rob Cohen, Nick Dybek, Nathan Englander, Arnault Finet, Peggy Frankston, Jeff Gracer, Nancy Gutman, Ellen Heller, Lindy Hess, Anne Higonnet, Patrice Higonnet, Betsy Houghteling, Lizzie Hutton, Mariko Johnson, Sandy Karam, Winnie Kao, Barbara Kean, Liz Kean, Théo Klein, Philippe Kraemer, Virginia Larner, Howard Lay, Adam Loss, Maja Lucas, Arnost Lustig, John and Risa Mann, Jean Martin, Peter Mendelsund, Dinaw Mengestu, Margaret Metzger, the Mindelzun family, Charles B. Paul, Nathan Perl-Rosenthal, Sharon Pomerantz, Deborah Quitt, Abel Rambert, Sandrine Rameau, Maxine Rodburg, John Rosenberg, Jesse Rosencrantz-Engelmann, Lionel Salem, Elaine Sciolino, Didier Schulmann, Claire Silvy, the Spatzierer family, Marcel and Vivian Steinberg, Laura Stern, Dan and Susan Suleiman, Margaret Taub, David G. Taylor, Emanuel Tanay, LeRoy Votto, Brad Watson, and Annette Wieviorka. Elizabeth Fishel and Bob Houghteling have gone beyond the call of family duty, from literary wisdom to welcoming me for months beneath their roof.

Caroline Clement has been my Parisian host, interpreter, and friend for many years. I could not have undertaken this research without Fred Davis's legal knowledge and historical expertise. I wish to thank Marianne Rosenberg for sharing her family's history with me; her grandfather, Paul Rosenberg, was the inspiration for this novel and her father, Alexandre, makes several appearances within. Seeing an invitation to a gallery opening at 21, rue de La Boétie written in her grandfather's hand and colored by Picasso's was an experience like none other. I am also thankful to Marianne for lending her keen eye to this novel. All errors, of course, on matters historical, artistic, and otherwise, are entirely my own.

I have been blessed to have a brilliant editor at Knopf, Jordan Pavlin. My agent Jennifer Joel has been a tireless advocate and friend. Special thanks also to Leslie Levine for her extraordinary help. Finally, I am grateful to Janet Baker, Nicolette Castle, Katie Sigelman, and Meghan Wilson.

My love and gratitude go to my grandmother Fiora, who first painted the pictures of Paris in my mind, to my father Peter who gave them a melody, and to my mother Susan who encouraged me to write them down. To them—and to my sisters Charlotte, Sylvia, and Pearl, and to Daniel—go my love and thanks beyond words.

ABOUT THE AUTHOR

Sara Houghteling is a graduate of Harvard College and received her Master's in Fine Arts from the University of Michigan. She is the recipient of a Fulbright scholarship to Paris, first place in the Avery and Jules Hopwood Awards, and a John Steinbeck Fellowship. She lives in California, where she teaches high school English.

A NOTE ON THE TYPE

This book was set in Janson, a typeface long thought to have been made by the Dutchman Anton Janson, who was a practicing typefounder in Leipzig during the years 1668–1687. However, it has been conclusively demonstrated that these types are actually the work of Nicholas Kis (1650–1702), a Hungarian, who most probably learned his trade from the master Dutch typefounder Dirk Voskens.

Composed by North Market Street Graphics, Lancaster, Pennsylvania
Printed and bound by Berryville Graphics, Berryville, Virginia
Book design by Robert C. Olsson